SPIRITS
BEFORE ENTERING THE
LIGHT

MARIE HARRIETTE KAY

BALBOA.PRESS
A DIVISION OF HAY HOUSE

Inspired by paranormal events.

Balboa Press books may be ordered through booksellers or by contacting:

Balboa Press
A Division of Hay House
1663 Liberty Drive
Bloomington, IN 47403
www.balboapress.com
844-682-1282

Because of the dynamic nature of the Internet, any web addresses or links contained in this book may have changed since publication and may no longer be valid. The views expressed in this work are solely those of the author and do not necessarily reflect the views of the publisher, and the publisher hereby disclaims any responsibility for them.

The author of this book does not dispense medical advice or prescribe the use of any technique as a form of treatment for physical, emotional, or medical problems without the advice of a physician, either directly or indirectly. The intent of the author is only to offer information of a general nature to help you in your quest for emotional and spiritual well-being. In the event you use any of the information in this book for yourself, which is your constitutional right, the author and the publisher assume no responsibility for your actions.

Any people depicted in stock imagery provided by Getty Images are models, and such images are being used for illustrative purposes only.
Certain stock imagery © Getty Images.

Print information available on the last page.

ISBN: 979-8-7652-2741-1 (sc)
ISBN: 979-8-7652-2742-8 (e)

Balboa Press rev. date: 04/12/2022

Contents

DEDICATION

I dedicate this book to my mother, the late Eva Kay, who by example and love of family, instilled in me honesty, compassion, and the ability to see all issues fairly.

I thank my three children, Jane, Robert, Steven, and son-in-law, Tom, for encouraging me to write, and for their help in successfully handling the computer problems.

I thank my mentor, teacher, and friend, the late June Black, who awakened me to my natural psychic ability. June guided me though seven years of basic psychic training and mediumship, teaching me how to rescue earthbound spirits and release them to the God light.

Most of all, I thank God for the privilege of helping others, and the spirit world for guiding and protecting me through each spirit rescue.

PREFACE

Marie Harriette Kay was born in Michigan, the seventh child of eight. She studied for seven years as an assistant to June Black, a psychic medium who came to the United States from London, England, where she had her training. Under Misses Black's guidance Marie visited haunted houses and assisted in the release of earthbound spirits into the God light. Marie has had an exciting journey this life-time, and now feels it's time to hand over the reins to the next generation. She feels a responsibility pass along the wisdom and knowledge she has acquired. Hopefully, the next generation of psychics will follow the examples of the spirit guides and approach each spirit with unconditional love and understanding.

SPIRITS.
BEFORE ENTERING THE LIGHT

is a collection of short stories inspired by extraordinary events to explain the unexplainable. They are enlightening, supernatural, and sometimes frightening. The paranormal events are unique, and have rarely, if ever, been addressed by the average psychic medium. The names, dates, and locations have been changed. Any reference to a living person or place is purely accidental, and should be considered fictional.

After physical death, the spirit reside in another dimension until its next incarnation. Many stories deal with the spirit's existence *after* physical death, but *before* it enters the God light. Each chapter ends with an explanation of why spirits are held in-between the earthly dimension and the spirit world.

Death is not an end, but merely the change of energy and form. Most people move from one dimension to another on the wings of death. But for some, existence after physical death may result in the spirit wandering in fear or darkness. The transition to the God light is not final until the thought pattern of fear that hold a spirit earthbound is broken.

SPIRITS IN THE ATTIC

Many people are able to recall their childhood memories because emotional events are stored in a part of the brain that retains emotion. Having grown up as a psychic child, I've had many unusual experiences. Psychic children are far more common than you think. Their awareness is still open to the next dimension, so it's natural for them to accept their own instincts. The following stories are intended to explain the unexplainable childhood memories.

A woman and her three children lived in a four bedroom wood-frame house on a culturally mixed neighborhood. Because it was an older home, there were no overhead lights on the stairs leading up to a long, dark hall. During the day, the upstairs hall was well lit by four open bedroom doors. However, when night came, the unlit hall took on an eerily spooky atmosphere.

The small bedroom where the child slept was unusually dark, dimly lit by one small window. As a youngster of three or four, she remembered watching the moonlight cast eerie shadows against the wall, and imagined the shadows changing form and come alive. Many times, as she was about to fall asleep, she sensed spirits moving about in the attic. Because she was young, she didn't feel threatened by them, but not knowing who or what they were, left her feeling uncertain. The child didn't feel they were hiding in the attic, they were just existing in their own space. She wasn't afraid of the spirits as much as she was afraid of the dark.

When the child was about the age of seven, she climbed the stairs to her bedroom. When she reached the top step, she stopped abruptly, stretched out her neck and searched the unlit hall.

An elongated blotch of light, the size and shape of a baby's sock, floated down the dark hall. The wispy apparition made a left turn, then entered a front bedroom.

The child gripped the handrail and froze in her tracks until the blotch of light disappeared. She had encountered these light spirits floating down the hall several times before, and didn't think of them as ghosts. They were more like disembodied residents coexisting in her house. Her sixth sense was still open to the spiritual dimension, making it easy for her to believe these spirits were real. She saw them as light, and sensed them as people. She never mentioned her ghostly encounters to outsiders, and accepted them as her own truth.

In retrospect, she looks back and wonder if she had been mistaken about the phantom light. Could it have been a natural occurrence, or an actual light? But after logical reasoning, she realized the light came from the dark end of the hall where it would have been impossible for outside light to reach at night. Also, the light floated down the dark hall and made a sharp turn into a bedroom. Natural light cannot turn. Light travels in a straight line. The only way light will appear to bend is when it moves over an obstacle. If it had been the other way around, the light coming from the bedroom that had two windows, she might have reasoned that a passing car light could have reflected against the window and created the strange blob of light. But, since the light came from the darkness, it had to be a paranormal light entity.

WICKER BABY CARRIAGE

Two very young girls were playing in the attic. In one corner of the attic was a wicker baby carriage covered with a white sheet. It had been there for years, gathering dust. Something caught the girls' attention in the darkest corner of the attic. They stared in disbelief as the sheet in the buggy slowly began to rise. It was as if a gust of air had lifted the sheet, then let it fall back in place. After the sheet floated back into the buggy, the girls dashed down the stairs, screaming to their mother that a ghost was in the attic. The mother grabbed a wooden stick and rushed to the attic. Just as the sheet was floating down, she struck it hard.

The sheet remained motionless.

The mother stood poised, ready to strike again, fully expecting an animal to jump out. But the sheet lay limp inside the buggy. After a while, she gingerly lifted the sheet. The carriage was empty. The frightened woman gathered her family and dashed to the neighbor's house where they spent the night.

THE YOUNGER YEARS

During the 1940s through the 1950s, electronic information was barely available to the middle-class citizens. Truckers used CB radios, known as ham-radios, to guide their big rigs through traffic jams in busy cities. Often, fear of committing what some people believed was a sin, prevented the average person from trusting their own experience. Therefore, most people didn't speak of their paranormal experience for fear of being ridiculed. Even if they had witnessed a paranormal event, they would deny it rather than be humiliated by their peers.

These archaic practices prevented many people from accepting their own truth-their own natural sixth sense. Oh, we accept the use of our five senses: sight, touch, hear, tastes, and smell. But when it comes to the sixth sense, we have been programed to believe it is something unnatural. Nothing could be further from the truth. The sixth sense is a natural ability to sense, and should be used daily in all matters.

2

GRADUATION VISITOR

Near the age of thirty, I witnessed a paranormal visitation in a mirror. I was attending a family gathering to celebrate a high school graduation. My nephew was the only grandchild my mother had seen when she was alive. All the other grandchildren were born years after her demise. Several family members were gathered in the living room. I was seated on the couch between my oldest sister and my nephew's paternal grandmother.

"My sister looked at me curiously. "You look so much like Mom tonight. I never noticed that before."

The paternal grandmother nodded. "Yes. I see the resemblance too."

As they spoke, I felt particularly proud of my nephew, as if he was my own child. I didn't give their comments a second thought, and continued chatting. Several minutes later, I left the room to go to bathroom. On my way back, I stopped in the bedroom to comb my hair. As I looked in the mirror, I gasped, and jumped back.

My mother's face was superimposed over my face. She was staring back at me. The transparent image of my mother's face appeared to be veiled over my face. Her blue eyes were intense, as if they were looking right through me. She wasn't ghostlike, as one might think an apparition would be, nor was she frightening. She appeared real—alive.

As I gazed in the mirror, I received a message as a thought in my head. *My mother was proud to be at her grandson's graduation.* Shaken by the visitation, I told no one for fear of trying to explain something that I knew nothing about.

At this time, I wasn't aware of my psychic ability, and didn't understand why I had witnessed a spirit. I thought other people had similar experiences, and that it was just something that happens. Since paranormal experiences were shunned by society and forbidden by some churches, I kept this strange incident a secret.

In retrospect, after having had many years of psychic training, I now understand what happened that evening. My sister, who was sitting beside me on the couch, was actually seeing my mother's energy (her soul) superimposed over my face. The paternal grandmother saw my mother's energy veiled over my face, and both recognized the resemblance. Because my mother's spirit was hovering close to me, I had sensed her thoughts that she was proud of her grandson.

I now realize that spirits often slip into the earthly dimension to join in the gaiety of a family occasion, or to check on their loved ones. My mother chose to join the family for this special graduation. She must have known I was psychic, and that I would see her face in the mirror. It was her way of telling me how proud she was of her grandson. Even though I saw my mother's face, I still didn't connect it as being psychic. It was going to take more than this experience for my guides to awaken me to my abilities.

BALL OF NEGATIVITY

Have you ever been in a house where you felt unwelcome? Or have you had the feeling your energy is being drained, either by the hostess or the room itself? Not all hauntings are caused by spirits. Some may simply be negative energy in a particular area. Extremely negative people can unwittingly create an atmosphere of destructive energy within their home. When their negativity continues over a long period of time, that energy can accumulate in a room and emit a strange, eerie feeling.

Many years ago, before I was aware of my psychic abilities, I often visited a woman who lived in a house filled with negative energy. She and her husband were pessimists and would dwell on negative thoughts daily. As a result, their constant brooding created a negative energy which had accumulated in the living room of their home.

Each time I visited their house, I felt uncomfortable. Often, disturbed by the dark overshadowing of the dreary room, I left their house feeling tired and distressed. As time passed, I begin to sense the negativity in her house more easily. I didn't realize that the destructive energy had attached itself to me and was draining my energy. After talking to several people who knew this couple, each claimed to have experienced the same depressive feeling while in their house.

One afternoon, upon entering their living room, I was struck by an intense feeling of depression. The living room appeared darker than usual, and the murky atmosphere felt heavy.

As I stood talking to the woman, I felt something draining the energy from my body. In my mind's eye, I envisioned a ball of gray mist, more than six feet in diameter, rolling in slow motion in the center of the living room. Because my psychic abilities were becoming more pronounced, I was able to see the ball of negative as moving vibrations. I sensed the gray, slow-moving vibrations were a result of the residents' dismal attitude.

I don't judge this family. There may be an underlying reason for their negativity. If I could, I would have warned them to stop dwelling on negativity. Then, in time, the destructive energy would dissipate, and the result would be a happier, healthier atmosphere. But I knew they would be insulted, so I remained silent.

In retrospect, after having participated in years of psychic phenomena, I can now recognize many forms of energy. I have seen negative energy as gray, wispy shadows drifting against a wall, and felt the gloomy atmosphere draining energy from my body. Violent energy was seen as erratic fast moving friction, causing me to feel uneasy or jittery. I have seen nervous energy as waves of vibrations, and erratic energy as a fast-pulsing friction, each leaving me feeling anxious. It's important to know that people who constantly dwell on negativity may unwittingly draw negative spirits into their homes.

3

MOTHER'S VISITATION

Two months before I was to be married, my mother passed away. I had already made wedding plans, and since my mother had approved of my husband-to-be, I was married one month later. During the first year of marriage, on days when I felt discouraged, a peaceful feeling would come over me and I would sense my mother's presence. It felt like she had her arms around me, hugging me, consoling me. At the age of twenty-one, I knew nothing of the paranormal, and wasn't aware that I could communicate with her.

While married and raising three children, I experienced many strange phenomena, such as sensing and knowing what was about to happen. Often, I would know when the phone was about to ring, and sometimes who was calling. There were days I would sense company would be arriving. This came in handy, giving me plenty of time to tidy the house before the guest arrived. There were times while driving the car, a thought would cross my mind. *Better slow down. There's a police car just ahead.* That brief thought was usually accurate. I remember sensing a premonition of bad news, and even though the omen came true, I dismissed it as a coincidence. Many times, I would sense sadness veiled over a friend's face and saw phantom tears that were only visible to me. Even though I empathized with their sadness, I remained silent. I didn't know I was psychic and accepted this sensitivity as normal. I now understand it was my psychic ability beginning to surface.

ASTRAL PROJECTION

At the age of twenty-five, I had my first out-of-body experience. I offer this experience to prepare the readers, and to lessen any fear they might have during their first experience. Astral projection occurs when the brain waves slow down and the physical body is nearly asleep. It's quite common for the soul to leave the body during sleep, giving the body time to regenerate. This happens to most people, but is seldom remembered.

Many years ago, a woman came to me with a serious problem, and I was hesitant to give an answer. At this time, I knew nothing of the paranormal and wasn't aware of my psychic abilities. That evening, I lay in bed wondering how I could help this woman. *What should I say to her? Will she accept my answer? And, if she does act upon my words, would I have offered the correct solution?* I was drowsy and about to fall asleep when I felt my consciousness slipping from my head. I actually felt my awareness moving slowly down until it reached my chest. Surprisingly, it didn't frighten me. Instead, a calming effect swept over me. I lay very still, analyzing this strange sensation. My consciousness continued moving down my body until it was at my knees, then at my feet. I felt my consciousness, which I now believe it was my soul, slipping out through my heels and rising up to the ceiling. Within seconds, I was floating peacefully above my physical body without recognition of time or space.

Still, I didn't fear this unusual sensation. I felt comforted by it, as one would feel guided by a loving presence. While hovering in midair, I received a message as a thought in my head. I had a sacred responsibility to this woman and was to give her a specific answer that would save her life. The answer that I received will remain private as it was meant for only one person. From that moment on, my perception shifted. I felt an intense responsibility toward all people, and knew that I would always be available to help others in spiritual matters.

The next day, I delivered the message as it was given to me. Several days later, I learned the woman had acted on my suggestion. Yes, it did make a difference. It changed her way of thinking. She followed the advice and as a result she has lived a long, happy life.

As I look back at this experience, I now understand it was my consciousness that astral projected out of my physical body. What an amazing way for the spirit world to get my attention. Even after this experience, I was unaware of the spiritual significance of the soul, and had accepted this as something beyond my comprehension. I'm sure my spirit guides were frustrated trying to get my attention to inform me that I was psychic. But I went on my merry way, not understanding my abilities and accepting each paranormal experience as natural, but unusual.

I have since learned that when the consciousness-the soul-slips out each night, the physical body is regenerating itself. During this time, it may travel on the astral plane. It may visit loved ones, comfort the needy, or solve problems that are often remembered as a dream. Ever since the first out-of-body experience, I accept the responsibility of helping others as one of my life missions.

KIDNAPPED BOY

Several years later, I had a paranormal experience that awakened my belief in angels. I was married, had three children, and lived in the northern suburb of Michigan. During the summer, the sidewalks were lively with children playing hopscotch and roller skating. Little girls pushed their doll carriages, and boys played with their toy guns. At night, the streetlight served as "home base" where the neighborhood children gathered to play hide-and-seek in the shadows. I had read about frightening tragedies in other towns, but never expected to find evil lurking in my neighborhood.

My daughter and son were in grade school and the youngest son in kindergarten, and I had just sent them off to school. I stood looking out the front window, watching them walk hand in hand down the sidewalk. The public school was located about three blocks away, so it was a short walk for the children. When I was sure they were well on their way, I returned to the kitchen to wash the breakfast dishes. Several minutes later, I was drawn back to the living room. As I stood looking out the window, I noticed a young boy in a red and white-striped shirt playing across the street on a neighbor's front lawn. He appeared to be a preschooler, younger than five. I had never seen this boy before and didn't know if he was visiting a relative or if he lived down the street. I watched him for a while, then returned to the kitchen.

Within seconds, something drew me back to the front window. This time, I saw the tail end of a car drive past my house. Now, this isn't unusual. Anyone could be driving down the street for any reason. But now, I didn't see the boy. A dreadful feeling of anxiety swept over me. I panicked, sure the boy had been abducted!

If I had acted logically, I would have thought the boy went home or ran behind a house. That would have used up precious time. It was as if someone had blocked the idle chatter in my brain. Somehow, I was prevented from second-guessing myself. The impression that the boy was in grave danger was overwhelming. I just *knew* the boy had been kidnapped.

Reacting to the vivid impression of danger, I dialed the police. I told the dispatcher that a young boy in a red and white-striped shirt had just been kidnapped. I told him the name of my street and where I had last seen the boy.

The dispatcher asked, "What kind of car did you see?"

I wasn't about to tell him I had only seen the tail end of a car passing my house. Not knowing what to say, I lied. I told him that I wasn't wearing my glasses, and I didn't know much about cars.

He voiced a disgruntled groan, then made a comment about women who are too vain to wear glasses and requested that I stay on the line.

I could hear the dispatcher's voice sending the kidnapping message out to the patrol cars. Within minutes, I heard the blaring sound of police sirens approaching. Two patrol cars raced past my house and continue through the winding streets of the subdivision. During the next hour or two as I watched out the window, a calmness sweep over me. Never once did I doubt myself. Never once did I feel I had made a mistake. I was positive that the boy was in danger.

Several hours later, a police officer knocked on my front door. He thanked me for making the phone call so quickly. He said the police caught the man who had kidnapped the boy, and that the boy was home safe. He further explained that the officers found the man driving aimlessly through the winding streets in the subdivision. They were able to apprehend him because he didn't have enough time to find his way to the highway.

Later that evening, the boy's parents came to thank me for saving their son's life. It was a warm summer evening and my husband and I invited them to sit on the porch and talk about the children. Soon other neighbors joined us. We set up lawn chairs and served pop and beer, which of course drew more neighbors. Soon it was a neighborhood get-together, with everyone discussing the abduction.

Later that evening, after the neighbors had left and my family was asleep, I sat in the living room, turned off the lights, and thought about this extraordinary experience. Strange thoughts crossed my mind.

It isn't the boy's time to leave this earth plane. This boy has a mission in life.

This message came with unusual words such as 'earth plane' and 'mission in life.' Words I wouldn't commonly use, nor had ever used before. I wondered, *where did these words come from? They certainly weren't from my vocabulary.* Even though I wasn't privy to what the boy's life mission would be, I sensed his life would be very important.

In retrospect, I think about what happened that day with profound interest. I now believe angels blocked the idle chatter from my brain. If I had taken time to think logically, it might have been too late to save the boy. The angels also blocked me from thinking about the legal ramification if I had been wrong, or of being accused of making a false police report. Nor did I think about being ridiculed if I had made a mistake. I believe the angels blocked those concerns from my mind. During the several hours that I had waited in suspense, there was absolutely no doubt, no second guessing. I was positive the boy was in danger.

I now understand why the neighbors never directly questioned me about the abduction. I feel certain the angels had again taken charge. They kept the neighbors busy, and no one thought to ask me what actually happened. The angels had guided and protected me in every aspect of this experience, and had protected me from lying. At that time, I didn't know I was psychic. I simply followed my natural instincts and accepted this as an extraordinary event.

4

MEETING MY MENTOR

I begin this chapter with the woman who became my best friend and mentor. June Black was a soft-spoken, compassionate woman who changed my life and awakened my psychic abilities. June was born in London, England, where she was trained in extrasensory perception (ESP). She arrived in United States as a soldier's bride. Several years later, she began teaching meditation. In search of like-minded people, June attended a lecture on the paranormal at the local community college. The following is a true experience of how I met my mentor.

MIMOSA

Since my children were now in high school, I now had more time to further my education. I never thought of myself as psychic, but attended a lecture on the paranormal at the local community college. At the time, I didn't realize I was being spiritually guided to attend this lecture.

I entered the large lecture room and, because I was timid, I found the least conspicuous chair in the last row at the back of the room. While listening to the instructor, a strong scent of flowers emanated from the floor. I leaned close to the girl sitting next to me and whispered, "Your cologne smells beautiful."

The girl whispered back. "I'm not wearing cologne."

Without thinking, the words poured out of my mouth. "I smell Mimosa." As soon as I said the word "mimosa," the potent fragrance forced itself on my face. Startled by the attack, I jumped out of my chair, dashed to the back of the room, and shouted, "There's a spirit here! It's blasting Mimosa in my face!"

The instructor acknowledged my comment with a slight smile and a nod. It was evident that he didn't know what to do. Offering no suggestion, he continued his lecture.

I returned to my seat, still shaken from the experience. Even though I had been aware of spirits all my life, I had never been attack by one. Also, I didn't know what mimosa was, or how it smelled. *I wonder why I said mimosa? I think it's a flower or a tree.* Since the instructor didn't appear concerned, I remained quiet for the rest of the lecture.

After the meeting ended, a petite, blond-haired lady came to the back of the room and introduced herself. June Black spoke with a charming British accent and asked if I would be interested in joining her psychic classes. I agreed, and the next day enrolled in the metaphysical workshop.

Several months into my studies, I heard a knock on the front door. It was June. She was having trouble with her car and stopped in to call an auto service.

"Marie. Would you like to be my assistant? Every time I drive the main street near your house, my car stops. This is the third time. My spirit guides want you to be my assistant, and I'm tired of my car breaking down when I pass your street."

I felt honored to receive the invitation and eager to work with Mrs. Black. It meant I would be attending day and night classes. I was to learn meditation, psychic awareness, automatic writing, hands-on healing, psychometry, mental telepathy, past-life regression, spirit communication, sensing and seeing a spirit within the mind's eye, and much more.

COUNCIL OF SPIRITUAL ADVISORS

Several months later, after learning how to meditate, my sensory perception had improved. With my eyes closed, I was able to visualize spirits within my mind's eye. This evening, I closed my eyes and listened as June gave to the opening prayer. In preparation to meditate, I began slow, deep breathing to slow down my brain waves.

The room grew solemnly silent.

After several minutes, while concentrating on my forehead, I envisioned ten or eleven men standing in a semicircle, hovering above the room. They had long white hair, long beards, and were clothed in pure white robes. Though I had seen many spirits within my mind's eye before, I had never seen these men. I sensed they were Spiritual Councils, highly evolved spirits with a mission in mind. With closed eyes, I focused on the figures hovering above me.

The men were looking down, studying me. It appeared they were pondering a question.

I sensed they were wondering if I would be faithful and would continue using my psychic ability. Several minutes later, by nodding, it appeared that they had agreed to accept me. Feeling this was an honor, I was grateful they had selected me. I had no idea what I had been accepted for, or what I was to do, but was soon to find out.

AUTOMATIC WRITING

The psychic workshop was now teaching automatic writing. It is a method by which the human mind can receive information from spiritual sources through writing. The students were seated at a table with a pen or pencil in hand, ready to communicate with their spirit guides.

June began the lecture. "When writing, always begin by imaging the white light around your body. This light will act as a protection and will ward off any mischievous spirits who want to interfere with your writing. Be patient if the writings are just scribble at first. Some spirits may not have done automatic writing before. Expect the first writings to be large print or garbled word usage. It may take time for the spirit to learn to direct your hand, or to put thoughts into your mind." June began the opening prayer. "We ask for protection, guidance, and direction. We ask for the very highest spiritual guidance we are capable of using."

The members closed their eyes and mentally surrounded their body with God's white light. Next, they mentally called upon their angels and guides for protection and guidance.

I imaged a circle of white light surrounding my body, then gripped the pencil firmly and waited to receive a message as a thought in my head. Instead, much to my surprise, my hands begin scribbling large circles. Even though I didn't accomplish much that day, I recognized that something had moved my hand, and was trying to communicate with me.

The following day, when I was home alone, I began automatic writing. I wrote several days a week, several hours at a time. Eventually, the scribbling turned into large print. After weeks of practice, the writing became more legible. Now my hand was writing fancy, curved script, writing archaic English words such as "thee" and "thou." Words I would not commonly use.

Often, when I placed the pencil in an upright position, my hand moved automatically, printing the word "OPEL." At first, I didn't understand why this name kept popping. My writings were usually in circular script. So why the large, bold print connected to the word Opel? After weeks of writing, I penned the question. Who is Opel? My hand raced across the paper, pressing hard in strong strokes and printed in bold letters.

"I AM OPEL. I AM YOUR GUIDE. I HAVE BEEN WITH YOU SINCE YOU ENTERED THE EARTH PLANE. I AM PLEASED YOU ARE WRITING. CONTINUE WRITING."

From that day on my writing often began with a same key phrase: "Opel is here. Let us begin." I was delighted that I had found a way to connect with my personal guide. Through automatic writing, Opel acted as my conscience, warned me of danger, and encouraged me to use my intuition. After several weeks, I began by asking about personal prophecies, current problems, and how I could help other people.

One day, the writing changed from Opel's straight bold print to a softer script identifying a second guide named Peter. This writing told of a male guide who was a gambler in his last incarnation. Now, Peter gives me courage, so I would not back away from problems. Several days later, the writing informed me of another spirit guide, a German woman who had been a street sweeper in her last incarnation. Although the woman never wrote or gave a message, I could sense when she was present.

Soon, I was receiving information about existence after death. The writings described souls as energies, and how people's thoughts existed in the atmosphere. The automatic writing described how thoughts accumulate in the divine ether and can affect the atmosphere and the earthly planet. The writings offered concepts beyond my understanding at the time. I dated and saved those writing. Perhaps they would be valuable in the future.

However, some days the pencil seemed stuck to the paper. Though I tried, my hand stubbornly refused to move. One afternoon, after waiting patiently for my pencil to move, I asked aloud, "Why won't the pencil move?"

But the pencil remained still.

On those days, the atmosphere seemed vacant, and I could feel a void in the space around me. I soon learned that when I felt that void, it meant the writing guides were not present, and I was to cancel writing. Apparently, they were aware I would be called away, or a telephone call would interrupt my writing. The guides knew I would be busy and had canceled the writing before it began.

SHATTERED LIGHT BULB

The event that convinced me of the value of automatic writing came one cold winter evening. After the family was securely in bed, I sat down to write. I placed an artist's canvas board on my lap, set a stack of paper on the board, and gripped a pen in my hand. I turned on the lamp beside me and began slow, deep breathing to slow my brain waves. Soon my hand began to write, answering each question that crossed my mind.

My cat, Misty, sat in front of me, his ears tipped forward and his whiskers humorously spread out. He had an inquisitive expression on his face while staring curiously at something above my hand.

Half an hour later, I had penned several pages of information from the spirit guides. All the time my cat sat still, curiously amused, and never took his eyes off my moving hand.

Though I didn't see anything, I sensed a ball of energy hovering over my hand. I wondered, *can the cat see what I'm sensing?* Every once in a while, I glanced at the cat to see if he was still interested. He sat motionless, seemingly entertained by what he was seeing.

Suddenly, a flash of light and a loud cracking sound broke the silence. A light bulb in the lamp exploded, scattering glass over my writing board, the chair, and the floor.

The cat jumped straight up in the air and bolted out of the room.

I jumped up as shards of glass flew across the writing board. I placed my hands on my face. Somehow, the shards of glass had not touched me. I set the writing board aside, cleaned up the pieces of glass, and inserted a new light bulb in the lamp. After settling down to write, it dawned on me. *Why not ask why the light bulb burst?* Even as I considered the question, my pen raced across the paper. My hand pressed down hard, and the message flowed in large, bold print.

"WE COME IN GREAT NUMBERS. WE ARE PLEASED YOU HAVE CHOSEN TO USE THIS INFORMATION. THE GLASS BULB SHATTERED BECAUSE OUR ENERGY IS GREAT. CONTINUE WRITING."

As I finished printing the last sentence, I became aware of a fullness in the room. *So this is what a room full of spirits feels like.* The feeling encompassing the room was peaceful, comforting, and pleasantly energetic.

This extraordinary experience strengthened my belief that angels and spirit guides do give off vibrations of energy, just as people emit energy from their aura. The accumulation of spirits in the room was powerful enough to cause the light bulb to burst. Also, the reference to a "great number" of spirits and the inspirational message reassured me that I was receiving communication from sources other than my own imagination. This amazing display of powerful energy encouraged me to continue writing.

Many years later, I learned that my sincerity to learn about the paranormal had illuminated my aura, drawing spirits guides to me. They were pleased that I was using my writing to communicate with the spirit world.

This experience also verified that animals can see above the normal visual sight that humans cannot see. Misty seemed to enjoy watching the energy hovering over my hand. The cat's amusing gaze convinced me that an unseen presence was assisting my writing.

JAMES JOYCE

During the time that I was learning automatic writing, I was also painting, selling many paintings, and began a creative writing class at the local community college. Prior to this, I had very little writing skills, and had never attempted to write a story.

My first class assignment was to write a short story. I didn't know where to start or what to write. I sat down with pen in hand, slowed down my brain waves, and began writing. Much to my surprise, the writing flowed effortlessly. As I wrote, I felt and visualized each scene as if watching a movie. Because the writing came easily, I felt that the information was coming from the spirit world.

Several months later, my story, *'A Day in Court,'* had won the top award from all the creative writing classes for that semester. I received a twenty-five dollar award and a Webster dictionary with my name embossed in gold on the cover.

Now, I wondered, how it was possible to write a winning story when I had never written before? Again, I sat down with pen in hand and asked the question. "Do I have a writing guide?"

My hand printed out in large, bold letters, "YES!"

Again, I asked, "Who is my writing guide?"

My hand moved effortlessly without hesitation and printed the name 'JAMES JOYCE.' I had heard of this famous writer but had never read any of his books. Because I was busy attending the psychic development class, teaching oil painting at the public school, and attending the creative writing classes, I temporarily set the name of James Joyce aside.

My next assignment was to write a short story. I sat down with pen in hand and wondered what I would call this story. I thought about my mother's name, Eva, and decided to make up a similar name. I would write about a girl named Evaline.

I was well along in my story when I decided to learn more about my writing guide. James Joyce was a famous writer and because he had been dead for many years, there were no current books available. I went to a used bookstore and bought three well-worn paperbacks that he had written. When I got home, I opened to a page in the center of the book and was startled to see the title of a short story, Evaline. A pleasant surge coursed through my body. This gave me confirmation that James Joyce was my writing guide and had inspired me to write the story, Evaline.

After reading several of James Joyce's stories, I realized that my writing was dry—too factual. I scanned the pages, studying how he presented each story. Following his work as an example, I added more detail, vivid description, depth, and emotion in my writing. My story became alive.

Years later, I wrote and published a book, *Awaken Your Psychic Abilities*, by Marie Harriette Kay. It's an easy-to-use instruction manual for a novice alone, or for class room participation. A lesson on automatic writing can be found in Chapter Twelve.

Many years later, I wrote a second book, *High Society Murder in Detroit: the Peacock-Tail Mirror*. It's a historical murder mystery sprinkled with scenes of the paranormal about the physical and psychological effects of unnecessary self guilt.

WE WON'T LET YOU MAKE A MISTAKE

A woman purchased a small foot stool which came boxed and unassembled. She was usually very good at reading directions and thought this would be easy to put together. Several hours later, she finished assembling the foot stool, but legs just didn't fit right. Surely the manufacturer had made a mistake in the directions. After several hours of trying and retrying, the legs still wobbled. She would have to return the foot stool as defective.

She placed the foot stool fully assembled and drove to the store. Surely the clerk would see the legs on the footstool were loose. She pulled into the parking lot and sat quietly for several minutes.

Why am I sitting here? Why don't I go in the store? She wasn't sure why she felt compelled wait, until she picked up the footstool and examined it carefully. *This just isn't right!*

Suddenly, a thought crossed her mind. *Look at the bolts.*

Well, I'll be! She had screwed the bolts from the outside of the legs, and the bolts must be screwed on the inside of the legs. Whew. She was glad she didn't go in the store and make a fool of herself. Suddenly she heard a booming voice in her head. "WE WON'T LET YOU MAKE A MISTAKE."

She hurriedly drove out of the parking lot and headed back home.

This may seem like a simple, unimportant story to the average person, but it was intended to show that spirit guides were always nearby. Many times in the past, while automatic writing, her spirit guides would write, "We are all here!" Again, the word "we" was used, indicating many spirit guides. This mere act of preventing her from making a mistake gave her further confidence that spirit guides really are nearby, and would try to prevent her or the living from making a mistake.

WHAT HAPPENS AFTER DEATH & IN BETWEEN DIMENSIONS

Many people have reported near-death experiences (NDE). Some claim to have had an out-of-body experience where they were greeted by deceased loved ones. Some mention traveling through a whirling tunnel toward a brilliant light, or being drawn into a compassionate, all-loving energy. Some claim to have entered a dimension of absolute harmony, an environment so beautiful that they did not want to return to earth. These reports reinforce my belief that the consciousness—the soul—survives after physical death. Existence of the soul is constant. Death is not an end to one's existence. It is a change of energy and form.

Through years of experiences, I have come to believe there are many dimensions of afterlife. That the spirit enters the dimension according to its spiritual awareness, thoughts, intentions, actions, and probably more than I could even imagine. Usually, and most often, the spirit is drawn by the God light into a dimension of celestial peace and unconditional love.

Most people cross over into the God light without a problem. However, some people, after experiencing a tragic death are unable to let go of the horrifying memory. They remain suspended in a state of shock, wandering in a void of darkness. They are earthbound, unable to make their final transition until the thought that holds them is released. This is where the rescue medium takes over.

THE RESCUE CIRCLE

This chapter will be of interest to those who are searching for information on mediumship and how to form a mediumship circle. Since I am entering my golden years, I feel obligated to pass on the valuable knowledge that I have acquired over the past fifty years.

A Rescue Circle consists of a group of mediums, five to fifteen or more, who meet for the sole purpose of releasing earthbound spirits into the God light. The chairs are placed in a circle and the lights dimmed. The circle formation is very important because the circular shape holds positive energy in and keeps the negative entities out. Each rescue circle has a time limit, depending upon the amount of energy the mediums are able to create. An average meeting may last anywhere from one to three hours. Time is precious. A negative, ill, or depressed medium sitting in the circle might drain positive energy from the circle, thus shortening the time available.

The members sit, alternating a student next to an experienced medium. They close their eyes and visualize the God light surrounding their body and the circle. Each medium will act as a conduit between the physical world and the spirit world. The meeting will begin with a prayer to create God's white light.

White Light is an energy created by the medium's prayer and sincere intention to help. The prayer I often use is as follows. "We sit with love and understanding. We ask our spirit guides for protection, guidance, and directions. We ask for the highest spiritual guidance we are capable of using. Thank you, God, for your love and protection."

Prayer sends out positive thoughts. Thoughts are energy, just as light is energy. It took me many years to realize the importance of the following statement: "Thoughts are things occupying a place in space." Therefore, a prayer is a thoughtful energy. White light is a spiritual energy—a protection which surrounds the rescue circle. The God light is an entrance into another dimension.

EARTHBOUND SPIRIT

Most often, immediately after physical death, the spirit is drawn by the power of the God light into a dimension of absolute harmony and unconditional love. However, some remain earthbound, unable to cross over into the light. There are many reasons why a spirit is earthbound. It might be locked in the memory of a horrendous death. Or, a spirit may not believe in the afterlife or accept that their existence is eternal. Usually, but not always, the spirit is held earthbound by its own earthly memories. Some spirits are guided to a rescue circle by their personal spirit guides or angels. Some are drawn in by energy of the God light which the mediums have created by prayer. Or an earthbound spirit is able to see the aura light surrounding a medium and follows that light to the meeting.

THE MEDIUM

A **medium** is a channel between the physical world and the spirit's environment. There are different types of mediums; natural mediums, experienced mediums, control mediums, trance mediums, and raw mediums. Each work differently, each intuitively. Hereafter, I will refer to the medium as "she."

A psychic may or may not, be a rescue medium. Some choose to be readers. They communicate directly with the spirit when giving or receiving a message. Some psychics choose to rescue spirits and send them into the light. Each profession is important, needed, and useful.

Most mediums mentally communicate with a spirit mind-to-mind. Some sense a spirit, but cannot see it, while others perceive the spirit as an image in their mind's eye. Commonly, mediums sense the spirit's thoughts, or see symbols which identifies the spirit's message. With the assistance of spirit guide(s) and/or angel(s), she will mentally tell the spirit to stand back while they are communicating. Through mentally communicating, she will learn why the spirit has not crossed over into the light. She will then assist the spirit in releasing its fear or disbelief and explain how it can enter the God Light. The medium doesn't judge a spirit. She acts with compassion and is willing to help all who come to the rescue circle.

Only one **head control medium** is selected to direct each meeting. She should be knowledgeable in all aspects of mediumship, well trained, and intuitively guided to direct a rescue. She is the only person allowed to leave her seat and move about the circle while assisting other mediums.

A **natural medium** *is* intuitive. She may sense a spirit's present by an icy chill, a coolness, or feel a slight pressure on her back where the spirit is standing. When a spirit is near, some mediums can sense the spirit's thoughts, emotions, mannerisms, and speaks in the spirit's voice. She will mentally communicate with the spirit to determine why it has not crossed over into the God light. This mental communication is a non-verbal exchange of emotions which will take only several seconds or a minute to guide the spirit into the light. Often the medium will see realms of angels guiding the spirit into the God light.

The **experienced medium** often calls upon her spirit guides and/or angels to assist, or mentally images a path of white light on which the earthbound spirit may travel to the light. She may send out thoughts which the spirit can see as flashes of light, or tentacle of color. The spirit reads the colors as we would read words. Mentally projecting a message to a spirit is as easy as sending a thought. Thoughts have energy, and energy can move a spirit.

A **trance medium** work quite differently. The trance medium's soul slips out (trances out), or partially slips out of her physical body. This act may occur with, or without, the medium's consent. It may occur willingly or unwillingly, or unbeknown or uncontrolled by the tranced medium.

When the trance medium's soul is out of her physical body, a spirit can easily slip in and take control. Because the soul has slipped out of the medium's body, she may or may not be aware of the spirit's thoughts or understand the spirit's predicament. She must rely upon the head control medium to take charge and assist in crossing the spirit into the next dimension.

A **raw medium** has the ability to sense or see spirits, but hasn't learned how to communicate with it. She may sense the spirit but doesn't know how to stop it from influencing her daily life. This often occurs in very young children who are 'raw,' still open to the spirit world. As a child grows up, she should learn how to use her sixth sense to its fullest ability.

A **control medium** works quite differently. She has the ability to breathe a spirit into her body, connect mind-to-mind with it, yet keep control of the spirit. Just because a spirit has entered her body doesn't mean she is possessed. The spirit can only temporarily coexist within a control medium for several minutes, or until she releases it. She can exorcise the spirit from her body at will. A control medium will connect with the spirit's thoughts, emotions, and speak with its voice. Using mental communication, she will learn why the spirit is earthbound, then instruct it how to release the memory that holds it earthbound. She will instruct it how to cross over into the next dimension, then release it from her body.

Allowing a spirit to enter the medium's body may seem scary or dangerous to the average person. However, to a control medium, it's quite spontaneous and intuitively natural to breathe a spirit into her body. With the protection of the spirit guides and/or angels, the control medium stays in control, mentally and physically. She is never frightened while coexisting with a spirit. She realizes that she is only a channel, and can exorcise the spirit from her body at will. She need only huff it out. Because she is spiritually connected she has the protection of her spirit guides, and of course, God.

Coexisting with a spirit may seem like a form of temporary possession, but it is not. The control medium can expel the spirit from her body upon command. My intuitive reaction to release a spirit is to raise my hands over my head as if taking off a sweater, then mentally thrust the spirit out of my body. This raised hands position allows the spirit to slip out of the medium's body easily. Each medium may use a different method to release a spirit, but usually acts upon the method she intuitively receives.

All mediums communicate with their guides and/or angels using the intuitive right side of their brain. A control medium never allows a spirit to access the right side of their brain, which is the intuitive side of the brain.

CAUTION: I don't recommend attempting control mediumship unless you have the natural ability and are trained by an experienced medium. I have taught, off and on, for nearly fifty years, and have never taught the technique of breathing a spirit into the body. Control mediumship should be a natural, spontaneous, and an intuitive reaction.

BEFORE ENTERING THE GOD LIGHT

The following story deals with a person's existence *after* physical death, *before* it enters the God light. The reader will observe the mediums as they communicate with the spirits and analyze the fear that holds them earthbound. As you read each story, keep in mind that spirits are disembodied people existing in another dimension. They deserve the respect as if they were a member of your own family. The following is an example of a rescue circle in progress.

SUICIDE

This was to be my first attempt at rescue mediumship. The mediums placed their chairs in a circle, situating their chairs between the students to balance the energy, and the lights were dimmed. This evening, June Black was acting as the head control medium.

June began. "Remember, students, stay seated. An empty seat leaves an open space where an uninvited spirit can enter. While seated in the circle formation, you are protected by the white light. Anyone sitting outside the circle is less protected. If I leave my seat to assist another medium, I will mentally ask my spirit guide or guardian angel to protect my empty chair."

The members closed their eyes and begin slow, deep breathing to slow down their brain waves. With each deep breath, they mentally drew the energy in, sending it through their body, then mentally directing the light outward, into the center of the circle.

June continued. "The energy should never come from your physical body, but *through* your body." June opened the meeting with a prayer. "We sit with love and understanding. We ask our guides to stand by for protection, guidance, and directions. We ask for the highest spiritual assistance we are capable of using."

With closed eyes the mediums visualized a white light, then mentally projected it around their body. Now they were ready. They sat quietly, waiting for a spirit to make its presence known.

Within minutes, a coolness spread throughout the room. The chill is an indication that many spirits are gathering outside the circle.

I felt an icy chill collecting on the left side of my body. I sat still and waited to connect with a spirit.

The room became icy cold and eerily silent.

An icy breeze touched my cheek with a feather-like contact. It felt like a spider web touching my face. I twitched to brush off the tickling. With closed eyes, I intuitively breathed in and mentally connected with a spirit. Immediately, I sensed the spirit's panic. My fingers curled as if gripping something tightly. I grimaced as my facial muscles tighten up.

June moved across the room, and in a pleasant British accent, asked, "Marie. You have someone with you?"

"I see a man hanging onto the window ledge. He's clinging to the ledge of a very high building. He's looking down at the street below."

June knelt down and touched my hands. "May we help you?"

I took a deep breath, and with this deeper connection, became aware of the spirit's fears, emotions, and mannerisms. I sensed his body as it was when he was alive. "The man is frightened. I think he wants to commit suicide. He's afraid of falling."

June continued softly and reassuringly. "I'm going to take your hands. Can we help you?"

I felt June's hands on mine and knew the spirit felt them as well. "He wants to pull his body up to the window."

"How long have you been there?" June knew that if she asked a question, the man might concentrate on the answer and forget his fear of falling.

"He's been here a long time, years, since the Great Depression of 1931. He lost a lot of money in the stock market. He's weak. He can't save himself. Fear of falling is the last memory."

June remained calm. It was time to release his fearful thought pattern. In a rhythmic, mesmerizing voice, she chanted. "You are safe. It's over. You are safe now. Let go."

I intuitively breathed the spirit deeper into my body. No one had

27

taught me how to do this. It came as a natural response. My voice turned masculine and panic stricken. "I can't let go. If I do, I'll die."

Knowing that spirits can be persuaded with words, June began chanting words that would convince the spirit to release his fear of falling. She continued in a mesmerizing chant. "Feel yourself drifting toward the ground. I'll guide you. See, you are drifting down. . . Drifting down."

"He let go. I see him floating down." Once the man believed he was safely on the ground, I felt my fingers loosen and a sense of relief spread across his mind.

"You're on the ground. You're safe. You're ready to go to the God light." June again chanted softly. "See the God light. Go to the light."

I intuitively raised my hands over my head, and my body released a slight quiver. I felt the spirit slipping out of my body. In my mind's eye, I envisioned the man as spot of energy, rising up and entering the light. I opened my eyes and smiled. The spirit had crossed into the next dimension. The rescue was complete.

Is rescuing earthbound spirits what the Council of Spiritual Counselor had intended? In retrospect, I believe I had been a rescue medium in many past lives because the act of mediumship came naturally, without hesitation or fear. Rescuing earthbound spirits may be one of my current life mission, my soul's purpose. I believe each person comes into this life with many missions to accomplish, mine is to help spirits.

THE RELUCTANT MEDIUM

Now that you have observed the way an average rescue meeting works, let's examine the inexperienced medium, and the problems that can occur.

Pearl became a natural healer, and although mediumship made her uncomfortable, she had agreed to participate. "I'm here to create energy, but I don't want to communicate with a spirit." Tonight she watched the mediums with apprehension, wondering if the mediums were making things up.

June sensed Pearl's disbelief. She wanted to assure Pearl that mediumship is real, but explaining it was not proving. Unsure of how to convince Pearl, she mentally asked the guides to handle the problem.

The spirit guides and angels were already handling the problem.

Pearl had been watching the mediums for quite a while when she began squirming and twitching uncomfortably. Suddenly, a masculine, rowdy roar came from her mouth. "Ha, ha, ha!" Pearl stiffened upright in her chair, as if trying to regain control over her physical body. Her eyes widened and panic set in when she realized a spirit had entered her body. "It's a fat man," she shouted, aware that she actually knew who it was.

June hurried across the room and took Pearl's hands. She sensed this was happening because of Pearl's doubt, and this experience was necessary for Pearl to believe in the truth of mediumship. So, although Pearl seemed frighten, June remained calm and confident.

"Ha, ha, ha. . ." Pearl's coarse laughter exploded again, and her face took on a masculine expression. "Get him out of me!" she bellowed in her own voice. She wriggled and twisted, as if trying to back away from the spirit.

June sensed the spirit guides were hovering nearby and were orchestrating this experience. She tightened her grip on Pearl's hands. "Watch your medium. Watch your medium," she chanted to the spirit guides. June held a reassuring pressure on Pearl's hands. "It's all right. It's just a man who . . ." She snickered at the impressions she was receiving. "He finds it very amusing that he's inside such a 'big-boobed' woman." June let out a faint chuckle. "Those are his words, not mine. Relax, Pearl. It's all right." June again addressed Pearl's spirit guides. "Watch your medium."

Pearl burst into another involuntary round of lusty laughter. "Ha, ha, ha, ha. . ." Within a second or two, Pearl forced the masculine expression from her face, stiffened up in her chair, and again demanded in her own angry voice. "Get him out of me! Get him out, *now!*"

June raised Pearl's hands up toward the ceiling, pulling gently with a slight upward motion to ease the spirit up and out. "Be calm, Pearl," June murmured as she projected a calming energy and asked the spirit guides to lift the male spirit up and out. "I'm sorry this happened, but your spirit guides had to assure you that these rescues are important, and they are real."

"Well, I didn't like it at all," Pearl grumbled when she realized that the male spirit had left.

June searched Pearl's eyes to be sure the spirit was gone. Often, a spirit's presence can be seen in the eyes as a mist or whitish film. Pearl's eyes were clear and sparkling blue. When June was sure the spirit had gone, she lowered Pearl's hands.

The class began snickering at the comment the male spirit said upon entering the body of such a well-endowed lady.

June raised her finger to her lips, quieting the group. "I'll explain all this after the circle is closed."

Pearl folded her arms stubbornly over her chest, and her lips pouted downward. She was angry and felt violated. She sulked for quite a while at the unwanted experience, before relaxing enough to lower her brain waves once again. Pearl spent a few minutes in mental communication with her spirit guides, making it clear that she did not appreciate this unwelcome invasion of her body.

Even though this experience was frightening to Pearl, June explained why this temporary possession had taken place. June sensed Pearl's doubts but felt certain that the spirit guides would take charge and resolve the problem.

If Pearl had continued thinking the members were untruthful, her body would give off negativity energy, thus draining the positive energy from the circle. Pearl had to be convinced that mediumship was real, and that earthbound spirits need help. She had to be convinced that helping spirits to the God light was a responsibility and a privilege to be taken seriously. The spirit guides had presented proof of mediumship by allowing Pearl to experience the existence of a spirit firsthand. They knew she would be safe because qualified mediums were present.

Even though Pearl objected to the uninvited brash male spirit, it validated her belief in mediumship, and gave her confidence in the protection of her own spirit guides. Pearl is now convinced that mediumship is real and was given the best proof by her experience.

THE BLESSING

Several days later, I was attending a psychic workshop where June would be teaching meditation. The women had placed their chairs in a circle formation and closed their eyes.

The room became pleasantly silent.

With my eyes closed, I felt the room assembling energy, compressing a force to fit the space within the circle. It was as if the atmosphere was growing solid matter.

June closed her eyes, scanning the circle within her mind's eye to find the source of energy. "Marie? You have someone near you?" she asked, sensing where the unseen energy was collecting.

I felt a sacred, compassionate energy compressing itself into my body. It felt like billions of protons, neutrons, and electrons were assembling inside me. Even though I sensed my body growing enormous, I had no fear, only an intense feeling of absolute love and perfection. The massive power continued to increase until my body felt huge. My arms felt as large as the trunk of a giant redwood, and my mind intellectually omnipotent. I sensed a Supreme Being was expanding within me. If this spiritual being was visible, it would have risen over the room, towered above the roof, and rose miles up in the sky.

June did not approach as she usually would have. She remained seated and bowed her head.

With this omnipotent power expanding inside me, I felt an unconditional love for all. The wisdom of the ages was flowing through my mind. As the power of love intensified, I knew I was in the presence of a supreme being. I sensed the being was a male angel. Intuitively rising to my feet, I stood with my arms extended outward and the palms of my hands open toward the circle of women. *A blessing!* I bowed my head, acknowledging the omnipotent presence.

June spoke softly. "Everyone, open your eyes. We are receiving a blessing."

The members opened their eyes.

Though I felt enormous, the members saw no physical change in my body. I don't know how many, or if all, the women felt the overwhelming feeling of unconditional love that I was experiencing. Realizing that I was in the presence of an archangel, I bowed my head as the blessing flowed through my hands. When the blessing was over, I felt my body settling back down in my seat. Slowly, the feeling of compassion and supreme wisdom was slipping from my mind. The truth of the ages was escaping me. Oh, how I wanted to hold on to the universal wisdom, but it continued to fade until I once again felt normal. I knew this angel was not of my dimension and the unconditional love was not of my dimension, either. When the angel was completely gone, I felt empty-hollow. I was left with only the awareness of this immediate lifetime. It seemed so little.

June's soft voice broke the silence. "We have just received a blessing from an angel. Mentally bless this being and thank him for coming."

The women bowed their heads and mentally prayed, each in their own way.

June waited several minutes, then began the closing prayer. "We thank you, God, for the glorious angelic experience and for your protection and guidance tonight."

I will never forget that evening. Now, I am certain that spiritual beings are in communication with God and had granted our group an extraordinary earthly visitation. An angel had visited our circle and had honored us with a blessing.

It's impossible to explain this experience in human terms. There are no words to convey the intense power of wisdom and unconditional love for all that flowed through me. The density of my body felt as if molecules of energy had compressed themselves into a solid mass within me. Within that density was a serene feeling of peace and the wisdom of the ages. It's difficult to explain unconditional love because very few people have actually experienced it.

MEDITATION

Meditation is the act of slowing down the brain waves to see images within the mind's eye. Meditation stimulates the pineal gland located in the interior of the brain, thus opening the third eye to sense or see images beyond normal sight. The third eye is located behind the forehead between the eyebrows. When the brain waves have slowed down, the medium is able to sense the higher vibrations of the spirit world. Meditation lessens anxiety, increases imagination, activates creativity, thus improves one's self-image and a positive outlook on life.

While in meditation, I have seen spirits manifest in different ways. Most spirits can be felt as an icy chill or a wisp of cool air. Friendly spirits often appear as misty shadows of light, blurry images, or fragments of a spirit. They transmit a positive energy, filling the atmosphere with comforting lightness. On the other hand, sinister spirits often appear as dark, shadowy images that permeate the atmosphere with heaviness and transmit a feeling of fear. Though I have seen different kinds of spirits, I had never seen one manifested itself in a three-dimensional physical form until I examined ectoplasm.

ECTOPLASM

Ectoplasm is a misty, greenish energy which is created by a group of mediums through long, intense meditation. This takes time, an hour or two of sincere, deep meditation. The mediums produce this energy with their mind, which then flows from their body. As the energy accumulates within an area, it forms a greenish haze called ectoplasm. This energy cannot be seen with the naked eye, but certain cameras have captured the ectoplasm on film.

When the spirit appears in the misty-green ectoplasm, it will manifest as a three-dimensional body. The spirit then can be seen with the naked eye. Because most mediums are not able to produce an adequate supply of ectoplasm, the spirit will not appear as a whole image, but may appear as a partial form or a misty image.

Nineteenth-century physiologist Charles Richey first used the term *ectoplasm* to describe a strange material that seemed to flow from spiritual mediums during a séance.

The dictionary definition of ectoplasm is as follows: "A supernatural, viscous substance that is supposed to exude from the body of a medium during a spiritualistic trance and form the material for the manifestation of spirits."

In addition to the dictionary definition, I believe ectoplasm is a powerful energy created by intense mediation. Through my own experience, the mediums did not enter a trance. They remained alert, conscious while in a meditative state of mind.

A TEST TO CREATE ECTOPLASM

Tonight, only the most advanced mediums were invited to attend this meeting. They were seated in a semi-circle in the living room of June's home. The living room was open to a dining room, and beyond that was an open door to a kitchen. The dining room table was shoved against the wall, clearing a space where three slats of wood were stacked upright to form the shape of a pyramid. This symbolic pyramid would collect the energy as it flowed from the mediums.

June began the meeting. "Today, we will go into a deep meditation to create ectoplasm. After you're completely relaxed and are deep in meditation, mentally direct energy toward the pyramid. Please be patient. This will take an hour or two. Eventually, the build-up of mental energy will create a greenish fog-like substance which the spirit uses to manifest itself into a three-dimensional form. During mediation, open your eyes from time to time and check on the space next to the pyramid. You will actually see the spirit with the naked eye."

The room quieted down as the mediums prepared to meditate.

June began with a prayer. "We sit with love and understanding. We ask our spirit guides to stand by for protection, guidance, and directions. We ask for the highest spiritual assistance we are capable of using. Our intent is to create and learn about ectoplasm."

The mediums closed their eyes and began slow, deep breathing.

This was my first attempt at intense mediation. I had never heard of ectoplasm before and wasn't sure what to expect. After achieving a relaxed state of mind, I concentrated on my forehead—the third eye. I had been meditating for about half an hour when I opened my eyes. Much to my surprise, I saw a greenish fog had filled the kitchen. I blinked several times. *Yes, it definitely is a green fog.* Again, I closed my eyes. A half hour later, I opened my eyes. The kitchen appeared foggier, and the green color more pronounced. I watched the greenish mist drifting from the kitchen until it filled the dining room. The mist was settling beside the pyramid.

While directing my concentration on the mist, a human shape began to form. *It's the outline of a man. This is amazing. I can see the form with my naked eye.*

June's voice broke my concentration.

"We are coming back. Take a slow, deep breath, then slowly exhale. Breathe in deeply and open your eyes. The meditation is now ended."

The mediums opened their eyes, amazed and impressed by the greenish mist that was now fading

"Let's discuss what we have just seen. Did anyone see the spirit?"

Each medium offered her interpretation of the ectoplasm, and what they had seen and learned.

"Why did greenish mist gather in the kitchen, the farthest distance from the medium?" I asked.

No one had an answer, but all were amazed that they had produced the ectoplasm. Because it was getting late, the meeting came to an end.

I never had another opportunity to participate in creating ectoplasm, so I may never know why the mist formed farthest away from the mediums. Nor do I know why it flowed toward the pyramid. The mental energy was not seen coming directly from the mediums, but the result was an accumulation of greenish fog confined within the room. Though it was an interesting experiment, I found it too long and drawn out. Also, it took too much time to produce an effect. It was easier for me to close my eyes, take a slow deep breath, and if the spirit was willing, it would step forward and I would see it in my mind's eye. I write of this experience to show what can be accomplished by intense meditation. There is no moral or conclusion to this experience. Just a fascinating experiment that satisfied my curiosity.

MESSAGES DIRECTLY FROM SPIRITS

I believe spirits enter the dimension according to their spiritual awareness, thoughts, intentions and/or actions. The following brief messages are from people shortly after their demise, and some directly after entering the God light. The stories offer knowledge gleaned from each brief message.

Thirty years after my mother's demise, a strong thought crossed my mind. I understood her to say to me, "I'm going to a school of higher learning. If you need me, I will be there."

I glean from this brief encounter that my mother was leaving her current dimension, and rising to a higher dimension. It appears she is able to tune into my daily life quite easily. Notice she didn't say, "call me." I believe this was a definite assurance that she would be present long before I even thought of calling for help. This suggests that spirits who have been in the God light for many years are capable of tuning into many people's thoughts simultaneously. This confirms my belief that there are different dimensions of afterlife. The School of Higher Learning could be a dimension where the spirit continues its education. Perhaps this sacred level might be required for some souls before they reincarnate into the earthly dimension.

The day after my friend Pearl passed away, I sat down to meditate. I wanted to make sure she had crossed over into the God light. I closed my eyes and in a matter of seconds, Pearl's image appeared in my mind's eye. She didn't appear in a female form as I would have expected. She appeared as a misty glow. I sensed Pearl was standing in awe of something before her. I didn't see what she saw but did sense the immense grandeur of the dimension she had just entered. I didn't hear words but sensed her thoughts.

"Heaven is more than I expected. It's beautiful."

Pearl was raised Catholic, so her perception of heaven may coincide with her beliefs. However, it seems she saw much more than she expected to see.

I mentally sent a message. *"Did you see your mother?"*

As Pearl received the question, I saw a mist of light speeding toward her from a great distance. I sensed her to call out, *"Mama!"* Then, I saw Pearl as an ethereal glow, moving with great speed toward the misty light in the distance.

I glean from Pearl's remark that she saw what she expected to see—a heavenly dimension. I believe she had not completely entered the God light yet because she didn't mention the compassion and love that a spirit feels when it is engulfed in unconditional love of the God light. I feel certain that as Pearl adjusts to the spiritual realm, she will enter the God light and experience the sacred power of love.

Several months after my brother passed away, I was sitting quietly in my living room. I had not closed my eyes but was completely relaxed. My brother's face appeared across the room, near the ceiling. His face wasn't misty or transparent. I can't be sure if I saw him with my eyes or within my mind's eye. He was smiling down at me, and I mentally picked up his message.

"I'm pleased you shared your inheritance with your children. I had a hard time during my passing."

I mentally blessed him. Then, as quickly as he came, he was gone. This encounter lasted only a few seconds, but I was so pleased that he was able to contact me, and that he now understands why I was interested in the paranormal.

I glean from his brief encounter that my brother knew what had occurred during his demise and also what is currently happening in the earthly dimension. Even though he had no interest in the paranormal or belief in the afterlife when he was alive, he was able to communicate with me. Evidently, he has now learned that psychic ability can be used as a means of communication. His joy at my sharing his inheritance shows that he is still the same good-hearted, decent person he was all his life.

Several years after a lady friend, Kitty, had passed away, I was sitting quietly in my living room. I wasn't meditating nor contemplating connecting with a spirit. My eyes were open, yet I saw Kitty hovering near the ceiling. Whether I saw her with my naked eyes, or in my mind's eye, I can't be sure because her face was lifelike and her features distinct. She appeared at peace and blissfully happy. I received her message as a thought.

"Now I understand." She smiled, pleased that I had recognized her.

Even though Kitty passed away at the age of ninety-four, she presented herself as she would have been in her youth. She looked to be about thirty years old. Her eyes sparkled with happiness. Her hair was no longer white. It was the same dark brown it would have been many years ago. Her face was beautiful, her skin absolutely flawless. Not a single wrinkle. When Kitty was alive, she had been skeptical of the paranormal, afraid of what she couldn't see or understand. Apparently the fear disappeared when she entered the God light.

I glean from this very brief encounter that Kitty, after being in the God light for several years, had acquired a new awareness. She now understood why I had studied the paranormal. There was no indication of the spiritual realm she now resided, but her presence gave an impression of being contented and happy.

This is not the last time I saw Kitty. Years later, while attending a funeral, I sensed Kitty standing in front of me. She had come to be among her friends and family. I could feel her joy as she mingled among the people. Several minutes later, I saw her standing beside her daughter. I wished I could have informed her daughter of her mother's presence, but it wasn't the right time, or the right place.

I attended the funeral of Mary, an elderly neighbor whom I had known many years. As I stood in front of her casket mentally offering a prayer, I sensed a male spirit standing behind me, specifically noticing his shoes. I sensed it was Mary's husband who had passed away many years before. Mary was standing beside him while he showed her how she looked in the casket. There was no emotion or sadness. She offered no regret or complaint about her passing. It was just a matter of observation.

I glean from this brief encounter that we meet with our loved ones in the afterlife, and that some accept their death without regret or emotion.

A young woman named Carrie joined a church that believed that upon death, the soul would sleep until God blew a horn, then all the deceased would rise from their burial sites.

When I heard of her death, and knowing of her misguided belief, I feared she would be held in a thought pattern of sleep, and would not be enter the celestial dimension of heaven. I went down into a deep meditation to make sure she crossed over into the light.

I was guided to begin in an unusual manner. I had never opened a meditation like this before, but sensed this preparation was spiritually necessary. I begin by imaging a sacred circle in the middle of my living room. After bowing my head in prayer and making the sign of the cross twice, I felt I was ready to communicate with Carrie. I put a pad of paper on my lap, held a pencil ready to write, and closed my eyes. After several slow, deep breaths, I searched within my mind's eye.

Grayish, misty clouds appeared, roiling and churning angrily.

Though I tried, I was unable to penetrate the mist. I mentally called out. *"Carrie! Are you here? Wake up."*

Through the darkness, I envisioned a whitish form tumbling in a vast space. Sensing it was Carrie, I tried to make contact by calling her name. After an hour of trying without success, I ended the meditation, determined to try again tomorrow.

The next day, I again set a pad of paper on my lap, held the pencil tightly, and begin slow, deep breathing. After entering at relaxed state of mind, I mentally called out her name. *"Carrie, are you here?"* This continued for more than half an hour. Suddenly, though I didn't see her image, I felt Carrie's excitement and heard her message as a thought in my head.

"Wow! That was beautiful."

My hand began automatically writing her message. *"The energy you see is what I know."*

Hum. That was a strange answer. I sensed Carrie was referring to the colors of energy emanating from my mind or hand as I wrote. My personal spirit guide took over my hand and wrote.

"Carrie is doing fine. She is very happy. She sees what she wants to see." There was a pause, then the writing began again. *"Carrie has left us now. She's not interested. Carrie saw your presence as glowing energy and doesn't understand some of this. Remember, all this is new to her. She will study. She has a lot to learn."* The writing stopped. My spirit guide was gone, and Carrie was gone as well.

I glean from the spirit message that Carrie had awakened to her new environment without fear. I sensed her amazement as she viewed the vastness of the dimension she had just entered. Perhaps, in time, she would adjust to this dimension and learn to communicate with her angels.

My job was done. I was sure Carrie had passed into the light because she was not frightened, just curious of her new surroundings. I believe she had not yet reached the most sacred spiritual sphere because she didn't mention the unconditional love that encompasses the heavenly dimension. She had not reached her ultimate heaven. She only saw what she expected.

Even though I wasn't privileged to view this heavenly dimension, I sensed its vastness and grandeur. There may be a reason that I couldn't see next dimension. Perhaps it was my inability to retain a deep meditative state, or my guides blocked me from seeing this dimension. Perhaps the dimension is to remain a secret until it is our time to enter the heavenly light of God.

One day, while automatic writing, I received a message from Sara, a young woman who had passed away more than seven years ago. I had known Sara for many years, and was interested in what dimension she now existed, especially in what she had learned. The message came through my mind as thoughts, and my hand automatically wrote her message.

"It is so beautiful here. We are all so happy. We all want you to be happy, too. We're here together with our family. We are working on all things that were left undone on the earth plane. Things we should have addressed while on earth. I have learned to have compassion for all. Tell all to take a look at the shoes others walk in. Then decide if you had walked in those shoes, what you would do? I no longer judge others. The worst of human faults is to judge. We are not all alike. We each came into the earth with different goals, different lessons. Let those lessons belong to those who seek out to learn. Be at peace. We understand what the true value of life is about. Be at peace because I am happy here. I am filled with love each and every day. I see what is necessary that I did not fulfill while on earth. So now, I strive to correct all that I missed. Be at peace."

After a while, Sara's energy started to fade. She was stepping back. I mentally sent her loving energy. Thinking of her in a positive and loving way had increased her energy, and I felt her coming back.

"Yes, now I have renewed my energy. I received it from your love. Do you understand that love is energy? Do you know how we exist in love energy?"

Before I could thank Sara, my hand stopped writing. Sara was gone.

I glean from this message that a person has the opportunity to correct the mistakes he or she made during its recent incarnation. I took special notice that Sara said the word "we" are working on our mistakes. I sensed Sara was referring to those family members, who now existed in the next dimension with her. So, it may be that there is a way to make corrections in the afterlife.

Upon hearing of a young man's untimely demise, I went down into mediation to make sure he had passed over into the God light. When he was alive, he had been a church elder, so I assumed he would know what to do.

In my mind's eye, I saw him frantically running in all directions, frightened because he didn't know where to go or what to do. I mentally sent a message. *"Relax. It's okay. You must go to the God light. Then, in time, you can reincarnate back into the earth plane."*

He continued running frantically, waving his hands in the air. I tuned into his thoughts. He recognized me, but even my voice didn't calm him. The word 'reincarnation' had scared him, and he was looking for a way to be born into a physical body. Again, I mentally sent a message. *"You're not going to be reborn immediately. You must go to the God light first."*

After the young man calmed down, he was able to see a light growing brighter in the distance. As it came closer, he began drifting toward it.

As I viewed the scene, the man's image changed into a misty, white cloud drifting toward the light. My work was done. He was heading toward the light.

I glean from this encounter that even though he was an elder in a church, he was unprepared to enter the God light. Apparently, this church did not discuss reincarnation. It certainly would have made his entrance into the next dimension much easier to accept.

In the middle of the night, I received a phone call that a prominent public figure had died in an automobile accident. The man had been drinking at a political affair and was driving over a bypass when his car careened off the bridge and fell into the bypass below. Having met this man several times, I was concerned that he might not understand what had happened to him. I closed my eyes, slowed down my brain waves, and tuned into the accident. In my mind's eye, I envisioned the man having an out-of-body experience. He was hovering in midair, looking through the darkness at his wrecked car. I tuned into his thoughts.

"I can't believe I did this."

Within seconds, the scene faded and I could no longer see or contact the man.

I gleaned from this brief encounter that even though he died in an accident, he felt no pain and wasn't frightened by his demise. I sensed that because he was an intelligent man; he had accepted his culpability in the accident. Though he acknowledged his mistake, he did not relate to it as a sin. He realized his unwise behavior was a lost opportunity to live out the entirety of his life. He had no guilt about what had happened, nor did he fear God would punish him. Since I could no longer see him, I surmised he had been drawn into the God light.

I was attending a memorial service for Martha, a close friend. Many years ago, Martha and I had attended psychic awareness classes, so she was well prepared for her transition into the next dimension. After she moved away, it had been years since I had seen her family and wasn't sure I would recognize her children at the memorial.

From across the crowded room, a young man called out my name.

Upon recognizing Martha's son, the words spewed from my mouth, calling out his name with immense joy. I reached out and hugged him. Though it was my arms that embraced the boy, it was Martha's soul that had slipped into my body. She was using my body to hug her son. As she held him in my arms, I felt the love flowing to her son. There were no words, only the feeling of a mother's deep maternal love.

I glean from this brief encounter that Martha, now in spirit, knew how to enter a medium's body. She used the medium's physical body to channel love to her son. This may have happened to you without your knowledge. You may have been prompted by a spirit to give a message or comfort a loved one. You may have been influenced to act in concert a spirit's prompting.

After passing into the God light, a spirit may experience the effects of karma. Spirits feel emotion and are affected by criticism from the living. There are many aspects of karma such as: The spirit may hear a friend or family member's gossip regarding their previous earth life. Gossip is another way karma confronts the spirit. The spirit may not like what it hears, but it is a way for the spirit to learn what he/she did while on earth.

Karma is not a punishment. It's an opportunity to recognize one's mistakes and correct those errors in preparation for the next incarnation.

When speaking ill of the dead, remember, they can hear you. They are emotionally affected when faced their own actions.

6

HAUNTING

After working with the paranormal for many years, I've learned that some people unknowingly create their own destructive energy. I don't judge why people create their own negative situations. I offer these stories so the readers can look deeper at their own actions and perhaps change their lives for the better.

Not all hauntings are caused by spirits. An extremely **over-active mind** can create enough energy to move objects or cause weird noises. A **disturbed person's mind** can, willingly or unwillingly, knowingly or unknowingly, generate energy powerful enough to nudge, push, or strike a person without any physical touch. One doesn't need to be psychic to feel the effect of an over-active mind. It can be felt by the average person as a nervous, tense irritation. This phenomenon, when active, is often mistaken for poltergeist activity, i.e. a noisy spirit, although an over-active or disturbed mind has nothing to do with mischievous spirits.

A person who is **constantly angry** can create a friction that alters the atmosphere within an area. If the anger continues, that friction can accumulate and emit an uneasy feeling in the room. A living person's extreme anger can create a violent energy which can be felt or sensed as tension or irritation. If the anger is intense and constant, that energy can accumulate and form a swirling tornado of energy within a room. This twisting energy may be accompanied by a crackling, thumping, or rapping sound, and can transmit a tense or edgy feeling. Over a long period of time, the twister can become a vortex, which will open a space in the atmosphere where like-minded angry spirits can enter.

A person's constant **negative attitude** can accumulation into a mass of negative energy and can be seen or sensed by psychics as a slow-moving ball of mist. It is usually gray or black, rarely has sound, and transmits a depressing, heavy feeling. The size of the misty energy depends upon the intensity and/or the accumulation of negativity. I have seen a negative ball of energy at least six feet in diameter, and it emitted a dull heaviness in the room. Negative people are susceptible to becoming pessimistic when they remain in its environment over a long period of time.

Spirits often have the same habits, thoughts, feelings, and flaws as they had when they existed on the earth plane, therefore, they are likely to be attracted to their likeness. A living person's positive attitude will attract a positive spirit, while a negative attitude will draw in a negative spirit.

Most people have a natural protection against possession, such as the clear white aura that surrounds their body. Prayer or positive thoughts will also create a protective energy. Prayerful thoughts have been seen by psychics as pure light, white light, blue or orchid waves of light. However, an evil spirit may be drawn into a home by the resident who dwells on evil intentions. The atmosphere in the house will be dark and sensed as heavy. The house will remain haunted until the person's evil intentions cease. The best way to protect yourself from evil is to walk in the light of the God consciousness. That means, being emotional engaged in or connected to unconditional love and concern for all. God *is* light. God *is* love. White light is a protection and, like a prayer, can be a comfort to those in need.

JOSEPH THE RESIDENT SPIRIT

A house may be haunted by the spirit of a deceased person, a relative, a friend, or even a wandering spirit. Many people have felt or sensed a disembodied presence while nearly falling asleep. So, we wonder, why are those spirits still hanging around? Why haven't they crossed over to the other side?

After physical death, most spirits travel through a swirling tunnel of energy into the God light. The spirit enters a dimension according to its previous thoughts, intentions, deeds, or actions. Commonly, the spirit is drawn by the light into the dimension of celestial peace, harmony, and unconditional love without a problem. However, if the person is unaware of an existence after death, or doesn't believe in the heavenly dimension, it may remain in familiar surroundings. Thus, it may haunt its own home.

During the time I was attending the mediumship classes, my family and I moved to the northern suburbs of Michigan. We had lived peacefully in this house without any problems for nearly a year. It was around that time when my teenage daughter complained that her twin-sized bed was too small. She claimed it felt like someone was lying next to her, nudging her to one side. Because she was half asleep, she brushed it off as an annoyance. After several weeks of restless nights, the nightly presence became more noticeable, and she was waking up more often.

At first, I overlooked her complaints, passing them off as teenage imagination. But, as I continued the psychic classes, I became more psychically sensitive, and noticed my daughter's bedroom seemed cooler than the other rooms. Everything I had been learning suggested there was something unusual about her bedroom, and I was determined to find out what it was.

One morning, after the family left the house, I laid down on my daughter's bed, fluffed the pillow, and closed my eyes. I did as I had been taught in class, took several slow, deep breaths to slow down my brain waves. When I felt relaxed, I closed my eyes and concentrated on my forehead, my mind's eye. I had been lying quietly for several minutes when I heard a scratching sound on the wall. My eyes popped open. *That sound is close to my head.* I scanned the room from side to side.

The faint scratching sound continued.

It sounds like an animal crawling behind the wall. This sound is real. Not something I'm sensing. My thoughts turned to logic. *Maybe the furnace turned on, and the heat ducts are creaking. No. The furnace isn't on.* I lay still and listened. *It sounds like the claws of an animal moving through the heat ducts.*

After a while, the scratching stopped.

I heaved a sigh of relief, closed my eyes, and lay very still. An uncanny silence permeated the bedroom, and an eerie coolness swept over my body. I shuttered, folded my arms across my chest and opened my eyes, again searching the room. Even though it was daylight, the bedroom took on an eerie haze. When I was sure there wasn't a spirit in the room, I took a deep breath and again closed my eyes.

I had been laying quietly for several minutes when suddenly, the strong scent of gardenias smashed into my face. My eyes popped open and in one leap, I was off the bed. I landed in the hall without my feet ever touching the bedroom floor. Now I was convinced. *There is something in this room. No wonder my daughter doesn't like sleeping here.*

Several days later, I arrived at the psychic workshop and poured out my unsettling experience.

June, having been an active psychic for over forty years, didn't seem surprised. "Go in the bedroom and mentally communicate with the spirit. Tell it to come to our rescue circle, so we can help it."

I nodded in agreement. I had never done this before and wasn't sure I could do it, but was willing to try.

The next day, I sat on the edge of my daughter's bed and closed my eyes. *Am I really living in a haunted house?* I took several slow, deep breaths until I felt relaxed. I concentrated on my forehead, and within my third eye, I saw the partial image of a man's white shirt fading in and out. Suspecting it was a male spirit, I mentally communicated with him. *"Can I help you?"* Even though I heard no voice, I sensed his thoughts. He was upset that I could see him.

"You can't see me!"

"Yes, I can, I mentally responded.

"No one can see me! I'm dead!"

"Yes. I can see you. You're a man."

The vague outline of the white shirt faded in and out until the vaporous image became more visible. The man was of average height with a heavy-set body. He seemed curious that I had made contact with him.

"Do you want me to help you?"

Again, his answer came as a thought. *"You can't help me! No one can help me out of this darkness. There's no place to go."*

"Don't you believe in God?"

The image shrugged, as if to say, "what's the difference?"

I continued mentally communicating. *"Will you come to our rescue circle? I have friends who will help you."* I sensed he wasn't sure what to do, and within seconds, his image faded away. I was surprised at how easy it had been to communicate with him, and that it had only taken a few minutes. I wasn't sure if he agreed. *I wonder if he understood.*

The following day, I mentioned the experience to my husband.

"That's nonsense! Don't go believing in that stuff." He wasn't ready to accept ghosts and wasn't willing to discuss the matter any further.

"But there is a man in the bedroom."

"What are we supposed to do about it?"

"I'll take the spirit to class next week. Then we'll see what can be done."

"Well, do whatever it is you're supposed to do. You're the one who went to school for this." He hurriedly walked away, unwilling to deal with the problem.

The following week, I returned to the bedroom and mentally relayed the message to the spirit. He was to follow me to class. Although I sensed the spirit's presence, I didn't know if he had agreed. It wasn't until I was driving to class that evening that I felt an entity in the back seat of my car. I smiled. *"He did hear my message. Could I actually be doing this? Is there really a ghost in the car with me?"* I entered the classroom and greeted June with a friendly wave.

June smiled and nodded. "I see you brought some spirits with you."

I nodded, then frowned curiously. *Why did June say spirits? I had invited only one.*

The members placed their chairs in a circle formation and began slow, deep breathing. With closed eyes, they visualized a white light, then mentally sent the light around their bodies and into the circle.

Tonight, Claudia was in training, and would act as head control medium. Claudia was a bright, cheerful lady with a severe handicap. She was born a partial paraplegic and had been confined to a wheelchair most of her life. Since her worldly activities were severely limited, the mediumship classes gave her a way to maintain an active life.

Even though I was doubtful of Claudia's ability, I sensed it was safe to continue because June would be present to oversee each spirit rescue.

Claudia recited the opening prayer. "We sit with love and understanding. We ask the spirits guides and the angels for protection, guidance, and directions. We ask for the highest spiritual assistance we are capable of using."

I closed my eyes and searched for the spirit in the white shirt to present himself. After a while, I opened my eyes and scanned the room. *Why can't I sense the male spirit?*

June raised her hand, motioning for Claudia to assist her.

"Yes, June. Do you have someone with you?" Claudia's wheelchair was placed in front of June. She held June's hands and connected to the spirit. Claudia spoke in a soft voice. "Can we help you?"

June, with eyes closed and head bowed, nodded. "It's a male spirit. He's been watching us. He thinks this is all very stupid."

"No, this isn't stupid. Can we help you?" Claudia smiled and applied a gentle pressure to June's hands, and her friendly touch drew the spirit closer.

June, being a control medium, breathed the spirit into her body and allowed it to use her voice. "What are you ladies doing?" the spirit asked in a deep, masculine voice.

"We're here to help you." Claudia answered.

"You can't help me. I'm dead."

A faint smile slipped across Claudia's face. "Yes, we know. Who are you?"

June, mentally linked with the spirit, sensed he was trying to remember his name. She waited patiently while the spirit mulled over the question. "Joe!" he called out in a masculine voice. "Yeah. Joseph's my name."

"Where did you come from, Joseph?"

"From my house. The house that lady lives in now," he said, pointing June's finger in my direction.

That's my spirit. He's the one I brought. I sat very still, curious why he didn't come through me.

"How did you get in that house?" Claudia asked.

June continued. "I used to live there. I have no place to go. It's dark everywhere."

"Why don't you call your guardian angels?"

June sat very still, giving the spirit time to mull over the question while the spirit projected a curious look across her face.

"Don't you believe in guardian angels?"

A frown appeared on June's face as the spirit again contemplated the question. "My wife was a bitch when I was dying. I couldn't get out of bed, and she was mean to me."

Claudia squeezed June's hands to assure the spirit. "Well, you're all right now, aren't you?"

June's body leaned forward in a manly pose, pulled her hands away from Claudia's grip and planted June's hands firmly on her knees. "When I was sick, my wife wouldn't turn the heat up in my bedroom. I got so cold, I put newspapers over me to keep warm." June leaned back, and the spirit slipped a satisfied grin across her face. "But I got even. I scared the hell out of that bitch after I died."

Claudia avoided the spirit's comment. "It's all over now. I want you to call your guardian angels. I don't care if you don't believe in them. Just call them and see what happens."

June smiled, then spoke in her own British accent. "He can jolly well see them."

"You can go with those angels if they are of the white light," Claudia told him.

"Yeah, but, listen! What if I don't want to stay where they take me? Can I come back if I don't like it there?"

Claudia smiled. She didn't know the answer, but assured him anyway. "Yes. If you ask your guardian angels, they will let you come back. But you must go with them now."

"Wait! I used to have fun in that house. Those people are real nice. I enjoyed being with them. Can I come back and visit them this Christmas?"

Claudia wasn't sure if this was possible, but felt it was important to assure him. "Yes. You can come back at Christmas."

"Okay then." June took a deep breath, opened her eyes, and her own facial expression returned. She raised her hands over her head and released the spirit from her body. "Wasn't he interesting?"

Claudia was pleased with the rescue and her wheelchair was pushed back to her place in the circle.

"Wait. Just a minute!" A high pitch voice called from across the circle.

I was surprised because the voice had come out of my mouth. As I spoke, I realized a spirit had slipped into my energy field. I sensed the spirit was a small woman, under five feet tall, and well over eighty years old. My voice changed, and I began speaking in short, rapid phrases, like a nervous person would do. "Joe's my neighbor. I used to live across the street from him."

Claudia's wheelchair was moved quickly across the circle toward me. "Marie. You have someone with you?"

I nodded. "It's an old woman."

"Where did you come from? How did you get here?"

The woman's voice came through me in short, quick spurts. "I saw a light around this lady from across the street, so I came here. My neighbor, Joe, lived across the street before he died."

Claudia was so surprised that this woman was aware of another spirit that she answered in a stammer. "Well, ah, do you want to call your guides?"

The woman's high-pitched voice again spoke through my mouth. "Yes, of course! Goodbye and thank you." I raised my hands over my head and felt the spirit slip out. In my mind's eye, I saw a ribbon of white mist floating toward a spark of light in the distance. When the ribbon of light was out of sight, I opened my eyes and lifted my hands over my head. I acted spontaneously, as if I had done this many times before. I never hesitated or wondered what to do. The whole process seemed so natural. "The woman went to the light."

Claudia closed the meeting with a prayer, thanking the angels for their assistance. The lights were turned on, and the chairs were immediately moved out of circle formation.

Several months later, on Christmas Eve, after putting gifts under the tree, I went to bed and fell asleep. A short while later, I was awakened by a light slap on my behind. Sensing a presence, I closed my eyes and searched within my mind's eye.

Joseph was looking down at me, smiling. From the vast space, I saw beautifully wrapped Christmas boxes hovering overhead. A feeling of joy filled my senses as I watched the gifts tumble down in slow motion. I mentally sensed Joseph's message.

"Hi, kid. I said I'd be back. I'm happy where I am." With his words came the overwhelming feeling of peace and contentment. As the image of Joseph faded away, I heard him say. "Thanks, kid!"

I lay awake for a long time thinking about the Christmas gifts that I had been given. They were the sincerest gifts I had ever received, and I would never forget the love that came with each beautifully wrapped package.

Several days later, I set out to confirm the evidence. Up until that rescue meeting, I didn't know that the spirit, Joseph, was the former owner. After inquiring in the neighborhood, I learned that Joseph had died in my house several years before we moved in. Only now did I realize we had purchased the house from Joseph's widow.

June knew nothing about the former owner, nor the circumstances of his death. Yet, she received the name "Joseph." Further confirmation came from the spirit's statement, "I got even with the bitch." When I moved into the house, there were three locks on the master bedroom door. One was a slide bolt, and two were hook and eye locks. The three locks confirmed that Joseph did frighten his wife just as he said. The woman had put the locks on the door to keep the ghost of her husband out of her bedroom. The three locks and his statement proved that he did frighten his wife after he died.

As to the identity of the old woman who lived across the street, I knew nothing of her until I spoke with the neighbors. They confirmed that an old woman had lived across the street long ago. They further agreed that the woman was just as I sensed her to be: a very pleasant, wiry woman.

This rescue solved the problem in the bedroom. Although I didn't tell my daughter of the spirit encounter, she no longer felt uncomfortable and began sleeping in her bedroom without complaint.

For days after the rescue, I was still bubbling with excitement. I wanted to tell someone, but it was 1970, and psychic phenomenon were looked upon with suspicion. So, although I was bursting with pride at my first house haunting rescue, I could tell no one. This rescue had released two earthbound spirits and allowed them to pass over into the God light.

In retrospect, if I hadn't developed my psychic ability, I might never have known our family was coexisting with a spirit. Joseph's disbelief in the hereafter held him earthbound, and because he didn't know what to do, he remained his home. When his wife, now widowed, sold the home and moved out, Joseph coexisted peacefully with my family, unaware there was another place for him to exist.

Many people have sensed the presence of a spirit as they are about to fall asleep. A person doesn't need to be psychic to experience a spirit visitation. Psychic awareness is heightened when the brain waves slow down and the mind and body are relaxed. Spirit have been known to pop in and check on their family from time to time. Spirit that visit occasionally are not usually earthbound, and can return to the next dimension at will.

DENIM JACKET

Claudia, a young woman in her early forties, was partially handicapped and had spent most of her life in a wheelchair. She had previously trained in the paranormal for one year under the watchful eye of June's classes. Even though she had attended only several rescue circles, she felt she was ready to begin training in the responsibilities of a head control medium.

Several months into Claudia's training, June phoned to say she wouldn't be able to attend the next meeting. Claudia was thrilled when asked to act as head control medium in June's absence.

The winter sun had already set and the moon showed little light this evening. Several members and I arrived early to practice psychometry before the meeting began. Psychometry is the act of sensing and then reading the vibrations on an object. The medium holds an object, such a watch, ring, glasses, etc., in her hand and mentally tunes into its vibrations. With closed eyes, she may sense information about the owner of the object.

David, a tall, lanky man in his late forties, was fascinated with the paranormal. He had previously participated in several months of psychic awareness training but had no experience with mediumship. He arrived at the meeting carrying a man's dirty denim jacket. He scanned the room, looking for someone to do tell him about the shabby jacket. "Marie. Will you do psychometry on this jacket?" he said, then tossed the jacket on the floor.

I picked up the jacket, closed my eyes and began slow, deep breathing. After a while I envisioned a shadowy figure of a man moving back and forth in the darkness. A sense of horror swept across my mind. My eyes popped open, and I hurled the jacket to the floor. "This man's dead!" I grumbled, startled by the unexpected, horrifying scene still vivid in my mind.

"Yeah, I know. Tell me how he died." David tossed the jacket back, grinning in amusement.

This time, I was prepared. I picked up the jacket, closed my eyes, and took a slow, deep breath. I mentally called upon the guardian angel to protect me from any intense emotion. As my fingers moved through the rough denim, images began to appear. "He's taken drugs," I said in a low, monotone voice. "I see a young, dark-haired man in his mid-twenties. He's wearing a denim jacket. He's slender to the point of being too thin." With eyes still closed, I watched as the scene unfolded. "He seems to be up high, like the ceiling of a garage. I see wood beams. He's got a rope around his neck. He's swinging back and forth. He's swinging…. Oh my God! He's hanging by his neck." My eyes popped open, and I scowled at David. "Here, take this," I said, then threw the jacket on the floor.

"I know how the man died." David grinned mischievously. "I wanted to see if you could tune into the jacket."

"I don't like doing this. It's awful!" I grumbled, disgusted by David's bizarre humor.

The members placed their chairs in a circle formation, alternating students between the experienced mediums. The lights were dimmed and Claudia begin the meeting. "Close your eyes. Mentally say a prayer for protection, then mentally cover yourself with white light."

The room grew quiet.

As I meditated, doubts of Claudia's inability crossed my mind. Though I felt she wasn't prepared to handle this meeting, I sensed it was safe to continue.

Claudia began the opening prayer. "We sit with love and understanding. We ask our guides to stand by for protection, guidance, and directions. We ask for the highest spiritual assistance we are capable of using, and that this meeting be a learning session. Please send only those we are capable of rescuing."

Several minutes passed as I waited for a spirit to present itself. After a while, I raised my hand to let Claudia know I wished to speak.

Claudia nodded, acknowledging the request. "Yes Marie? You have a question?"

"I think David's going to bring through the young man who committed suicide." I relayed the message as I had intuitively received it from my spirit guides.

Claudia turned toward David, but seeing nothing unusual, she shook her head. "No, he's not. I don't see anyone around him."

"Well, I believe he will," I replied politely.

"No! No! There's no one with David," Claudia insisted. She wasn't ready to accept what she couldn't see.

David remained strangely quiet most of the evening. Suddenly, he stretched his neck out and began flailing his hands in the air. "Whee, I'm flying!" His eyes remained closed, and his body swayed from side to side. It was apparent a spirit had entered David's body.

Ellen, Claudia's personal assistant, hurriedly pushed Claudia's wheelchair in front of David.

Claudia tried to grab David's hands, but he was a big man and his hands were held high, nearly out of her reach.

David's body began swaying in a slight circular motion. With his hands over his head and his neck extended, he started gasping for air, as if he were choking.

Claudia had never seen a medium out of control before and didn't know what to do. When his hands were within her reach, she grabbed them and hung on tightly. "Calm down. You're okay. You're all right now."

David continued swaying from side to side, then his body gained momentum until he was reeling out of control. His eyes popped open when he realized a spirit had entered his body. Stricken with fear, he tightened his grip on Claudia's hands and squeezed them tightly. He wanted to tell her that he was frightened, but a spirit had taken over, and with his neck stretched out, he couldn't speak. David's eyes closed and his body slumped down in his chair. His head fell to his chest and his body went limp, giving the appearance that his soul had slipped out of his physical body.

A startled silence spread across the room. The new students were wide eyed and terrified. They had never witnessed a medium trance out before. An atmosphere of fear permeated the dimly lit room.

Claudia panicked when she realized David had tranced out of his body.

Knowing that she couldn't communicate with David because he was no longer in his body, she wasn't sure what to do.

David's body swayed from side to side, and the spirit within tightened its grip on Claudia's hands.

"Help me! He won't let go," Claudia cried out, twisting and turning, trying to wrench her hands free from David's vice-like grip. "He's hurting my hands." As her fear rose, her lack of confidence begin to siphon off the positive energy in the room.

Ellen tugged and pulled, trying to wrench Claudia's hands free them from David's vice-like grip. But David was strong, and wasn't about to let go.

Suddenly, my spirit guides took over. I was on my feet, forcing myself between Claudia and David. I grabbed David's hands and yanked them off Claudia's hands. As soon as Claudia's wheelchair was rolled out of David's reach, the spirit guides begin directing my movement. I placed my left hand on David's forehead, holding him upright. "You. . . are. . . slowing. . . down. Your head is. . . not spinning. Your head is… not spinning." The words flowed from my lips in a low, commanding voice. "You are slowing down. You are calm. . . You are calm. . . There! Now you are still." Even though I had never seen a medium trance out before, I had responded intuitively. "You are slowing down. You are not spinning. You are not swinging."

David seemed unaware of anyone else around him. His neck stretched out and his head rose as if he were hanging. "Whee! I'm flying," David shouted as his body swayed in slow motion from side to side.

In my mind's eye, I saw the image of a boy dangling by his neck at the end of a rope. *This is the spirit that tagged along with the denim jacket.* Being influenced by my spirit guides, my voice continued in a soft rhythmic chant. "Slowing down. . . Slowing. . . down." I shifted my hand to David's shoulder to brace him upright. "You are slowing. . . down. You are quiet. You. . . are. . . all. . . right."

After a few minutes, David's body slowed down, and he was now swaying in a slight circular motion.

"Watch your medium! Watch your medium!" I warned, cautioning the spirit guides to protect David. Even though all this was new, the words came spontaneously. "Your mind has stopped spinning. You're at peace. You are at peace."

David, responding to the repetitive soothing chant, stopped swaying. Suddenly, his head dropped to his chest and his hands fell limp at his side. His slouched body signaled that the spirit within him had fallen into a stupor.

The spirit guides mentally informed me, that even though the boy died, he was still under the influence of the drugs, and its effect had not worn off. Knowing that his quiet state of mind was temporary, I had to move fast. "This boy will complete his drug withdrawal on the other side." I intuitively begin chanting softly. "You are calming down. You are calm."

David's body went limp, and he appeared non-responsive.

When the new students saw David slumped in his chair, their fear rose, depleting the energy in the room. With less energy, the guides would find it difficult to relay any communication.

I sensed this spirit should be guided out of David's body quickly while he was still dazed. Within my mind's eye, I saw two white figures standing at a distance, waiting to take the boy to the light. I continued in a soft, mesmerizing voice. "Look behind you. You see two white angels. Go toward them. You. . . will. . . go. . . to. . . the angels. Go." I opened my eyes and waited for any movement from David.

David slumped into a lifeless position. This slouched position indicated that the spirit had slipped out of David's body. After a second or two, David's awareness slipped back into his body. He opened his eyes, straightened upright in his chair, and glanced around the room. "What happened? Who got shot? Did somebody kill someone?"

I nodded to Claudia, acknowledging it was time for her to take over.

Claudia hurriedly ended the meeting with a prayer. "Class, mentally thank God and your guides for protecting us during this rescue. Thank you, God. Quick! Move your chairs out of circle formation.

The group mentally thanked their spirit guides for the privilege of rescuing the earthbound spirit. The chairs were moved out of the circle formation, and the meeting came to an end.

After class, Claudia explained to David what happened after he tranced out. David claimed to know nothing of swinging by a rope, the overdose, or the suicide. He recalled a scene that involved a gun. He felt someone had

---

been shot. No one in the room sensed a gun, but then, no one witnessed the death scene from David's out-of-body perspective.

David unknowingly had brought the spirit to the meeting with the denim jacket. He didn't realize that spirits can tag along with personal items. It's also possible that the guardian angels had guided the boy to the meeting for the sole purpose of being rescued.

Since this was the first time I assisted a drug-induced spirit, I don't know if all people who die while under the influence of a drug must complete a withdrawal on the other side. Though I sensed, in this specific case, a withdrawal was necessary. The spirit guides informed me that the spirit would sleep for a while, and when he awoke, he would become aware of the angels hovering around him. Even though this suicide appeared to be a drug overdose, it may or may not have been intentional.

This rescue demonstrated the importance of having an experienced head control medium. Claudia's physical handicap didn't hinder her ability to act as a control medium. However, her fear and inability to handle this tragic situation had drained energy from the circle. If Claudia had more experience, she might have prevented David from trancing out completely. She might have coached him to remain in his physical body, so he could assist in sending the spirit to the light.

In retrospect, I wonder if the spirit guides had presented this difficult case to prepare the mediums for similar rescues in the future. If so, it certainly proved to be an emotional training session.

You may wonder why was an earthly contact was necessary to release this spirit to the light.

Through many years of experience, I have learned that some spirits, while in between dimensions, are unable to release their emotions. They may feel sad, but are unable to cry. The same principle may apply to the release of a drug-induced state. It took several minutes of soothing, repetitive chanting to alter the spirit's disoriented state of mind. After the spirit had released some of the drug's effect, he was able to follow the spirit guides into the God light.

Several days after this rescue session, I still felt exhilarated and regenerated with energy. I was overwhelmed with the feeling of joy that the boy had been helped, and grateful for the knowledge I had learned to help drugged spirits.

been shot. No one in the room sensed a gun, but then, no one witnessed the death scene from David's out-of-body perspective.

David unknowingly had brought the spirit to the meeting with the denim jacket...

REINCARNATED TOO QUICKLY

All people, you and I, have personal spirit guides that assist us throughout our lifetime. They have been with us since our birth. They guide us daily by sending mental messages as thoughts within our mind. However, when life becomes unbearable, some people are unable to hear the message.

Tonight, several new students joined the psychic workshop. I noticed the new student, Pattie, hadn't spoken to anyone and seemed ill at ease. Feeling a need to befriend her, I placed my chair next to her.

June usually started the meeting with a lecture on the benefits of meditation, but today her lecture was on suicide. June had never lectured on why a person would take their own life, so I was surprised when, for the second meeting, she again addressed suicide as a wasted lifetime.

The room became quiet as June began the meeting. "We sit with love and understanding. We ask God for protection, guidance, and the highest spiritual intervention we are capable of using. Sometimes we don't realize the importance of each lifetime. This life should not to be taken for granted, nor should it needlessly be thrown away. Each life in important. Remember, you may not get another chance to reincarnate as quickly as you would desire."

After the meeting ended, I made an effort to welcome Pattie by inviting her to the local restaurant for coffee. While we chatted, I sensed a frailty within her, and that she was dealing with a serious matter. Even though I encouraged her to talk, she only spoke of trivial matters.

Several weeks later, I received a phone call from June. "Marie. I just heard from Pattie, the new student. I was mopping the kitchen floor when a song kept playing across my mind. *This time we nearly made it, didn't we girl.* I sensed someone was trying to communicate with me, so I closed my eyes and tuned into whoever was present. Within my mind's eye, I saw the new student, Pattie. She came to thank me for trying to help her. She said she couldn't handle this life any longer and had committed suicide."

Later that day, I learned that Pattie had closed the garage doors and sat in the car with the motor running. By morning she was dead. Though I didn't know the girl very well, nor the circumstance of her health or life situation, her suicide took me by surprise. I now assume she had come to the meetings to find peace in meditating. Sensing a need to contact Pattie, I closed my eyes, took several slow, deep breaths. After feeling completely relaxed, I mentally called Pattie's name. In my mind's eye, I saw her crouched on the floor of her bedroom, terrified of the birds outside her window. I sensed Pattie's fears had intensified beyond her control, and she chose to leave the earth-plane rather than live in fear.

Though I heard no voice, the message was clear. *"I reincarnated too quickly. I didn't select a strong enough body. I'll get a stronger body next time, so I won't commit suicide again. Thank you for trying to help me."*

Pattie's image began to fade. I took another deep breath and drew her back.

"I tried to commit suicide several times before but failed each time. I finally did it. Tell my husband that I'm sorry. I just couldn't stay any longer. He doesn't realize how frightened I was." Pattie's words faded, and her image faded as well.

I share this story to pass on the knowledge that I've learned from this tragedy. Because there wasn't enough energy for Pattie to remain in the earthly dimension, I didn't take time to ask for the details of her passing. I assume from Pattie's message that she had entered the light because she didn't say she was in a dark, scary place. Therefore, I assume she had passed into the light without fear of reprisal. After Patty entered the light, she became aware of her higher self—her soul. Now that she was in spirit, she recognized her suicidal tendencies as a trait she had carried through many lifetimes. I truly believe that God's love is absolute, and his compassion is infinite, and that He wouldn't judge her actions negatively. God knows what anxiety she was dealing with. *He* is the only one who understood her fear and reason for her actions.

I make no judgment on Pattie's suicide. I'm grateful that she returned briefly to the earthly dimension to thank June. However, don't think Pattie walked away from this quite so easily. There is karma to her actions. She still has to face this imperfection in her character. She still has to overcome the defect in her next incarnation. I don't condone suicide, nor do I take her actions lightly. I'm just relaying the encounter as it occurred. I feel suicide is a waste of a valuable lifetime.

With Pattie's new enlightenment, she now recognizes that only a part of her came to earth for the physical experience. Her true self-her soul-remained in a higher celestial dimension, while her physical body experienced an earthly existence to overcome the flaw in her character. The soul is eternally omniscient, but the physical body exists for only a limited number of years on the earth.

THOUGHT PATTERNS OF FIRE

A spirit may be earthbound because it can't release the memory of its horrifying death. It may haunt the place where the tragedy occurred, often reliving the same horror over and over again.

Claudia was still in training and had never investigated a haunted house before. She was pleased when she received a phone call asking for help.

"Hello. I understand you're psychic, and. . Ah. . . . I've got a ghost in my house. Can you help me?"

"Who is this? What's the problem?"

"My name is Hazel. I hear strange eerie noises in my house. There's a scratching sound in the living room. It's coming from behind the wall."

"Maybe there's an animal between the wall."

"No," Hazel replied impatiently. "It isn't an animal. Last week I saw a mist over the bathtub. But when I stepped into the bathroom, it disappeared. There was no reason for the bathroom to fog up. It was dry."

"Tell me more." Claudia said. Her curiosity had been piqued.

"When I put my hand in the bathroom, it felt icy cold. But, when I stepped into the room, the cold disappeared. I'm sure there's a ghost. I'm so frightened I'm ready to sell this house."

"Has anyone else said the house is scary?"

"I talked to the neighbor about my house. He said new owners move in every few years." Hazel lowered her voice and whispered. "No one mentioned ghosts."

"I'll make arrangements to have a rescue circle come to your house."

"What's a rescue circle?"

"A group of mediums will sit in a circle in your living room. We'll meditate, and tune into the house's vibrations. We'll try to find the reason for the strange sounds."

"Thank you so much."

Claudia was thrilled at the prospect of rescuing a spirit from a haunted house and immediately telephoned June. "I have a request to clear a haunted house. Are you available next week?"

"No, I'm sorry. I've already made appointments for next week."

"Do you think I can do this alone? Most of the mediums will be new students. Marie is the only one who knows about haunted houses."

"I'm sure you'll have no problem," June said, sensing there would be no danger. "Hold the meeting in the evening when there is less natural light. It's easier to see spirits in a dimly lit room."

Claudia telephoned the members and invited them to Hazel's house.

Twelve members and I accepted the challenge. I wasn't sure if Claudia could handle the haunting, but sensing no danger, I agreed to assist. If I had sensed anything evil, I would have warned her.

It was autumn, and the setting sun cast long shadows across the living room. As the members arrived, they walked through each room with their hands held out, feeling for cool spots in the air. Several students stood in the bathroom waving their hands, feeling for an icy spot, but the room remained a normal temperature.

While waiting for the sun to go down, Claudia cautioned the students. "Be sure to listen for strange sounds. If we can't find an answer, Hazel may have to sell her home."

The members placed their chairs in a circle, alternating experienced mediums between the students. The lights were turned off, except for a small light in the kitchen that barely lit the living room.

"Hazel, I want you to join us in the circle. You should stay and watch," Claudia said.

Hazel nodded in agreement. "Why are the chairs in a circle?"

"Because the circle will hold the energy that we create with our prayers."

Hazel dragged a chair across the room and placed it in the circle formation.

After Claudia's wheelchair was moved in the circle formation, she began the meeting with instructions. "No one is allowed to leave their seat. An empty chair could leave an opening for uninvited spirits to enter. Mentally fill the room with white light and ask your guides for assistance and protection."

The members drew in a deep breath, then exhaled, slowing down their brain waves. They imaged a white light entering their bodies, then passed it through their hands, and into the center of the circle. With bowed heads and eyes closed, they waited for a spirit to make its presence known.

The room grew eerily quiet.

A faint scratching sound came from behind a wall.

My eyes popped open. I scanned the wall, then closed my eyes and searched within my mind's eye but saw nothing unusual.

Everyone else had opened their eyes and were staring at the wall where the scratching sound was heard.

The room grew icy cool, and a feeling of terror permeated the atmosphere.

Even though the students sensed the fear, they closed their eyes and listened, unsure of what had caused the scratching sound.

Something is in the living room with us. With closed eyes, I visualized a woman at the kitchen doorway, peeking in the living room. She appeared to be about forty years old with dark hair and dressed in dark clothing. A single strand of pearls encircled her neck. She appeared curious and moved from behind the doorway.

The pearls immediately drew my attention. I sensed they represented a gift given with love. The word *stepmother* came to mind. I mentally conversed with the woman. *"Come! We're here to help."*

The woman remained at the doorway, reluctant to come forward.

Again, I mentally spoke to her. *"We're here to help. Can we help you?"*

The woman didn't appear to be afraid, only curious. After a minute or two, she disappeared.

I opened my eyes and spoke softly, letting Claudia know what I had seen. "There was a woman standing by the kitchen door. She was watching us. She's gone now."

Claudia turned toward the kitchen door, but seeing no one, she answered. "I'll watch for the woman."

Several minutes passed in silence, and the students shifted nervously in their seats.

With eyes closed, I envisioned a teenage girl standing across the room in the darkness. "Claudia. We have a teenage girl here. She's watching us."

"Tell her to come into the circle."

"She's confused. She won't come any closer." I began conversing mentally with the teenager. *"We're here to help you."*

The girl stared suspiciously but didn't reply.

The guides instructed me to respond with specific words. My voice softened as I spoke. "Send love and peace to this young girl. Pray that she sees the truth of her situation."

The group prayed silently, each in their own way.

"She's coming closer to the circle," I whispered.

"What does she want?" Claudia asked, squinting to see the image.

"She's standing in the center of the circle wondering how she got here." Realizing the girl was confused, I again communicated mentally. *"We're here to help. Do you know you are dead?"*

The girl appeared to be analyzing where she was. A frantic expression crossed her face when she realized she was no longer alive.

Sensing the girl's panic, I mentally sent a calming message. *"It's all right. You're all right now. See! You're whole. You don't hurt."* I waited several minutes, giving the girl time to focus on her predicament.

The girl was now standing in the center of the circle. She appeared calmer, but still puzzled.

Suddenly, an eerie scratching sound came from behind the wall.

The girl's eyes grew wild, and she stared at the wall.

She's concerned about her brother. "Do you have a brother? Can we help him?"

Panic swept over the girl's face. Her eyes darted from one side of the room to the other.

A sudden flash of heat penetrated my body. "Oh my God! The girl died in a fire," I said, just loud enough for the group to hear. "Her brother is in a toy box against the wall!" I pointed in the direction where the scratching sound was heard. "He was burned alive."

The student's eyes popped open, and they stared at the wall.

Claudia's frantic voice called out. "Tell them there was no fire."

I knew it would be difficult to convince the girl there was no fire when she was reliving the last frightening moments of her life. Softening my voice, I chanted rhythmically. "It's all over. You're all right. Your brother is all right, too. The fire is over." I waited until the girl had calmed down, then said, "Call your brother. Tell him to come out."

The girl appeared terrified, still frantically searching the room.

The girl is concerned about more than one child. The spirit guides prompted me to speak, and words flowed from my mouth. "Everyone is fine. Tell them to come out! Call them!" In an effort to calm the girl, I mentally created the image of a peaceful white light wrapping around her body.

Several minutes later, a medium called out. "I see a small boy in the circle. He's looks like a five-year-old."

I vaguely heard Claudia's excited voice in the background giving directions, interrupting my train of thought. Again, I mentally directed a calming energy to the center of the circle.

A medium whispered across the circle. "I see something blurry in the center of the circle."

With closed eyes, I frowned, searching through the darkness. Several hazy images were now milling about in the circle.

Barbara, being more experienced, broke the silence. "I see shadowy figures of two children. I don't know if they're boys or girls. They're being drawn toward the circle. I get the impression they're still frightened."

Even though the students didn't see the images, they followed their maternal instinct and began praying, mentally sending peace and love to the spirits.

"They're afraid," Barbara whispered.

Claudia's voice quivered with tension. "Ask your spirit guides to help them."

Hazel frowned, uncertain of what was happening. She wasn't psychic and wondered what the women were seeing, if anything at all. Still, she was curious, so she sat quietly and watched.

The blurry image of a teenager moved in the darkness.

She's looking for two other children.

The face of the woman with a pearl necklace peeked from behind the kitchen door.

I sensed the woman's thoughts. *The necklace was given to her by her husband. That's why I noticed it so clearly.* I spoke softly to Claudia, so I wouldn't startle the spirit. "The woman is standing by the kitchen door again. She died in the fire."

Claudia turned toward the kitchen door. "Come out. Let us help you."

The woman seemed unsure and didn't move.

"Come! Bring your guardian angel with you," Claudia coaxed.

An icy chill spread across the room as the misty figures moved within the circle of darkness.

Claudia, feeling the atmosphere turning cooler, whispered to the members. "Send more light! Send love into the circle."

As I watched the blurry figures milling about the darkness, I realized they were feeling the soothing effect of the white light and were starting to release their fear. *They followed their sister into the circle. They believe the fire is over.*

Within seconds, the shadowy figures began fading from the circle.

Although I didn't see the children, I sensed they had followed their sister into the light. The woman was gone, as well. The circle was empty. I spoke softly. "The God light has opened the entrance into the next dimension. They're gone. They're okay now."

The mediums stirred uneasily but remained seated. Somehow, they sensed it wasn't over yet. Several minutes passed, and the room had become eerily quiet.

With closed eyes, I noticed a male spirit at the front door. He leaned in the doorway and searched the living room.

He's the father. He must have died recently. He's checking on his family.

When he was satisfied all his family had left, he disappeared as well.

"They're all gone, I said aloud.

"Break circle," Claudia called out, relieved that the spirits were gone, and the meeting had come to an end.

The members quickly moved their chairs from circle formation and began milling about the rooms with outstretched hands, feeling the atmosphere in the house. When they first arrived, the rooms felt dismal and unusually cool. But now, as they investigated, the house seemed warm and peaceful.

"The house does feel different," Hazel agreed. "Maybe I won't have to sell the house."

The memory of the fire had trapped the spirits, binding them to their earthly state of mind. They existed in the *now* of what they believed was their reality. The teenage girl had been so engrossed in saving her brothers and sisters that she wasn't aware the fire was over, or that she had died. The children, still trapped in their individual traumas, didn't hear their sister's voice until the mediums filled the room with white light. Then, and only then, did they see their sister and believe the fire was over.

The mediums agreed that the man at the front door could have been the father, and that he had died years after the fire. So, even after his own death, he still felt a parental responsibility, and didn't rest until his family was released to the light. It's possible that in concert with his angels, the father orchestrated this rescue. It's also possible that his deep concern for his family had sent a message to the universe. Any sincere cry for help, whether it comes from a living person or a spirit, projects a colorful display of energy, much like a human aura. His concern would have been seen by the spirit world, and the angels were eager to help. Perhaps there is more assistance from the world beyond than we realize.

THE DOLL HOUSE

Intense arguments can create an irritating feeling throughout a house. If the arguments continue, they can create caustic pulsating vibrations. This may cause the residents to feel irritated, angry, or even vindictive. If the resident's anger continues over a lengthy period of time, friction can build up and create an opening in the atmosphere. This opening is called a vortex—a portal from which entities from another dimension can come and go. The more severe the argument, the larger the portal opening.

June received a phone call to investigate the strange atmosphere in a teenager's bedroom. The woman claimed something unusual was affecting her daughter and the whole family. June agreed to investigate.

The following afternoon, June and I arrived at a large colonial house in an upper-class suburb of northern Detroit, where we were led into a large family room. I stood at the doorway and closed my eyes, searching the room within my mind's eye. *This room doesn't feel scary. I don't see a ghost, just sense a jerky vibration in the atmosphere.* I opened my eyes when I heard June and the woman talking.

"Who lives in your house?" June asked.

"My husband and I have three school-age children and two older children," Pauline answered.

June sensed the jittery energy thrashing through the family room, but that wasn't her main concern. She turned abruptly, and though she had never been in this house before, she started up the stairs. Guided by her intuition, she headed straight for a bedroom at the front of the house.

Pauline trudged up the stairs, and I followed close behind, into a long hall with four open bedroom doors.

Without hesitation, June headed toward a room at the end of the hall. She stood with her hands on her hips, peering into the room. A disgusted expression crossed her face when she sensed a vortex of swirling energy in the center of the room. "Is this your teenage daughter's room?"

Pauline nodded, "Yes, it's Martha's room."

"Has she been arguing a lot? Is she more defiant than usual?"

"Yes. She's having problems at school, and we argue about her boyfriends. She wants to stay out late at night, so we fight about that, too."

"Marie, tell me what you see." June said, encouraging me to use my natural intuition. "I want to confirm my own impressions."

I stepped to the doorway, closed my eyes, and took a deep breath to slow down my brain waves. "I see flashing energy swirling through the ceiling. There's a black hole. It's a vortex. It's an opening to another dimension." The words spewed from my lips even though I knew very little about vortexes.

"Yes, that's right. This opening was caused by the constant arguing. The teenager let her temper get out of control in this room. What else do you see?"

"I sense a whirling motion in the center of the room."

"That's right. What does it look like?"

"Just a spiraling mass of energy! It's dark and negative, like a black hole." There was no doubt in my mind what I was seeing, but it was not what I had expected. I was still in training and found this an unusual kind of haunting.

"You expected to see a ghost, didn't you?"

With a nod of my head, I opened my eyes and asked. "Shall we take this dark force out?"

"There's not much point in that." June turned to Pauline. "Do you and your husband argue a lot?"

Pauline edged her way to the door and peeked in cautiously.

"Sometimes, but it's just our way. We don't mean anything by it!" Pauline replied, dismissing the matter with a casual wave of her hand.

"You'll have to change your ways. Your arguments are causing an irritating friction in this house. Are your children extremely active? Do they bicker a lot?"

"Yes! A lot of the time." Pauline frowned, irritated by the personal questioning.

"Hum! I see."

Pauline looked up at the ceiling. "I don't see anything. How can we get this ghost out of here?"

"It's not a ghost," June replied, then stepped into the center of the bedroom. "It's an energy force."

"It's bothering my daughter. Martha is always arguing with her brothers and sisters."

"As long as she continues to argue, the vortex will remain open."

"What's a vortex?" Pauline asked, staring suspiciously at the ceiling.

"It's an opening to another dimension. If we neutralize this negative energy, we can't be sure what might come in its place. No! Your daughter has to change her ways if she wants the vortex to close."

"Okay. I'll talk to her," Pauline mumbled.

"When your daughter stops arguing, phone me. Then we'll see what else needs to be done." June knew that the teenager's temper had intensified the destructive energy. "If she doesn't stop arguing, this force will grow stronger. This can get worse. It's up to your daughter. She can change her ways, or your whole family will have to live with this agitating energy!"

Pauline grimaced, taken aback by the accusatory criticism. "What about the other kids? She fights with them all the time. Can you do something about that?"

"These are your children. It's up to you to stop them from arguing. If you don't, you'll continue having trouble." June shook her head in disgust, closed the bedroom door, and headed down the stairs.

Having never encountered this kind of haunting before, I thought I had the answer. "You can start by filling your house with white light," I said to Pauline.

"How do I do that?" Pauline asked as she made her way down the stairs.

"Just imagine a beautiful white light all around you. Then mentally cover your house with the light. That will be your protection," I said, sure that was the correct solution.

"That's fine," June answered. "But what will happen when they start bickering again?"

I stopped in my tracks. "I hadn't thought of that."

"When the children act up again, their anger will siphon off white light."

"Oh, I see! The protection has to start from within the house," I replied, confident this time I had the right answer. At the time, I didn't connect the teenager's hostility with the jerking motion in the family room. But now, as I studied the situation, I realized that all the children the had contributed to the irritating vibrations.

"No," June answered. "The protection starts within the soul. Even if you put white light around this house, it will be depleted when the arguments escalate. Peace starts from within. Love is the energy that will protect this house." June turned to Pauline, and looked at her sternly. "Change your ways and you won't have so many problems."

"What about that evil spirit upstairs? There's still something in that bedroom."

"It's not evil, and it's not a spirit. It's negative energy. Try being less argumentative."

"Okay. I'll talk to the kids," Pauline grumbled, disappointed that the problem wasn't solved.

On the ride home, I questioned June. "Couldn't we have taken the negative energy out?"

"No! I feel the teenage girl will have another temper tantrum. If we remove that dark energy, there's still an opening in that space. We don't know what else will come in. It could be worse."

"Can more than one spirit come through that portal?"

"Yes. Not just spirits. Different kinds of dark energy can enter. If we nullify this energy, the vortex is still open. Marie, listen to your guides and use your intuition. The spirit world is just as complex as our own world. That bedroom isn't the only room that's affected. The family room has an unusual irritating vibration. I'm sure Pauline will phone again. Her family isn't ready to change their ways. It's going to get worse."

Several months later, Pauline again telephoned. But, because she was taken aback by June's blunt criticism, she called upon me. "I'm having a problem in little Robbie's bedroom. She's only five years old, and she won't sleep in her bedroom anymore. Her sister, Nancy, who is thirteen, shares the room. Nancy doesn't seem to be bothered."

After agreeing to investigate, I telephoned June and explained the situation.

"Just as I predicted," June replied, then agreed to investigate.

The following morning, Pauline was waiting at the front door and led us into the family room.

I closed my eyes and searched within my mind's eye. The room was neat, clean, and visible pleasant, except for the same jittery energy I had experienced on the last visit.

June scanned the room, then she looked up at the ceiling. "There's a sinister force upstairs," she muttered. Without asking where the little girl's bedroom was, she climbed the stairs and headed toward a bedroom in the center of the hall.

Pauline and I followed up the stairs.

June stopped at the doorway. "They're in here. There's more than one." She entered the bedroom, closed her eyes, and scanned the room within her mind's eye.

I peeked through the doorway expecting to see, or at least sense a spirit, but the room appeared strangely quiet and empty.

The morning sun shone brightly against the blue walls of the bedroom. Twin beds were arranged on opposite sides of the room. At the foot of a neatly made twin bed was a doll house. Across the room was another twin bed and a dresser with an attached mirror, decorated with football pennants and photographs of school friends.

"My daughter, Robbie, says her doll house has bad things in it. It scares her. She wants me to throw it away."

June closed her eyes and mentally tuned into the doll house. "There's a dark energy making a cackling witch-like sound. It's nonhuman. It's hiding in the darkness." June opened her eyes and turned to Pauline. "You're right. There's evil energy in there," she said, pointing to the doll house. "I wonder what made it hide?"

While Pauline and June were discussing the doll house, I felt drawn toward a closet. I moved across the room and stood in front of a closet door. With closed eyes, I searched inside the closet. I sensed a slender man squatting on a top shelf. *He's angry. He's swearing.* I raised my hand, palm forward, to protect myself, and mentally sent a message. "Stop swearing! I don't want to hear those words."

More vulgar words erupted from behind the closed door.

I turned toward June. "There's a male spirit on the top shelf of this closet," I said, pointing to the closet door. "He's swearing. He doesn't want me to invade his territory."

June cast her eyes down, searching the depths of her mind. She also sensed the entity. "We'll take that spirit to our rescue circle next week." She turned toward Pauline. "In the meantime, I want you to burn this doll house!"

"Why can't I just give it to the little girl next door?"

"Would you give poison to the girl next door? No, of course not! I recommend you burn it. Don't give anything evil to anyone." June sensed the force inside the doll house wasn't a soul, nor was it a spirit. It was a destructive energy, and it would be difficult and time consuming to neutralize it. She knew from experience that in order to destroy nonhuman energy, it would have to be burned.

"Why burn it?" I asked.

"Like the phoenix, the fire will nullify the evil, and a positive energy will be reborn."

Pauline seemed satisfied that the ghosts were to be removed. "Will you come back and get the ghost out of the closet?"

"We don't need to come back here. We'll draw them out by mental telepathy."

"How will you do that?" Pauline asked.

"The psychics will mentally tune into the spirits. Since spirits move on thought patterns, it would be natural for them to follow our thoughts to the rescue circle. They'll come to our meeting without question."

I raised my eyebrows curiously. *Why did June say "them?" Is she implying there is more than one spirit in the room?* Again, I scanned the room, but sensing no other spirits, I followed June and Pauline down the stairs.

Pauline stopped at the front door. "By the way, how do you think that spirit got in the doll house? Little Robbie doesn't argue."

"It isn't a spirit. It's an energy. It could have happened a number of ways. Perhaps the constant arguing broke down the natural protection of your home."

"I thought all houses have a natural protection," Pauline replied.

"They do. But your family's bickering could have opened another vortex. Spirits often seek like-minded vibrations to hide in. We've seen spirits attach themselves to furniture or mirrors. It's believed that spirits are drawn to their own reflection in a mirror. You'd be surprised how many mirrors are possessed by spirits." June reached for the doorknob. "Don't worry. Where're no spirits in your daughter's mirror.

Pauline gave a weak smile, momentarily relieved,

"Whatever is inside the doll house, isn't a spirit. It's non-human. It doesn't have a soul. It's a destructive energy scaring your daughter. This is something you can take care of."

"How? I don't know how to do this spooky stuff."

June sensed that the force was non-human, and would be difficult and time consuming to neutralize it. She knew from experience that in order to destroy nonhuman energy, it would have to be burned..

"Again, I will repeat. You must take the doll house outside and burn it in the trash."

Pauline shrugged her shoulders. "Okay. I'll do that. What else do I have to do" She didn't understand any of this. All she wanted was someone to exorcise her house.

"Just burn it! That will destroy what ever is inside."

The following week, a group of experienced mediums gathered in the living room of June's home and placed their chairs in a circle. When the room was quiet, they closed their eyes and slowed their brain waves. Each imagined a cloud of white light surrounding their body for protection.

June bowed her head and began the prayer in a soft, rhythmic voice. "We sit with love and understanding. We ask our guides to stand by for protection, guidance, and direction. We ask for the very highest spiritual assistance we are capable of using. We ask for God's blessing in this circle. We make a special request to bring the entities from Robbie's bedroom. Thank you, God."

The dimly lit room grew silent. The women closed their eyes and searched in their mind's eye for a spirit to present itself.

Within seconds, I sensed someone standing next to me. I raised my hand and informed June in a soft voice. "I have a spirit near me."

"Yes Marie. There is a woman standing next to you." June crossed the room, knelt down, and took my hands, drawing the spirit closer.

I was surprised when the spirit slipped into my body so easily. I had expected the agitated energy of the swearing spirit. But instead, I felt myself coexisting with a peaceful feeling, much like my own energy.

June, sensing the gentleness of the spirit, asked, "Who are you?"

"I protect Robbie," a timid female voice spoke through my voice. "Can I go back?"

June had never intercepted a spirit guide before and was pleased by its gentleness. "Are you Robbie's guide?"

"I love little Robbie. Can I go back and watch over her?" the spirit pleaded softly.

"Yes. Yes. You can go back. Are you Robbie's guide?"

"No. I ain't no guide. I love little Robbie. I come to protect her cause I want to. Can I go back now?"

"How did you get here?"

"Something drew me out. I don't want to be here. Send me back."

"I'm sorry. We didn't mean for you to come out of the bedroom. Yes. Go back. Protect Robbie."

After the spirit slipped out of my body, I opened my eyes, fascinated with the new experience. I had no idea a medium could draw a protective spirit out. *Perhaps the guides had allowed this as a learning experience.*

Dorothy, who had been sitting quietly across the circle, began to shift anxiously in her chair, irritated by an entity hovering near her. She gestured to June. "I have a spirit near me."

June, sensing the urgency, took a deep breath and breathed in white light energy. With her chest expanded, she prepared for a confrontation. There was no time to explain. She knew this spirit was about to attack Dorothy, and it had to be stopped. She mentally directed her energy, drawing the spirit across the room. She needed a stronger medium. "Marie! You can handle this. Take it!"

"O'mph." I felt something slam into my body with great force. My forehead frowned and my face contorted as the spirit made its violent entry.

"Son of a bitch! Let me out of here," a gruff, masculine voice shouted from my mouth.

June knelt down, grasped my hands, and tightened her grip. "There's no need for that kind of language. Calm down. We're here to help you."

"It's none of your damn business. Let me out of here." My body twisted and turned as the spirit struggled to escape.

"No. Not until you stop swearing," June replied sternly.

I felt my jaw muscles clenching and my lips tighten. Whoa, *he's angry!*

June remained calm as she spoke. "Tell us why you're hiding in that closet?"

"I don't know," my voice retaliated in a masculine voice.

"Do you know you're dead?" June asked.

A frown of curiosity slipped crossed my face. I sensed the man was thinking. Within seconds, I felt the muscles in my face loosen, stunned by the realization of his condition.

"Yes. You're dead."

"But I don't hurt! How could I be dead?"

"Well, you are. See! You're with a group of people who want to help you."

"Help me what?" my gruff voice replied.

"To pass over to the other side."

The spirit reflected a bewildered look on my face. "The other side of what? It's just dark here."

"It's dark because that's how you're thinking. Why don't you see yourself in the sunlight, perhaps in a beautiful meadow?"

"I can't. I've been pretty bad all my life." The spirit's voice turned apologetic. "I don't think I could go there. I've done some hateful things. They might not want me. I swear a lot, you know."

"Yes, we know." The faint hint of a smile slipped out, then June's voice turned serious. "You don't have to swear. You can change your ways. Why don't you go out in the sunlight?"

Within my mind's eye, a scene began to unfold. In the darkness, I saw a male figure standing in front of two huge wooden doors. They appeared to be more than ten feet high. The man cautiously pulled a heavy door open just a crack. He hesitated suspiciously, then stretched his neck and peeked through the partially open door. After a while, he glanced back over his shoulder and looked both ways, as if expecting someone to stop him. He waited. No one stopped him. Slowly, cautiously, he edged the door open a little wider. A streak of sunlight pierced the darkness. The light grew stronger, more intense. He moved forward, drifting, as if being drawn by the power of the light, until he disappeared into its brightness.

I opened my eyes and nodded to June. "He's gone to the light."

June gave a short prayer, thanking the spirit world for its assistance. The women quickly removed their chairs from circle formation and the room took on a joyful atmosphere.

The following week, Pauline telephoned June. "My husband burned the doll house in our back yard. He did it while Robbie was in school."

June was pleased that they had followed her advice. "That's good, but there is something that is still bothering me. Why do you call your daughter little Robbie? She's not a baby anymore. You're putting a negative thought in that child's head. She will always think of herself as little until you change those words. Remember, words can create thoughts, and our thoughts create our actions."

"Hum. I guess there is something to that," Pauline replied.

"Please take this seriously. You don't know the damage words can do, especially when the words can hold a child back from maturing."

Let's look at the important issues of this haunting. The irritating friction in the family room was created by the family's constant arguments. Though this irritating energy wasn't dangerous, it contributed to the disharmony in the home. The vortex in the ceiling of the bedroom may have been created by the family's constant arguing and the teenager's unbridled anger and rebellion.

The nonhuman mass in the doll house was an accumulation of negative energy created by all members of the household. This negative mass could not exist in the light of the protective spirit, so it confined itself by hiding in the doll house. Since it was not a spirit, nor did it ever exist in human form, the mediums had no way to send it to the light. The only way to destroy this destructive energy was to neutralize it by fire. Much like the phoenix, the destructive energy will be extinguished and new energy will arise. The reason I wasn't fearful of the entity in the doll house was because my spirit guides were protecting me and had blocked any fear from my mind.

The swearing spirit was earthbound, existing in the 'now,' a dimension where time doesn't exist. He hid in the darkness where he felt comfortable. June mentally created the image of white light for the spirit to enter the next dimension. The swearing spirit's own belief that he wasn't good enough created thoughts of a barrier—the image of wooden doors. When he opened the door, he was affected by the unconditional love and compassion of the light which drew him into the next dimension.

On the other hand, the friendly spirit may have been drawn in when it saw Robbie's aura emitting fear while frightened by the entity in the doll house. Spirits see thoughts as energies of color. Each thought emits a variety of hues and colors, ranging from brilliant to dull. Each color emits a vibration of sound. The friendly spirit read Robbie's thoughts by observing the various colors around the child's aura. The protective spirit claimed it came by its own choice. Therefore, it wasn't earthbound. It could return to the next dimension at will.

In this case, the teenager's anger created a vortex similar to a whirling tornado of energy in the ceiling. When, and if, the teenager is able to control her temper, the negative energy will dissipate and the vortex will close. The room will then return to its natural positive energy.

Usually, most vortex are seen coming from the earth. However, in the past, I have seen negative entities coming from a vortex in the floor of a house, and in another case from a basement. Spirits travel back and forth through these vortex openings. I have also experienced a vortex of positive vibrations in which the resident stood near the opening and used it as a source of healing energy.

However, not all spirits are earthbound. Many have entered the God light, then returned into the earthly dimension to visit loved ones. They often stay a very short time, a matter of several minutes. They don't stay long because it takes a great deal of energy to remain in the earthly dimension. Spirits who are not earthbound can return to the light at will.

I've never charged for the service of removing earthbound spirits from haunted houses. My payment was the overwhelming feeling of happiness I felt after releasing a spirit to the God light. Besides, who ever heard of a spirit paying a fee? My reward was the information I gathered to write this book.

7

SPIRIT ARTIST

While raising three children, I studied oil painting at a local art studio. Even though it started as a hobby, the sale of those painting helped pay the bills. After years of painting, I was motivated to study the brush strokes of the Great Master's paintings. At that time, I didn't know I was being influenced by spirits who had been artists in their previous lives. Many days I would sit at the easel and feel myself settling into a calm tranquility. I became one with the canvas and my paintings became alive. I suspect the spirit guides did their best to teach me to paint.

After having attended June Black's psychic workshop for several years, I began to sense when a spirit was presence. I would place a blank canvas on the easel, close my eyes, and sense a spirit standing behind me. Soon I was able to visualize the guide and the clothing it wore. Occasionally, a guide would control the brush, or move my hand across the canvas. I chuckled to myself when my hand would slam into the pallet and retrieved a heavy dose of paint and spread it lavishly across the canvas.

The artist spirit guide I remember most was a heavy-set monk dressed in a light-brown burlap garment, similar to a toga. Several years later, I sensed a second art guide—a tall, regal looking man in a turquoise robe and a turban wrapped around his head. He guided me to use paler colors, and my painting technique again changed. I don't recall the third artist guide;

it was so long ago. In fact, I may only have sensed its presence and never visualized it at all. Under their guidance, my painting techniques changed from time to time, and the paintings improved. I have since learned that psychic people are usually creative, that would include inventors, music, painting, and writing.

Swiss Alps: Oil painting by Marie Harriette Kay

This painting took about three or four weeks to complete. First, I sketched with a paintbrush the skyline, the horizon, the size of the mountains, and the foremost plot of ground on the right side of the canvas. Several days later, after the paint dried, I painted a wash coat. This requires applying only the background without any details, such as the blue sky without clouds. There was no change in color or hue. Each sitting I applied more detail, overlaying the paint to enhance the scene. I learned this technique by examining the Great Maser's paintings with a magnifying glass to discover how to overlay the paint with delicate strokes of the brush. This painting, in particular, was requested many times. It was painted with different colors and sold four times

You're probably wondering, well, what about me? What applies to people who are not psychic? And, if you believe the average person has guides, where did you get your information?

The knowledge comes from my personal experiences. I'm not any different then you are. So, you most likely have had spiritual assistance, just as I have. Because you can't see them, doesn't mean they're not present.

It's my belief that there are many spirit guides who assist us daily, such as personal guides, talented spirits offering their expertise, guards, protectors, totems (spirit animals) and, of course, a wide array of angels. Possibly more than I will ever know. Many years ago, I had a reading from a psychic who spoke of angels. She said to me, "You have three groups of angels with you, Seraphim, Cherubim, and Dominions. I have never met anyone who had this many angels with them, as you do." Up to that time, I knew very little about the names of angels, or that they offer assistance to others.

So, whatever profession you have chosen, you may also have angels or talented spirits assisting you. When you 're in need of an answer, they place an idea in your head as a thought. It just pops in out of the blue. I will present several examples and perhaps you'll recognize that you also have spirit guides.

1. Often, when sewing, I have difficulty threading the needle. After several tries and my patience exhausted, I would mentally or vocally ask for help. "May I have a spirit guide help me? I can't thread this needle." Immediately, on my very next attempt, the thread slipped through the needle easily. If this had happened only once, I might say it was a coincidence. But this occurred time after time. And too, I always sensed an unseen presence when the problem had been solved. Of course, I remember to thank who ever helped me. Though this seems impossible; the fact that it repeatedly happened when I asked for help is tangible proof that I received help. Therefore, I cannot and will not deny my own truth.

2. After watching a television program on teleportation, I doubted that an object could move without any physical means of propelling it. That evening, I noticed a wooden lead pencil on the living room floor. *Where did this come from? Have I been influenced by the program to believe it had been teleported to my floor?*

Yet, it was strange. The lead pencil was purple and obviously new. *Where did it come from? No one had been in my house all day, and I never owned a purple pencil.* I picked it up and intuitively felt I should place it in a kitchen drawer. *Wonder why it's important that I place it in this drawer?* At the time, it seemed necessary, so I shrugged my shoulder and placed it in the drawer. That evening, I decided to ask for an answer in my dreams.

The next morning, I was startled to see the purple pencil again on the living room floor. No one had been in my house during the night, and the cat certainly can't open a drawer. So, how did the pencil get on the living room floor? I believe my spirit guides had answered my question by proving teleportation is possible. Teleportation is a phenomenon, an unproven science, that humans do not yet understand.

The reason I call your attention to this story is to show the reader to how to mentally ask your spirit guides for an answer when you don't understand or believe a paranormal event. The answer may come in a dream, or it may be set right before your eye, just as the pencil appeared for me.

3. While in the hospital recovering from cancer, I awoke in the middle of the night and through the darkness, I saw a shadowy figure at the foot of my bed. Immediately, I sensed a calming protective feeling about its presence. *It's a guardian spirit protecting me while I slept.* As soon as I lifted my head off the pillow, the image floated across the room and passed through the closed door.

If this had been a nurse or a real person, I would have seen the door open, and the light from the hall would have lit the room. But since the room remanded dark I was sure that the image did not leave through an open door, it passed through the closed door. I now realize we have spirits guarding us, even if we are unaware of their presence. This adds to my belief that we all have spirit guides who assist and protect us daily. They will answer your questions by placing a thought in your mind if the request is the best for all concerned. Remember, be courteous. They're here to guide and protect us, not serve us.

DECISION TIME

I enrolled in a creative writing class at the local college. At the same time, even though I painted often, I still managed to attend nearly every psychic workshop and rescue circle. Today had been exceptionally busy, and I had just sat down to unwind for a few minutes when I heard a strong message running cross my mind.

"Are you ready to make a decision?"

My head jolted upward and my back stiffened. It felt like someone had placed me firmly in a chair to get my attention.

"Which profession do you choose? Painting or mediumship?"

This wasn't my own thought, because the question was addressed to me in the second person. If it had been my own thought, I would have heard, *am I ready to choose?* Without hesitation, I responded, *"Mediumship. This is what gives me the most pleasure."*

Even though I wouldn't be earning money by selling paintings, mediumship was my primary interest. There were far too many spirits who needed to be rescued and not enough mediums. Also, it is something the average person wouldn't do.

Then I wondered, *Am I spreading myself too thin? Do I have too much on my plate?* Releasing earthbound spirits to the light was extremely important. Many of the new students were working mothers with children, so they had little time to attend haunted houses or rescue spirits. As the years passed, even though the painting commissions declined, I never completely stopped painting.

In retrospect, the spirit guides knew I would begin a career in writing, something I hadn't anticipated at the time. Apparently, they knew I would be penning my memories many years before I began writing.

8

ANGEL RESCUE

While attending the psychic workshop, the paranormal experiences were coming more often, or perhaps I was noticing them more clearly. My next experience confirmed that we indeed have angels watching over us.

Many years ago, I was caring for a woman who had an allergic reaction from newly laid carpeting. I invited her to move into the spare bedroom until the carpet was removed from her house. She was to occupy a bedroom on the upper floor of our tri-level home. There were only eight stairs leading up to the bedrooms.

Several days later, I went into her bedroom and picked up several glasses and set them on a tray. As I started down the stairs, I stumbled and fell forward. It happened so fast that I didn't have the presence of mind to try to catch myself from falling. Nor did I drop the tray, as one might normally do.

I could feel my knees hitting each step on the way down. Strangely, even though the glasses clinked together, they remained upright on the tray. My body remained upright as well. How is this possible?

While all this happened in a matter of seconds, I felt a calmness sweeping over me and an angel hovering behind me. I felt its hands under my armpits, holding me upright. Much to my surprise, I landed on my feet, still holding the tray. I remember looking up at the heavens and saying,

"Thank you." I was grateful that I had been protected from getting hurt. I accepted this rescue as a divine intervention.

In the past, I had promised the angels I would help others, and now they had helped me in return. I'm so glad I decided to walk the spiritual path. It had more rewards than I could have imagined. With this new confidence of knowing angels were protecting me, I felt more at peace and will continue to help others.

CAR OUT OF CONTROL

Several years later, an angel again intervened, and this time, it actually saved my life. One winter afternoon, I was driving home through heavy workday traffic. It was dusk, and the headlights of oncoming traffic sent glaring prisms of light against the window. I had stopped at a red light, waiting to make a left turn.

The light turned green.

Since there was no oncoming traffic ahead, I started to make a left turn when, all of a sudden, out of the darkness, a car was speeding directly at me. *It's going to crash into me.* What happened next can't be explained with logic.

I felt my hands tighten its grip on the steering wheel. There was no time to get out of the path of the oncoming car. Time ceased. Everything seemed to slow down. Strangely, I didn't panic.

The car's glaring headlights continued racing toward me.

I felt the steering wheel turning, and my car swerving, winding its way behind the oncoming car. I was still gripping the steering wheel when I realized I had passed behind the car and was safely on the road, heading toward home.

How did I do that? I heaved a sigh of relief, slowed down to normal speed, and merged safely into the traffic. I looked up at the heavens and said, "Thank you." It was only after I was through the traffic, and able to breathe a sigh of relief, that I realized someone had taken over the steering wheel. I am convinced an angel maneuvered me safely between the oncoming traffic and saved my life.

In retrospect, I look back at the near accident with gratitude. If I had been in control, my instinct would have been to slam on the brakes. This would have put me directly in the path of the oncoming car. And, being so frightened, I couldn't have maneuvered my way in front of, or behind, the oncoming car. Either way, my own reaction would have put my life in danger.

THE MODEL HOUSE

An area of ground that gives off disturbing vibrations is often referred to as unholy ground. If the area had experienced violent battles, tragic deaths, or natural disasters in the past, a negative residual may still remain. These agitated vibrations can encompass an area as small as a room or extend for miles. Even though an area is known as unholy ground, it is not necessarily unholy, nor is it evil.

My next experience deals with a plot of ground that gave off an unusual vibrating energy, causing the atmosphere to quiver in an unusual way. An enlightened psychic may sense the vibrations, while a novice may not sense anything at all. I have been in many haunted houses, but I must admit, this house really took me by surprise.

My niece, Mickey, and I had been attending the psychic development classes for several months, and seemed well-matched in similar psychic abilities. One afternoon, we decided to tour model homes in search of new decorating ideas. We headed toward the suburbs, passing vacant farms, overgrown fields, and rickety, weather-worn barns that leaned precariously toward the ground.

In the distance, an OPEN sign caught my attention. I turned off the main road and down a street lined with newly built houses and stopped in front of a colonial house.

The model house was freshly painted and the newly laid sod meticulously manicured. On the front door hung a sign: Come in and browse.

Mickey opened the door and stepped into a small, dimly lit foyer. "Hello!" she called out, expecting a salesperson to greet us.

I followed her into the living room and stopped dead in my tracks, afraid to step forward because the brown-speckled carpet seemed to be quivering beneath my feet.

The dimly lit room appeared oddly slanted, and the walls were painted in khaki green. On one wall, the wallpaper quivered like heat waves radiating from sun-baked metal. The large front window was shaded by a huge tree on the front lawn, and the morning sun barely shone through. A strange silence encompassed the dreary room.

"Look at the wallpaper," Mickey said, grinning mischievously. "It's psychedelic. The pattern looks like it's moving. Do the walls seem slanted to you?"

"Yes. Everything looks strange, like it's haunted," I answered as I followed Mickey across the room.

"Look at that bronze statue," Mickey said, as she headed toward a small table across the room. "It's weird. I can't explain it, but it feels evil."

I edged my way closer to the table. "Look at the grotesque face on that statue. Everything in this room is slanted, just like that statue."

"The face looks like it's melted," Mickey giggled. She paused at the foot of the stairway and gazed up at the narrow, strange looking steps.

I edged my way past Mickey and a curious frown wrinkled my brow. The staircase appeared confining and the steps tilted at a threatening pitch. I gripped the handrail, and started up the stairs, moving cautiously as each step seemed oddly slanted. The ceiling seemed extremely low, and I found myself ducking to avoid hitting my head.

"Hey, wait for me," Mickey called out, as she followed close behind.

After reaching the top landing, I stepped into a long dimly lit hall. I gasped, stopping abruptly, startled by the eerie feeling in the murkily lit hall. "Oh. This is scary."

The narrow hallway was unusually dark, and the only light came from the open bedroom doorways. One small window at the end of the long hall cast eerie shadows against the olive-green walls.

"This place is spooky," Mickey whispered as she followed cautiously down the hall.

I peeked in the first bedroom. The walls appeared to ripple with agitation, and the room gave off an unfriendly feeling.

Mickey slipped past me and entered the bedroom. "Look at the ugly wall. It's painted khaki green, just like the hall. Yuck!"

Even though the carpet seemed to be vibrating beneath my feet, I stepped cautiously into the room. "What kind of house is this?"

Mickey again brushed past me and hurried to the next room. "You think that's strange! Look at this," she chuckled as she entered the next bedroom.

The second bedroom was dimly lit and gave off a heavy feeling of anxiety. The walls were papered in grotesque patterns of snarled, grayish-white flowers scattered on a dark burgundy background.

Mickey leaned against the wall, laughing until tears came to her eyes.

I entered the room and started laughing. "Boy, whoever did this decorating should be shot! I wouldn't want this person decorating my house."

"Wow! Now that's ugly," Mickey chuckled, then hung on my shoulder, giggling.

"This is the strangest house I've ever seen." I headed down the hall, curious as to see the third bedroom. And indeed, all the bedrooms seemed equally grotesque. We were still laughing when we finished touring the house.

"I wonder what kind of person would buy this house?" Mickey said as she stepped out into the bright sunshine. She closed the door, still giggling. "Well, they say there's something for everyone."

"Yeah, but whoever buys that house has really got to be strange."

At the time, I considered this just a humorous excursion, not understanding the uniqueness of our experience. But I was soon to find out.

Several weeks later, we decided to visit that weird house again. I drove down the street toward the same house. The OPEN sign was placed in the same spot as it was before. I parked in front of the same brick colonial, grinning in expectation.

Mickey snickered as she turned the doorknob. "I hope the salesman isn't here." She entered the small living room, and her jaw dropped in amazement.

The sunlight seemed brighter today, casting a cheerful glow in the living room. The pale green walls seemed pleasantly different, and the gold thread that ran through the patterned wallpaper now gave off a pleasant glow.

I followed behind. "Is this the same place?" I approached the bronze statue for a second look. It wasn't as weird as I remembered it to be.

"It's got to be the same house. It's the same wallpaper. The same curtains. Every thing's the same, yet it's different." Mickey smiled, pleased at the attractive decorations. She stepped further into the living room. "The walls aren't slanted, and the carpet doesn't vibrate like it did before."

I raised my eyebrows curiously. Suddenly, it dawned on me. "Yes, it's the same place, but do you know why it looks so different?"

"No. Why does it look nice now? Is it haunted?"

"I now realize what happened on our last visit. This house isn't haunted with a ghost, it's haunted with. . ." I hesitated, mulling over the extraordinary difference. "I think it's been built on unholy ground. That's why everything appeared distorted and twisted the last time we were here." I closed my eyes and slowed down my brain waves, attempting to enter the same dimension as before.

Mickey watched quietly, understanding what I was attempting to do. "What do you see?"

I drew in a deep breath, then exhaled slowly, lowering my brain waves even deeper. I could feel my eyelids fluttering. Symbols flashed across my mind. "I can't seem to get to the same level as before. I'm visualizing symbols, but nothing seems logical." I opened my eyes and shrugged my shoulders.

Mickey started up the stairs. "This staircase doesn't look the same. I thought it was dark and narrow, but it's really bright."

The sun shone through an upstairs window, brightening the steps.

"These walls are a pale green," Mickey called down. "I can't explain it, but I'm sure it's the same hall."

I hurried up the steps, slipped past Mickey, and headed for a bedroom. "Oh, it's the same, but look at this."

The wallpaper appeared to glisten with delicate silver threads woven within the billowy white flowers, scattered against a pale blush-pink background.

Mickey stood in the bedroom doorway. "It's actually quite charming. What made us think it was so repulsive before?"

"I think we entered in an altered state of mind." I paused, trying to visualize what dimension we had entered that day. "I think we were in a different dimension of time," I said, as I intuitively received the answers. "I sense a lot of people were killed in this area long ago."

"Why can't it just be the house that's haunted?"

I quoted the impressions I was receiving. "I don't think the house is haunted. I sense the area is haunted. I wonder if a battle took place on this ground?"

"Are the other houses haunted just like this?" Mickey asked.

"I don't know. Let's try to figure this out another day."

Because we were both psychic, it was not unusual to sense the eerie vibrations. But it was unusual that we both entered the same dimension at exactly the same time.

Many years have passed since we visited that strange model house. Now, rows of houses covered the acreage where the antiquated wood barns and twisted trees once spread across open fields.

I was curious as to what had happened in this area a long time ago, so I began to investigate. The first clue came from a lady friend who drove a school bus.

"Oh, that subdivision has a lot of mischievous children," Judy answered. "They seem to be troubled, unruly kids. Sometimes it's difficult to handle them on the bus."

I jotted down notes as Judy continued.

"The experienced bus drivers come early in the season to make out their yearly bus schedule. They don't want to pick up the kids in that subdivision."

"Why? What's so different about that area?"

"No one wants that route. Some of those children are rebellious."

"Does the area look different?"

Judy thought a bit. "No. I can't say anything looks unusual about the houses, just that some kids act like they're irritated or high-strung."

Through my research at the library, I found no historical event had occurred in that area. However, I suspect there had been a tragedy that caused the turbulent vibration that continues to affect the children. It's not known how long this negative energy will affect the area, or if it will dissipate in time.

Allow me to explain what really happened the day we toured the model house. I now realize both Mickey and I had the psychic ability to reach a deep level of awareness. When we slowed down our brain waves, we were able to see the house psychically, rather than physically. We saw the wall tilted because we were viewing them through negative vibrations which had caused a distortion in the atmosphere. The carpet appeared to quiver because we were seeing the energy vibrating beneath our feet. For two people to dip into the same dimension at exactly the same time is rare indeed.

THE SOLDIER

Spirits don't haunt a house just because it's old. They often haunt when they are in need of help. Even though the spirit means no harm, their presence often frightens the residents.

Lila lived in an old house where strange creaking sounds were a common occurrence. In the past, she had been too busy raising a family of seven children to question the strange noises. But now that the children were at school and the house was quiet, she began to take notice. Lila was in the kitchen when she heard the sound of a ball softly bouncing. She hurried to the living room, where the sound had come from. Seeing nothing unusual, she dismissed it as inconsequential and went about her daily chores. Several days later, she again heard the soft thumping sound. This time, she traced the sound to the stairway leading up to the bedrooms. She stood at the bottom of the stairs and listening.

The thumping sound moved slowly down each step. It was apparent that something, or someone, was trying to attract her attention.

After hearing the strange sound several days in a row, Lila needed to talk to someone. She didn't feel threatened, nor did she get a fearful feeling from the unusual sound., but she needed an answer. She dialed the phone. "Marie! I hear funny sounds in my house.. It's like someone is bouncing a ball."

I listened to her story, immediately sensing a spirit was trying to attract her attention. "Perhaps it's a ghost," I replied with a giggle. "I don't think it's anything dangerous."

Lila snickered, belittling the mention of ghosts. "I don't believe in ghost, but I can't find a logical reason for the bouncing sound. I don't know why I phoned you in the first place." Lila preferred to dismiss the experience, rather than admit it could be paranormal.

Since Lila wasn't ready to accept a metaphysical explanation, I didn't press the matter any further.

Several days later, Lila's daughter, Debbie, was looking in the bathroom mirror while brushing her long blond hair. She noticed the partial image of a man's boots reflecting in the mirror. She shivered, having an eerie feeling that a soldier was watching her. She turned quickly. There was no one behind her, and the boots she saw in the mirror had disappeared.

Thoughts of an American soldier from the Vietnam war came to mind. Because society wasn't ready to embrace the paranormal, neither was she. Unaware that a soldier was asking for help, she dismissed the incident from her mind. Several days later, she saw the misty fragments of a soldier reflected in the mirror, his boots being most prominent. Because she was a young, active teenager busy with high school activities, she again dismissed the matter.

Days later Debbie's older sister, Annie, confided that she, too, saw a soldier's boots and fragments of his uniform reflecting in the mirror. Even though both girls had seen the images, they each denied their own truth, and refused to accept the strange phenomenon. They weren't ready to accept the paranormal, and feared they might be ridiculed if they told anyone.

One afternoon, while visiting Lila, her teenage daughter, Annie, arrived home from high school before the other children. She tossed her schoolbooks on the kitchen table and paused as if to speak. She didn't intend to share her story, and though she didn't realize it, her spirit guides had prompted her to speak. The words poured out of her mouth. "I think I saw a soldier's boots in the mirror. It's probably my imagination, but I had to tell someone."

In my mind's eye, I saw a soldier standing in the corner of the living room, next to the fireplace. Even though I was in the kitchen, I had visualized him as if there were no walls obstructing my view. "It's a young boy who was in the Vietnam war."

"How did you know? That's exactly what my sister and I thought." Annie's eyes widened, and her curiosity had been piqued. "Sometimes it looked like he was wearing an old-fashioned army uniform."

Thought flooded my mind. *There must be a special reason why this soldier came to this house. Maybe he had attended the same high school. Maybe he returned to search out his friends. I wonder if the soldier saw the light of Annie's aura, and hoped she would help. Did the guardian angels have a specific reason for leading him to Annie's house?* "Do you want to help him?" I asked.

"Yes," Annie answered, even though she had no idea what I was about to ask her to do. She knew nothing of the psychic world, yet this soldier was able to make his presence visible in the mirror. Not thinking of this as a paranormal experience, she accepted the challenge.

"Come. Let's sit in the dining room," I said as I led the way out of the kitchen, out of her mother's sight. The dining room opened to the living room, in clear view of the soldier. Annie didn't see the soldier standing next to the fireplace, so I made no further reference to the spirit.

Lila followed us into the dining room. Within minutes, whether consciously or by spiritual suggestion, she made an excuse to return to the kitchen. If she had stayed, her disbelieve would have created negative vibrations, and the negative energy would have made it difficult for the soldier to communicate.

I set several sheets of paper on the table and handed Annie a pencil. "Have you ever done automatic writing before?"

Annie grasped the pencil without question and shook her head. "I don't know what that is."

"That's okay. Let's try this. Close your eyes and think about the soldier that you saw in the mirror, then mentally tell him you want to help him."

Annie closed her eyes and projected the thoughts of helping.

"Now, I want you to draw a straight line, horizontally across the paper, just as you would if you were shaking your head from side to side to say 'no.' Mentally, tell the soldier that this line across the paper means' no."

Annie drew a line across the paper, then closed her eyes and relayed the message. Again, she opened her eyes and waited for further instruction.

"Good! Now draw a vertical line, up and down the paper as if you would shake your head up and down to say 'yes.' Tell the soldier this line means yes."

Annie drew several vertical lines up and down the paper, closed her eyes and mentally conveyed the message. She opened her eyes and glanced up, waiting for more instructions.

"Good! Hold the pencil upright, so the side of your hand isn't resting on the paper. We need the pencil to be free of any obstructions."

Annie held the pencil in an upright position on the paper.

"Now, close your eyes. Mentally ask the soldier if he wants help."

Without hesitation, Annie's hand sprinted up and down on the paper. Her eyes popped open, startled by the automatic reflex of her hand. "Yes! Yes! He wants me to help," she replied, her voice rising to a high pitch of excitement. "Did you see that! My hand moved by itself."

"Um-hum. Now, close your eyes again. Try to stay calm. Ask him if he is lost?"

Again, Annie closed her eyes as her hand moved rapidly across the paper, scribbling several horizontal lines. "He says no," Annie replied while keeping her eyes closed, trying to quiet the excitement within her. "I think he's blind. I think he has bandages over his eyes. Could that be?"

"Yes, it can." I softened my voice to keep the peaceful, meditative mood. "Ask him if he knows that he's dead."

Annie's fingers tightened its grip on the pen and her hand pressed hard, scratching several lines up and down in strong, quick strokes.

"Good! You're doing fine. Now, in your own words, mentally say a prayer. Ask for God's help. Tell the soldier to call his guides or guardian angels."

Annie, being Catholic, found this a very natural thing to do. Seconds later, she opened her eyes. "He's gone," she said, surprised by what had just happened. Even though her answers had come spontaneously, she didn't question why she knew. She just accepted it as a fact.

"Good," I told Annie. "The soldier was able to see the angels because you told him they were there." In the quiet of my mind, I mentally said a prayer thanking God for His assistance.

Within minutes, the quiet mood in the house changed to an active, busy household. The screen door slammed, and several teenagers darted through the kitchen. The loud ringing sound of the telephone attracted Annie's attention, and she darted out of the dining room.

Lila returned to the dining room, unaware of the amazing rescue that had just taken place.

I smiled within. It was awe-inspiring to see how the guides had managed to keep the house quiet long enough for Annie to rescue the soldier. This simple, beautiful rescue had taken only a few minutes, and went completely unnoticed by the rest of the household. I set this rescue in the back of my mind, not fully understanding why this had occurred at this house and to this teenager.

As I look back at this experience, I noticed that the two girls and the mother never sensed fear, so they never thought of this as a haunting. The soldier was not fearful, therefore, he didn't emit vibrations of fear. He merely needed help to cross over into the God light.

In retrospect, I now understand why this spirit visitation occurred as it did. Many years later, Annie joined another religion. This church believed that after physical death, the soul would sleep until judgment day. Now Annie could draw upon her experience of knowing that after physical death the soul remains alert, and it does exist in the next dimension. Annie will take a second look at God's universal law. Each religion may interpret the afterlife differently. It's up to Annie to use her own life experience to justify her own belief system.

Annie had long forgotten her encounter with the spirit. Even though she had firsthand knowledge that souls *do* exist after physical death, she had dismissed her interaction with the soldier and denied her own truth.

Throughout history, many countries mention having had interactions with spirits and ghosts. It is my belief that the soul is eternal. After physical death, the spirit will exist in another dimension, and may, in the future, reincarnate to experience another earthly life. Each lifetime allows the spirit an opportunity to work out its life missions, and to rise spiritually toward oneness with God.

GILDED CAGE

Not all hauntings are caused by spirits. Some are merely a misinterpretation of facts, or a vivid imagination. This investigation took place many years ago when I was in training to be June Black's assistant, where I learned not to jump to conclusions too quickly.

Peaceful landscape surrounded a stately colonial house in the rolling hills of Birmingham, Michigan. Lillian Cromwell's (not her real name) home seemed peaceful, that is, until the shadows of night fell. Lillian had only one child late in life. Her daughter, Clarice, was born mildly handicapped. As the child grew, her facial features failed to develop normally. Her spine curved, forming a hump on her back, bending her narrow shoulders forward until her arms dangled in front of her stooped body. In Lillian's obsession to protect her daughter, she isolated the child from other the girls her age. Thus, the child developed slowly under the watchful eye of her overly protective mother, and without friends, became socially backward as well.

June received a phone call from Lillian, pleading for an answer to the ghostlike voices in her daughter's bedroom. June agreed to examine the child's bedroom.

Since I was still in training, June invited me along to investigate the haunting. The following day, June and I drove to Lillian Cromwell's house.

"Let me do the talking," June said. "I'll ask for your opinion only to verify what I'm getting psychically. Above all, don't offer this woman any advice. I feel this is a matter of life or death. I sense this woman is very possessive of her daughter. Just follow my lead. Don't offer information that she can't understand."

At the time, I didn't understand why I was asked to stay in the background but would soon find out.

June slowed the car while searching the street signs. After a while, she turned into a long, curved driveway and coasted to a stop in front of a huge mansion-like house. As we approached the porch, I noticed a woman peering suspiciously through beveled glass windows. Within seconds, she opened the massive, oak door.

Much to my surprise, the woman was matronly with gray hair. I had expected the woman to be younger because her daughter was a teenager. Lillian Cromwell was well dressed in designer's high fashion clothes, and by the size of the house and the clothing, it was apparent she was very wealthy.

The woman introduced herself, then led us through a large foyer toward a spacious living room. "Do you want to see my daughter's bedroom first?"

June shook her head. "Not yet," she replied, then followed Lillian into the living room. June moved about the room, touching several chairs with her fingertips. She paused several times, reading the vibrations off the furniture. "We'll go upstairs in a minute. First, tell me what your daughter is seeing at night."

"My daughter not only sees the ghosts. She talks to them! This all started when she was a teenager. I heard her whispering in the middle of the night.

"You heard her whispering from your bedroom?" June asked.

"My bedroom is next to her room. We have adjoining bedrooms. At first, I wasn't too concerned. I thought Clarice was mumbling in her sleep. But when the whispers grew louder and became more audible, I crept to her bedroom and peeked from behind the half-closed door. Clarice was moving around in the dark, muttering. She was answering the spirits."

"What did you do?"

"Nothing. I assumed Clarice was sleep walking. But, several days later, I again heard her mumbling, like she was answering a ghostly visitor. The next morning, I asked her who she was talking to last night. She said she has friends that visit her in the nighttime. I'm frightened. Something scary is in her bedroom."

"Did you ask her who these people are?" June asked.

"My daughter said they don't have names. They're coming more often, and I hear her answering them."

"Have you asked for professional advice?"

"Yes, of course. I talked to medical doctors, but they claim that's not their expertise. I phoned many services—sleep disorder clinics and mental clinics. No one offered a satisfactory answer. That's why I called you to investigate. My daughter is sleeping in a room full of ghost! Her mumbling wakes me up all hours of the night."

"What does she say?" June asked.

"I don't actually hear the ghost's voices. I just hear Clarice answering them. I think she wants to go with them. Can you see what is haunting her bedroom? I made sure her father takes Clarice out for a walk while you're here. I don't want to upset the child with this," Lillian said as she fingered a delicate linen handkerchief nervously between her fingers.

I stood back silently, watching and learning. I wanted to assure Lillian that June could handle a ghost, but remained silent as June had requested.

I wondered, *why is June being so evasive? Why doesn't she assure Lillian that she could exorcise a ghost?*

Tears filled Lillian's eyes. She turned away, embarrassed by her own fears. "Tell them to go! Please make them to go away!"

Still in training and fairly new at hauntings, I wondered. *Perhaps there is more than one spirit. Now that would take some doing, wouldn't it!*

June turned and made her way across a massive foyer, toward the wide, curved staircase. "Show us your daughter's bedroom." She stepped aside, allowing Lillian to lead the way. When they entered a long hall, she said to Lillian, "We want to investigate it alone."

By the time I reached the top step, I heard voices below. I glanced down and caught a glimpse of a girl stumbling clumsily through the foyer. She was being led, hand in hand, by a short, gray-haired man. *Obviously, it's her father.* I paused for a few seconds, watching them heading toward the front door. When they were out of sight, I followed June down the long hallway.

Lillian paused, waiting for June and I to catch up, then pointed to a large room. "This is my bedroom. Clarice's room adjoins mine," she said, pointing to the doorway on the left.

"Thank you!" June replied brusquely, indicating that she now wanted Lillian to leave.

Lillian hesitated, as if to speak. She frowned suspiciously, turned abruptly and made her way down the stairs, and toward the living room.

The bedroom was massively large, beautifully decorated, and wallpapered with pale apricot flowers. The floor was covered with pale apricot carpeting. The high ceiling offered a feeling of grandeur to the chandelier hanging in the center of the room.

I peeked in the door. *I don't sense this room has a problem.* June slipped past me, and I followed her into the spacious bedroom. I closed my eyes and studied the energy more closely. After mentally searching the room, I opened my eyes. "There's no ghost in this room."

June walked slowly through the room with her left hand in the air, feeling the atmosphere for a ghostly presence, or a cool icy area. She used her left hand, because it's connected to the right side of the brain-the intuitive side of the brain. "Tell me, Marie, what do you see?"

Again, I closed my eyes and concentrated on my mind's eye. "I see a man being pushed in a wheelchair."

"Yes. What does that mean to you?" June asked, wanting to confirm her own impressions.

"The man is an invalid. He lets a woman push him," I answered, then opened my eyes.

"Yes. That's right. Lillian is the woman, and the man is her husband being pushed around," June whispered.

"But he's not dead, and he's not an invalid. I saw him downstairs. He was taking his daughter out the front door."

"Oh, he's not a physical invalid. The wheelchair symbolizes that he's being pushed around, unable to stand up to his wife."

Ah! I was beginning to understand not all images seen in the mind's eye are spirits. Some are mental imprints left by people who occupied that room. Each symbol represents a clue, an impression of what is actually occurring.

"I think I know what this is all about. Let's examine the child's room, just to be sure." June led the way through the adjoining open door.

Clarice's bedroom was slightly smaller, decorated in the same pale apricot carpet and flowered wallpaper. Two large bookcases lined the wall. The first bookcase displayed beautiful dolls and delicate figurines. The second bookcase was filled with books, neatly arranged according to color and size. In the center of the room was a large bed covered with a white lace bedspread and a matching ruffled canopy.

June closed her eyes. "Like a gilded cage," she murmured under her breath, shaking her head in dismay. "What a shame."

I closed my eyes to search within my mind's eye but saw nothing. *Where are the spirits?* "I don't sense anything here," I whispered.

"No. You won't. There's nothing evil in this room, and there are no spirits. Let's go downstairs and talk to Missus Cromwell. I'll do the talking. Listen closely so you can learn, and don't jump to any conclusions."

Lillian was waiting in the living room and jumped up when she saw June enter. "What did you find? Did you chase them out?" Lillian pleaded, gripping the arm of the couch to brace her trembling body.

June sat down and took Lillian's hand, drawing her down on the couch. "There are no spirits!" She looked deep in Lillian's eyes, and paused, letting the message sink in. "Tell me, why do you feel you must protect your daughter?"

A puzzled expression crossed Lillian's face, and she frowned curiously. "She's not like other girls. She needs to be taken care of," she answered, brusquely defending her actions.

"No. She doesn't need to be supervised. Not like this," June softened her voice.. "Your daughter needs more freedom. She feels like she's caged. Let her go," June pleaded, hoping Lillian would understand.

"What! Clarice can't be let loose like other girls," Lillian grumbled, striking back sharply.

June shook her head. "If you don't relax your grip on her, she will leave."

Lillian, unable to grasp the full meaning, retaliated angrily. "Leave! She can't go anywhere."

June, struggling to impress the seriousness of the situation, gripped Lillian's hand firmly. "She will leave if you don't free her."

"She can't! She has nowhere to go," Lillian repeated, still not understanding the severity of the warning. "Who does my daughter talk to in the middle of the night?" Lillian demanded, intentionally changing the conversation back to ghosts.

June, keeping her voice firm but gentle, chose her words carefully. "There are no spirits in her bedroom."

"But she talks to someone," Lillian interrupted.

"No! She hears her conscience—her own higher self. She just imagines those voices are separate from her, that they're someone else. You've prevented your daughter from having normal childhood friends, so she conjured up a part of herself to act as a friend.

Lillian scowled and jerked her hand away from June's grip. "She's not like other girls. She's different."

"If you insist on holding on so tight, she will leave," June repeated softly, hoping Lillian would understand the significance of her statement.

"Leave?" Lillian mumbled under her breath, oblivious to the deeper meaning.

June hesitated, then said firmly. "She will leave this earth plane."

"No! You mean die! No! She's not going to die," Lillian shouted angrily.

"No. I'm not saying that, my dear. You won't let her live a normal life. She wants to be with friends. Release your grip on her."

"Who does she talk to?"

"Your daughter is speaking to her subconscious. She's answering her higher self." June searched Lillian's eyes, hoping she would understand.

Lillian stood up and began pacing the floor, angered by what she deemed an insensitive response. It was clear she was incapable of accepting the true meaning of June's words.

"Let Clarice be with other girls her age. Try to let her do more normal things."

"Can't you get those voices out of her bedroom?" Lillian pleaded, refusing to acknowledge any other solution.

June shook her head, resigning herself to Lillian's inability to comprehend. "No. There are no spirits in her bedroom. There's nothing more I can do." June stood up and started toward the foyer.

"Okay. What do you charge for this?" Lillian replied sharply as she followed June toward the front door. It was obvious by the tone of her voice that she was annoyed and considered this day a waste of time.

"I never charge for spiritual investigations. I do this because I want to help." June watched Lillian fumbling through her purse. "I don't take donations either." June hurried me toward the front door. "We're done here Marie. We should leave." She closed the door behind her before Lillian could pursue the question of money any further.

On the drive home, I asked June, "Why are you so sure there were no spirits in the house? Why are you sure it was just a figment of the child's imagination?"

"It wasn't exactly a figment of her imagination. Clarice was responding to her higher self for companionship. She's lonely. She's making a decision whether to leave."

"But there were voices."

"No. The child was answering her inner thoughts. Talking to herself. Lillian only assumed there were voices. She thought the voices were spirits, but, in this case, it was Clarice responding to her inner thoughts. I feel the child is preparing to leave this earth plane."

"Is she going to die?"

"Not immediately, but she may not live out a normal life span. She's already withdrawing into herself. Lillian doesn't understand, but she's destroying any positive motivation for Clarice to live a normal life."

"Why didn't you come right out and tell her that?"

"I tried. Lillian isn't ready to release her daughter. Even if it means she would lose her daughter to death, she won't release her grip on Clarice." June shook her head. "I'm afraid Clarice won't stay long on this earth plane."

"Shouldn't we explain that more clearly to Lillian?"

"No. Lillian refuses to accept that she has caged her daughter. She doesn't realize her daughter is creating her own surroundings by conjuring up imaginary friends."

"That child has a beautiful home. She has everything she wants. In fact, she has more than most girls her age."

"As beautiful as a gilded cage, but still a cage. My only concern is that one day Lillian will understand what she did and blame herself for her daughter's early death.

THE RAGING SPIRIT

The following story is based on my investigation of a plot of ground that affected many innocent lives. The location and names have been changed to protect those involved. It was necessary to create dialogue to clarify this frightening event as it actually happened.

Rita, a young woman in her early forties, joined the psychic workshop because she was curious about spirits. After several months of basic training, she felt she was ready to try her hand at automatic writing.

Since I was still in training to be June's assistant, my assignment today was to teach automatic writing. After the students were seated at a table, I began the meeting. "Take a slow, deep breath, then exhale slowly. This will slow down your brain wave. Imagine God's white light surrounding your body. Mentally ask your guides to stand by for protection and guidance while writing." I placed several sheets of paper on the table in front of each student. "Hold your hand upright. Don't let your hand drag across the paper. If the pencil doesn't move right away, scribble free-flowing circles until your hand starts to move on its own.

Rita closed her eyes, held her pencil in upright, and waited. The pencil began moving as if it had a mind of its own. Rita was fascinated and allowed her hand to move at will, drawing circle after circle. After scribbling for a while, Rita's hand moved rapidly, scrawling short, odd-shaped marks of illegible script. After she had written several lines, her pencil drew a slanted downward stroke, then came to an abrupt stop.

"Marie, come here," Rita called out, beckoning with a crooked finger. "Look at this chicken scratch."

I leaned over Rita's shoulder. "That's beautiful. Let's see what it says."

"What is that? It looks like scribbling to me."

Startled by her answer, I straightened upright in surprise. "Why! That's shorthand. Can't you read shorthand?" I answered, taken aback by Rita's question.

Rita stared at the lines, trying to figure out what she had written. "It's what?"

I bent closer to the paper and scanned the page. "That's the most beautiful shorthand I've ever seen."

"But I can't do shorthand. I've never written shorthand in my life."

"What!" I replied, again taken off guard by Rita's response. "Well, you've just written in shorthand. It's so perfect it looks like it belongs in a schoolbook."

Rita studied the scrawling script. "What does it say?"

I began, "Woman, beware…." I stopped reading when I realized the message was personal. "Let's move to the corner of the room where there's more privacy." I hadn't used shorthand in years and wasn't sure I could read it. The last time I used shorthand was in high school, and that was a long time ago. After we moved to a more secluded area of the room, I leaned close to Rita's ear and read the message in a whisper. "It says you must change the path you have chosen. There is misfortune if you continued in this direction." I stepped back to see Rita's reaction.

The scowl on Rita's face expressed her displeasure. She frowned, neither denying nor agreeing if the writing was true.

Leaning closer to Rita's ear, I whispered. "This could be a message from your spirit guides. I suggest you take this seriously."

Rita laid her hand over the paper, covering the script from prying eyes and looked auspiciously across the room, wondering if anyone had noticed. She nodded, assuming it had some value since it was written in shorthand.

"Let one of your friends read it, just to be sure I read it correctly." I moved across the room, giving Rita space to consider its value. My spirit guides didn't reveal the meaning of the message, nor what improper path Rita was taking. I sensed this message was very important and hoped Rita would take it seriously.

Rita picked up the paper, folded it, and tucked it into her purse. Then, turned abruptly on her heels without a comment, and returned to her seat at the table. This was Rita's first psychic experience, but there was more to come.

Almost a year later, I received a phone call from Rita.

"I think there's a ghost in my house." Rita's voice trembled as she spoke.

"Why? What makes you think it's a ghost?"

"Because, lately I. . . I'm losing control of my temper. I feel like throwing knives and other things, too. And that's not all. So does my next-door neighbor, and the lady across the street. In fact, the neighbors are still talking about the neighbor who went after some boys with a butcher knife. It's only a matter of time before someone gets hurt."

"A knife? When did this happen?"

"My God! It was Halloween! The kids came up on my neighbor's porch. She chased them away, waving a knife in the air. The neighbors are frightened. There's something strange going on with all these knife attacks. Can you help me?" Rita's voice trailed to a frightened whisper. "I scared. My son thinks something is in his bedroom. I'm afraid a ghost will attack him."

"Does your son feel threatened?"

"You bet he does. Even the air in his bedroom feels heavy. He told me that he hears strange sounds at night. He's sure a ghost is in the closet. He's so frightened that he removed the closet doors."

"How old is your son?"

"He's eighteen."

"Does any other room bother you?"

"Yes, the furnace room scares me. I'm afraid to go down there."

Even though Rita mentioned knives, I sensed no immediate danger.

"My teacher and I will come to your house tomorrow and investigate. In the meantime, say a prayer. Ask for God's protection." I knew Rita didn't attend church, but felt inclined to warn her to pray anyway.

The next afternoon, June and I arrived at Rita's home. As we approached the tri-level house, I noticed a blurred haze over the front windows. *Perhaps the windows haven't been washed in a long time.* As I moved closer to the house, I could see the windows were clean, but a dingy film covered the glass. "Do you see a haze over the front window?" I whispered to June.

June, always teaching, explained the veiled presence. "The haze you sense is an indication of paranormal activity. Its negative energy. Most people don't see that haze. You're sensing it, not actually seeing it. It's a way to sense a spirit's presence long before entering the haunted area. You'll learn to know the difference between a dirty window and one that is veiled with a spirit's presence."

"What causes that veiled appearance?"

"A dense atmosphere. It's unhealthy, dull like a sick person's aura. Negative energy often draws in troubled spirits. We'll understand more when we tune into the spirit."

"Can the haze obstruct our communication?"

"Mental communication isn't barred by a wall or a piece of glass. Space or time have little effect on mental communication."

Rita met us at the door and led us into the living room. Even though the afternoon sun filtered through the large front window, an eerie haze hung heavy over the room.

Upon entering the living room, I froze in my tracks. "O'mph!" It felt like someone punched in the stomach. *Something just attacked me. It doesn't want me there. If I can feel the hate, then June feels it, too.* My attention was drawn toward a shadowy image against the wall. Although I couldn't sense if the spirit was male or female, I felt its smoldering hatred coming at me. *It's threatening me.* Before taking another step, I mentally surrounded myself with white light, took a deep breath, then followed the two into the living room.

Rita, unaware of the malevolent presence, chatted non-stop as she led us into the kitchen.

"Tell us what kind of problems you're having," June asked.

"Well, first of all, I'm having trouble with my husband. He started running around. I think he's having trouble facing old age. Maybe it's his male menopause."

I watched June moving about the kitchen, touching the table with her fingertips. *She's reading the vibrations of the room.* I felt the presence of an enraged spirit. *It followed us in the kitchen. Step away from me!* I stepped back to watch June as she worked.

"I figured my husband was running around again, so I waited up for him one night. When he came home early the next the morning, I started throwing pots and pans at him. I just had to throw something."

"Have you always thrown things when you're angry?"

"No! I don't know what came over me. I kicked him out of the house the next day."

"Why did you feel a need to throw things?"

"It started a couple of years ago. I even thought about throwing a knife at him. It's getting harder to control my temper."

"How long have you lived in this house?" June asked.

A surprised look flashed across Rita's face. "A couple of years. Why? Do you think this house has something to do with my anger? If it is, I want to find out before something bad happens."

Without giving Rita an answer, June caught my eye and gave a slight nod.

Again, I sensed the raging spirit demanding that I leave, and the hair on my arms bristled in response.

"There's a spirit downstairs," June said as she made her way through the kitchen, toward the stairs leading to the lower level. She knew where to go even though she had never been in this house before.

"Can I watch?" Rita asked as she followed June down the stairs.

"Yes. Sure," June replied.

The stairs led to a spacious foyer with a door on each side, and opened to a large, brightly lit family room.

June entered the foyer and stopped abruptly, as if someone had obstructed her way. She closed her eyes and searched within her mind's eye. "It's here," she said, pointing to the door on the left.

"That's the furnace room," Rita answered.

Opening the door cautiously, I stepped into a dark room, made a quick turn, and ducked. *Whoa! Someone's throwing something at me.* I jolted backward and dashed out of the room. "It's an angry woman," I shouted while slamming the door closed. Even as I spoke, violent threats blasted through the closed door. "She threw something at me. I never experienced a spirit actually throwing an object before."

June agreed with a gentle nod, then entered the dark room with her hand up, palm forward in front of her. "Bless you," she said, then gave a quick jerk and ducked. "Yep. She's throwing things!" June stood in the darkness for several minutes and mentally communicated with the spirit. *"Come upstairs so we can help you."*

Again, I sensed swear words erupting within the small room. The spirit refused to move out of the darkness.

Rita wondered what we were talking about. She didn't see a woman or hear anyone swearing. "I don't know what this is about, but I'm afraid to go in that room, especially at night."

I could feel Rita's doubt. She was wondering if we really knew what we were doing. After all, she didn't see anything unusual.

June emerged from the furnace room and closed the door behind her. "We'll bring her through upstairs in the living room." June started up the stairs and headed toward the living room. Rita and I followed close behind.

June pointed to a chair. "Marie, I want you to sit here, facing north."

I turned the chair toward the north and sat down.

Rita leaned against the door jamb, hesitating to enter the living room. Even though she didn't see anything, she felt the tension building in the room.

June took a deep breath, expanding her chest, drawing in the white light energy. She sent a mental message to calm the spirit by sending peace and love. Again, she took a deep breath, drawing in more white light energy. She needed the extra energy to keep this spirit under control.

I clutched the arms of the chair, closed my eyes, and tuned into the woman's thoughts. "It's a raving mad woman. She's against that wall. She's angry because we're here." I took a deep breath, drew in the white light, then imaged God's light surrounding my body. "The woman wants to strike out. She wants to hit me."

The spirit's anger penetrated the living room, and the atmosphere turned cold and hostile. The feeling of violent hatred erupted from the shadow against the wall.

"Marie. Bring her through," June instructed, expanding her chest as if preparing for a battle. Again, she inhaled deeply, planted her feet firmly, ready to defend herself.

With eyes closed, I relayed the spirit's thoughts. "She won't come near me. She's mad at her husband. He burned her newborn baby. Oh, God! She hates him. She hates men." As I spoke, I felt the force of raging madness pushing against my chest.

June's voice turned gentle. "Come along," she coaxed the spirit. "We're here to help you."

"The spirit hates everyone. I see images of pioneer woman living in a log cabin on this property. That was long before this house was built. She still roams this area. . . It's her farm. I see her holding a knife. She wants to kill her husband."

June interrupted. "Clear yourself Marie. She's not going to come through today. We'll have to wait until next week and bring her to a rescue circle. We're going to need a lot of love and compassion for this one. She became insane when she lost her baby."

A bewildered look crossed Rita's face. "Why can't the spirit be exorcised from my house today?"

I opened my eyes and explained. "Sometimes it doesn't work like that. This spirit thinks she lives on this property. We can't get her to leave unless we change her way of thinking."

June nodded, encouraging me to answer, but was ready to interrupt if I offered a wrong suggestion. June turned toward Rita. "We'll investigate this next week at our rescue circle."

The following week, the chairs were placed in a circle formation, and the lights dimmed. The mediums closed their eyes and began slow, deep breathing to lower their brains waves. After they felt relaxed, they mentally covered themselves in the God's white light for protection.

June began the meeting with the usual prayer, and today she included a special request. "We ask our guides to bring the spirit from Rita's house to the circle."

A hush of silence fell over the dimly lit room.

June was sitting, facing north, when a blast of swear words bombarded her mind. The raving mad spirit had approached from behind. *"Stand back,"* June mentally demanded.

The atmosphere in the room grew icy cold and more intense.

All of a sudden, the spirit slammed into June's body. Before June could control the spirit, she had taken her ring off and hurled it across the room.

I ducked as the ring whizzed past my ear. If it had struck me, it would have raised quite a welt. I mentally thanked my guides for protecting me.

June, in contact with the spirit, felt its frenzied anger. She took another deep breath, drew in more energy, and braced herself for a battle. Her body twisted and turned as the spirit within struggled to escape. June was determined to help this spirit and wouldn't release it from her body until it had calmed down. She mentally communicated with the spirit. *"Relax. . . Be calm."* June imaged a cloud of white light encompassing the spirit. Then projected a feeling of love and peace. *"Bless you. Bless you,"* she mentally repeated over and over.

Within seconds, the spirit succumbed to the blessing, lessening her anger.

When June was sure the woman was under control, she opened her eyes and nodded. "Marie, you can take her now."

"O'mph!" The spirit slammed into my body with tremendous force. Suddenly, my spirit guides interceded and clamped my hands together in prayer position. I felt a sense of relief knowing my guides were protecting me. I couldn't move my hands apart, and the spirit couldn't use my hands to strike out. With my hands clasped in prayer position, the raving spirit couldn't leave my body. While the enraged spirit struggled to wrench my hands apart, I mentally began a calming chant. *"You are loved. You feel God's love,"* When the woman had calmed down, I allowed her the use of my voice. My facial muscles tightened, and the spirit used my voice to scream. "I hate him! He burned my baby." Though it was difficult to control the spirit's anger, my voice came through in short spurts. "Her baby died at birth. Her husband burned it. The ground was frozen. He couldn't bury it. He threw it into the wood-burning stove."

The spirit's voice broke through and shrieked, "I'll kill him! I'll find him and I'll kill him!"

June knelt down but didn't take my hands as she normally would have done. There was no need because my hands were clasped in prayer position. "Bless you." June said, then turned to the circle of women. "Send this woman love and peace. Help her to forgive. Help her to understand."

Each medium acted with the compassion of their maternal instinct. They understood the spirit's anguish and turned their hands, palms up on their lap to release their prayers. Each mentally sent their own personal message, asking God to help this spirit.

Within seconds, a peaceful feeling began to permeate the room.

Tears streamed down my cheeks as I felt the spirit absorbing the love, releasing its anger.

June addressed the spirit calmly. "Your husband didn't know what to do. He didn't realize how this would affect you. There were no neighbors for miles." June continued to change the woman's thoughts by confronting her with questions. "We can bring your baby to you. Would you like that?"

The word "baby" was powerful. The spirit's "yes," came as my head bobbed up and down.

June, knowing that spirits respond to suggestions, held out her arms as if holding a baby. "Is this a boy or a girl?" she asked, making the image stronger by requiring an answer.

An overwhelming feeling of immense joy swept across my mind, and my hands unfolded from prayer position. "A girl," the spirit answered, then folded my arms as if cradling the precious baby.

"You may take your baby with you," June instructed softly. "Go with the angels."

The spirit slipped out of my body, and I felt a feeling of maternal love as I watched her drifting peacefully toward a brilliant light.

After the meeting, I relayed the impressions I had psychically received. "The woman and her husband had been pioneers in the area many years ago. The man couldn't bury the baby because the ground was frozen. Since he was uneducated, he didn't realize how his actions would lead his wife to madness. The woman, having a strong maternal instinct, was unable to forgive her husband. She roamed her farm in a thought pattern of insanity far beyond her death."

In retrospect, it's easy to see how this spirit could have been mistaken as evil because her acts of violent had influenced the neighbors. When a subdivision of homes was built over her farm, the woman's presence was still felt. But now that the spirit has crossed over into the light, her negative influence will no longer be felt.

When June gave the appearance of presenting the baby, it changed the woman's thoughts. Thoughts can create changes in a spirit's environment, just as they do in the earthly world.

Consider Rita's husband's position. It's possible that he felt the spirit's hatred and mistakenly feared it as his wife's anger. This could have influenced him to stay away from the house? This was never examined, but the damage was done. Within the year, Rita had filed for divorce.

It was interesting the way the spirit guides got Rita's attention. Her first attempt at automatic writing was presented in shorthand for a reason. Because Rita couldn't read nor write shorthand, another person would have to verify the message, and perhaps urge her to change her ways.

I wasn't privy to Rita's possible indiscretion. The message was for Rita, and only she could accept or reject the warning.

It doesn't matter who you are. Anyone can be influenced when they're in the path of a raging spirit. People can be influenced by a spirit hovering nearby, whether they believe in ghosts or not.

9

ALIEN RESCUE

When an unidentified flying object crashed in Roswell, New Mexico in 1947, the United States government denied the event, and classified it "Top Secret." My contact with an alien occurred nearly thirty years later, 1974, when the existence of extraterrestrials still remained Top Secret and all evidence was barred from public viewing. But now that many nations are declassifying some UFO sightings, I feel free to relate my experience.

January 1974, June received a phone call from a woman who lived near either Arizona or Colorado. This happened long ago, and I since I had no direct contact with the woman, wasn't privy to the exact location. The woman explained that for the past several weeks, she saw a small spirit hovering at the foot of her bed. She contacted many psychics, but none seemed qualified to help with her unusual request. After an extensive search, she was given June's name as a psychic that might be able to help. June listened intently as the woman told her story.

In mid-November of 1973, the woman was awakened in the middle of the night by the thunderous sound of a distant explosion. She bolted upright, startled by a blinding flash of light that lit the sky behind the mountains, lighting her bedroom like daylight. The burst of light was brighter than anything she had ever seen. She jumped out of bed and hurried to the window. Though she saw nothing in the immediate area, she watched for several hours at an occasional burst of subdued blue light in the distance. When the activity ceased, she went back to bed.

The following morning, she arose early, expecting the television to explain the explosion. But nothing was mentioned of the flash of light or the sound of the explosion. The woman, curious about the unexplained event, questioned her neighbors and friends. Many claimed to have heard the explosion. Some had seen the sky light up, but no one had an explanation. Days later, rumors spread like wildfire that a spaceship had crashed, and four or five extraterrestrial beings were found at the crash site. They didn't know if the aliens were dead or alive. Even though no official statement was made by United States investigators, the area was barred from public access.

Several days after the unexplained explosion, the woman claimed she was awakened in the middle of the night by the presence of a small male figure standing at the foot of her bed. It had somehow awakened her and held her attention. Strangely, she had no fear of the misty image and made no attempt to get out of bed. When she raised her head off the pillow to get a better view, an unusual calmness swept over her, and she mentally received a message.

"There is no danger," it assured her.

She listened for a voice, but instead received another thought in her head.

"Help me," the blurred image seemed to plead.

She laid back down and studied the image. It had long arms and a large head in comparison to its slight body. Its skin was smooth with a peculiar, pale-green tinge. Even though it was an eerie image, she was amazed at the calmness it projected and felt confident it was friendly. Not knowing what to do, she mentally relayed a message. "I don't know how to help you." She was astonished when she realized it had understood her, and that she had communicated by mental telepathy.

Several minutes later, the small image disappeared.

She slipped out of bed and turned on the lights. First, she checked the spot where the image had stood, but found nothing unusual. She searched each room for evidence that someone might have entered the house, but the doors and windows were still locked, and nothing had been disturbed.

Several nights later, the image again hovered at the foot of her bed and mentally repeated the same message.

"Help me."

Nearly a week had passed and during that time, the alien had visited the woman four or five times, always asking for help. She marveled at the calmness that swept over her each time it appeared. The woman had never thought of using telepathy before and was amazed that during each visit, they conversed mentally. Now it seemed natural. This alien had selected her for some special reason, and she felt compelled to search for help. By now, she suspected this was an extraterrestrial who died in at crash site.

June listened to the woman's unusual story. She believed in extraterrestrials and wasn't surprised by the woman's description. Though she had no experience rescuing alien spirits, she accepted the challenge. Being a spiritual person, she felt confident that she could draw upon the spiritual realm for assistance.

After agreeing to help, June instructed the woman over the telephone on the basics of meditation, then told her this: "Next Wednesday at exactly five o'clock in the evening, close your eyes and meditate. That will be eight o'clock Michigan time. Visualize the alien as you saw him. When his image is clear in your mind, mentally communicate that you are going to help him. Mentally direct him to the address that I've given you. We'll take over then. A group of women will be meditating at that exact time and will tune into you. These thoughts will pass through time and space, and will provide a channel on which the alien can travel."

June, accepting the concept that collective thoughts are energy, knew that when two or more minds join together in concentration, they create a flow of energy by which the thoughts are transferred. These thoughts would be used as a path, like waves or patterns of energy. In this way, the alien's thoughts would be sent to June, and she, in turn, would direct her thoughts to him. This would enable the alien to travel without knowing the actual geography. June intuitively believed the rescue would be spiritually guided and all the mediums would be protected every step of the way.

The time and place was set, and June contacted the members, informing us of the unusual circumstances. She tuned into her spirit guides and received unusual preparations for the meeting, which she passed along to the members. "Dress carefully. No bright clothing or sparkles that would be distracting to the alien. No gaudy jewelry that could jingle or clink. We must prevent the slightest hint of noise. Be exceptionally clean. This alien is sensitive to sound and smell."

Wednesday arrived, and a larger than usual group, more than twenty-five women, placed their chairs in circle formation. The telephone was taken off the hook and the doors locked. A woman was posted outside the room to insure there would be no interruption. A small lamp, shielded by a scarf draped across a cardboard box, was placed on the floor in a corner. All other lights were turned off.

Each medium took her place, alternating the powerful psychics to be seated between the students, thus balancing the energy evenly within the circle.

June continued channeling the instruction from the spirit world, cautioning the members. "An alien who died in a spaceship crash will be visiting us. He asks for help to return to his proper dimension. There will be no smoking before class. No impurities in the air. Please be extremely quiet… Not even a whisper. My guides informed me that this alien isn't accustomed to voices. Mental telepathy is his way of communicating, and any sound would be unbearable to him. This alien will be aware of our thoughts, so keep your thoughts pure and direct a gentleness of heart to this being. Please be absolutely silent. Don't move about in your chairs. No noise and above all, don't cough. If you're wearing jewelry that might clink together and create even the slightest noise, remove it now. Because this is an unusual rescue, I will sit facing east. Marie, I want you to sit facing north."

I moved quietly across the room and sat facing north. This was all new to me and even though I didn't know what to expect, I was excited to begin.

At exactly 7:50 in the evening, the members closed their eyes and began slow, deep breathing to slow down their brain waves.

"Send peace, love, and gentleness to this alien. This will strengthen the energy within the circle." June slipped off her shoes for a closer connection to the earth and laid her hands in her lap, palms up. She closed her eyes and recited the opening prayer.

"We sit with love and understanding. We ask our guides to stand by for protection, guidance, and directions. We ask for the very highest spiritual guidance we are capable of using. We request God's assistance to guide this alien back to his spiritual home. Thank you, God, for this opportunity to help."

The room fell silent while the group meditated for a full ten minutes.

Shortly after eight o'clock, June moved silently into the center of the circle and knelt down, thus offering a non-threatening posture. Within minutes, a mist-like apparition began to take form.

With my eyes closed, I visualized the alien hovering in the darkness. He was about four feet tall with smooth skin. I couldn't see his feet, but that wasn't unusual. Most spirits don't usually appear in full form, and their feet are seldom seen. My attention was drawn to the compassion in his eyes. They were round, slightly larger than a silver dollar, with crystalline turquoise speckles and no irises. I was curious as to why he never blinked until I noticed that he appeared to have no eyelids. Of course, he may have had eyelids, but I was unable to see them. It's difficult to see details in a ghostly image when viewing in the mind's eye. I sensed a gentleness within his eyes, and that his power was his wisdom and his compassion.

I studied the alien's features. His nose was large, and somewhat wide for the size of his face. Not that it protruded, but it spread across his face, reminding me of the snout of an animal. He had a small, underdeveloped chin, and because he was in darkness, I couldn't see if he had a mouth. Yet, I sensed a slit where his mouth would be. His head was bald, with no protrusions where ears would be. *I wonder how he could be sensitive to sound without ears?* After some thought, I realized that each pitch or tone gives off vibrations and the alien will feel the vibrations. He had squared shoulders and long arms, and his smooth skin was a pale green. Although his body was not clearly visible below his waist, I sensed his feet were off the ground.

The room grew eerily quiet.

From time to time, I opened my eyes to watch June, who was kneeling in the center of the circle. I sat still, quietly observing. Suddenly, I begin making a circle on my forehead with my index finger. *Why am I doing this?* I motioned to Emma, who was sitting across the circle, and pointed to my forehead.

Emma pointed to the center of the circle and nodded, indicating for me to enter.

I moved quietly into the circle and knelt down in front of the alien image.

June, sensing someone had entered the circle, opened her eyes, nodded her approval, and closed her eyes again.

With closed eyes, I tuned into the misty image. After a while, I envisioned several children's alphabet blocks floating in the darkness. *The alien is trying to communicate by imagining a set of blocks.* Although the letters formed unrecognizable words, I knew he was trying to communicate grammatically in an earth-like language. The feeling of love and compassion that he projected was overwhelming. I sensed his wisdom, compassion, and superior intelligence were far above the earth's humans.

The mediums had been sitting in silence for more than half an hour with their palms up and hands extended, transferring love and energy to the center of the circle. They sat mesmerized by the calmness that he projected. Some mediums saw nothing but sensed his gentle presence.

June, still kneeling in the center of the circle, mentally informed the alien. *"Use the circle's energy to summon your spirit guides."*

More than an hour passed, and the energy within the circle began to wane.

The alien's eyes revealed his helplessness as he realized he wouldn't be released from his earthbound confinement. His image faded in the darkness until he had completely disappeared.

The members sat motionless in absolute silence.

After a while, June rose from her kneeling position. "Turn on the lights. Break circle, girls. He's gone," she said softly. "We've done our best, but he hasn't been released. He's still earthbound. We'll meet tomorrow and try again."

The lights were turned on and the mediums moved their chairs quickly out of circle formation. A hushed sadness filled the room.

On the drive home, I wondered if it was possible to help this alien? The look of gentleness within his eyes was still overwhelming. I had never seen, nor sensed, such compassion in anyone's eyes before. It was well after eleven o'clock that evening when I arrived home. *This is an image I don't want to forget.* I went directly upstairs to a bedroom that I use as my painting studio and laid a clean canvas on the easel. *I have to paint the alien's face while it's still fresh in my memory.* After I finished painting, I made it a point to paint the date on the canvas for later verification.

The following evening, the class arrived early, bubbling with excitement. After placing their chairs in a circle, the dimly lit room fell silent. Once again, June opened with a prayer. "We ask God to send guardian angels to guide this gentle spirit back to his spiritual home. We ask for the very highest spiritual guidance we are capable of using."

Each medium prayed in her own way, mentally projecting white light to create energy.

I closed my eyes, and after several minutes of absolute silence, I again saw a mist forming fragments of the alien. *His image is beginning to take shape.*

The alien had emerged from the opening where June had been seated before moving to the center of the circle.

Once again, I focused on the image hovering in the center of the circle.

The alien remained motionless, pleading with his eyes, begging to be helped.

The room took on the ambiance of being embraced in his aura of compassion.

No one stirred. No one spoke.

Several minutes passed, and again I felt compelled to move into the circle and kneel beside June. I sensed that I had to be in contact with part of his mind, while June would be in contact with the other. *Perhaps the alien's complex mind would be too great for one human to withstand alone.*

While the group meditated, a feeling of compassion flowed from his turquoise-speckled eyes as he waited helplessly for the divine light to release him. After fifteen or twenty minutes, the alien began to fade. His eyes twinkled a message of thanks, and his thoughts projected an expression of gratitude. He understood he was leaving.

Before the alien faded out of sight, I received his mental message. *"Compassion for all mankind."*

A hushed silence fell over the dimly lit room. After a while, June rose from her kneeling position, and moved her chair out of circle formation. "He's gone. Turn the lights on and break circle. He found his way."

The women hurriedly moved their chairs out of the circle formation and the room came alive with an excited chatter at the amazing rescue that had just taken place.

When I left that evening, I was still bubbling with excitement. I went straight up to my painting studio and again painted the alien while his features were still fresh in my mind. I wanted to preserve his face exactly as I remember. Sensing the date would be important future reference, I painted 1974 beneath my name. Naturally, I wanted to tell everyone, but the government was still denying the existence of extraterrestrials. So, I kept the rescue a secret. As the years passed, newspapers began printing articles about flying saucers and describing alien beings. Feeling more confident, I showed my closest friends the face of the alien that I had painted in 1974 and revealed my unusual experience.

At the next meeting, the members discussed their experiences. Since they were novices to matters of outer space, they offered their logical assumptions. Perhaps the alien had large eyes because he came from a subterranean habitat, or a planet with less sunlight. Since his eyes were large, any light may have been irritating. The unusual green tinge to his skin could be the result of copper in his blood, if he had blood that oxidized to a tinge of green, or it might be due to a photosynthesis of chlorophyll caused by the earth's sunlight. The alien appeared to have a slit for a mouth, reflecting the possibility of a different, or smaller, intake of food than humans. After seeing the alien had no protrusions where his ears might be, and mentally conversing with him, they assumed mental telepathy was his method of communication. Without ears the alien still could feel vibrations, just a deaf person can feel the percussion of a drum. The alien spirit made no attempt to coexist with the medium's mind. Perhaps he only transferred his thoughts because he knew a human mind could not assimilate his superior intellect.

I glean from this rescue that this alien had a soul because he accepted the God light as a path to his spiritual home. Is it possible that the God light is universal? Since earth-born spirits can travel on the energy of a thought, then it would be reasonable to assume an alien spirit might travel on a thought as well.

Consider that some aliens could be earth's ancestors, and through millions of years, they developed more spiritually than earth people. If this were so, then the afterlife they enter might be extraordinarily different.

Perhaps more beautiful and heavenly than an earth-born person could imagine. Also, consider the possibility that each species of aliens have evolved differently. If this were so, then the beings who exist in different galaxies might also have a soul. But if it isn't a religious belief or ideology that prevents an alien spirit from entering his proper spiritual dimension, then we must consider the possibility of different afterlife dimensions existing for different galaxies.

On the other hand, consider a species of aliens that had not developed spiritually, or had lost contact with the God consciousness within their soul. The members wondered, would their afterlife be according to their spiritual development? If so, do they have a different spiritual belief? Are there different levels of afterlife for beings from different galaxies? If so, might the afterlife they enter be different, or more glorious, than an earth-born person?

Aliens and afterlife are an intriguing issue. As long as people deny the existence of life in other galaxies, then we cannot probe the question of afterlife for all. We will always wonder if aliens enter the same dimension after death as earth-born people do, or if they enter a different dimension. We will always wonder where we go after death.

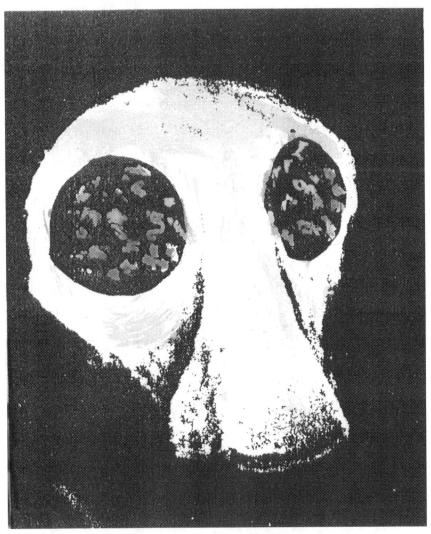

ALIEN: Painted by Marie Harriette Kay, 1974.

10

COINCIDENCE OR INTERVENTION

Have you ever said, "Boy! Wasn't that a coincidence? Lucky I was there at the right time." Did you brush it off as a coincidence? When a serious problem needs to be addressed, a spirit guide will create said meeting. Imagine the synchronicity of the timing, location, and need, for two strangers to meet at the right time. It would take a mastermind to orchestrate such a meeting. Some coincidences may just be by chance, but many are brilliantly arranged by spiritual beings.

Through the years, I often found myself at a place where someone was in need of help. I have since learned that I had been guided by spirits to help others. The following experience wasn't a coincidence. It was a magnificently synchronized event beautifully orchestrated,by spiritual intervention.

TRUCK OUT OF CONTROL

Late one evening, I was driving home from my sister's house. She lives about five miles away, and I had visited her often over the past twenty years. I always took the same easy route home. Tonight, for some strange reason,

I found myself driving in the opposite direction. As I was traveling down the dark road, I wondered, *How did I get here? Why did I take this street?*

This four-lane road is seldom used because it doesn't lead to a main street. The only drivers who use this road are local residents. Tonight, there was no traffic.

I would soon be approaching a small bridge where the two west-bound lanes turn into a single lane. There is only one west-bound lane ahead to cross the bridge. I had just moved into the single lane when I looked in my rear-view mirror and saw headlights coming down the right lane behind me.

The headlights were approaching fast, so I knew it was traveling well beyond the legal speed limit. The lights were high, so I assumed it was a truck barreling through the darkness. *It should have moved over by now so it could cross the bridge.*

But the truck continued traveling at a high rate of speed in the right lane.

If it doesn't move to the center lane soon, it's going to crash into the creek. There was nowhere for me to go. I had to stay in the center lane. *The right lane will end soon.* My thought ran wild. It's surprising how many thoughts can cross your mind in a matter of a few seconds. *That trucker isn't aware the right lane ends ahead.*

The headlights were approaching fast, getting closer and closer.

Time seemed to slow down. *I think that trucker fell asleep. What do I do?* The truck was traveling too fast to pull directly behind me.

Maybe if I slow down, he can move ahead of me. I slowed down my car so the truck could move ahead into the center lane.

Headlight continued approaching fast in the right lane.

He's traveling too fast. I have to do something to prevent him from falling into the creek. Again, I applied the brakes gently to slow the car.

The truck plowed past me, speeding down the right lane toward the creek.

I remembered my niece's husband say that truckers are alerted by blinking lights. I waited until the truck was slightly ahead of me, then blinked the headlights several times.

Instantly, the truck's brake lights blinked on and off. The truck veered into the center and sped safely across the bridge.

Now I understand why I'm here on this road at this time. I resumed normal speed, As I crossed the bridge, I looked up to the heavens and said, "Thank you for allowing me to prevent an accident." I believe I was guided by unseen hands to that road, and that this event was orchestrated by spiritual intervention to save that trucker's life.

FACE OF A SPIRIT DRIVING A CAR

It's not a coincidence when you feel drawn to glance in a certain direction. Spirits have the ability to project energy to attract your attention. Thoughts, whether by a spirit or a human, have enough energy to draw you to see something you might not otherwise look at. Such is the case of a spirit driving a car.

I was visiting a friend at the hospital when her two daughters entered the room. They were obviously shaken by what they had just seen.

"What's the matter. You look upset," I asked.

"We just saw a ghost!" Marilyn stepped forward. "Oh, Marie. I'm glad you're here. Maybe you can tell me why we saw a ghost."

The girls were not teenagers. They were well-educated adults in their early thirties, so I was sure they had seen something unusual. "Where did this happen?"

"My sister and I were driving here, to the hospital, when we saw a ghost in the car next to us."

"How do you know it was a ghost?"

"It was our friend. A girl who died a few months ago."

"Maybe it was someone who looked like your friend."

"No! It was her. Her eyes were looking right at us. It was like she was staring right through me. It scared the hell out of me. We both saw her staring at us."

"She wasn't looking ahead at the road," her sister chimed in. "She was looking at us."

"There's no reason to be frightened. Let me explain how this can happen. Your friend was sending thoughts to attract your attention. She used the driver's aura energy to superimpose her essence over the driver's face. Think of it as putting a veil of herself over the driver's face."

"But it was our friend's face. Her eyes. She was staring at us."

"This is how it can happen. The spirit of your friend needed extra energy to make itself visible in our earthly dimension, so she hovered near a living person and used that person's aura energy. Your friend merged with the driver's aura and used it to make her presence seen.

"How did she know how to do that?"

"Once a spirit has passed into the light, it may be enlightened. Apparently, your friend has learned how to use energy. Spirits see energy as waves and vibrations of color. They read the color. Spirits know more than we understand."

"Why were we drawn to look at that car?"

"It was your friend using mental telepathy to attract your attention. She knew I would be here, and that you would get your answer today."

"We didn't see anyone else but our friend's face. If it was her, why wasn't the driver affected?"

"Using the energy from the driver's aura didn't affect or harm the driver. Aura energy is naturally discharged from a person's body every minute of every day. There's no reason to be frightened. It was just your friend letting you know she's all right and still cares about you. I believe it was no coincidence that the spirit happened to show herself today.

GUESS WHO'S CALLING

It's not a coincidence when you know someone will be phoning you. It's simply your ability to tune into someone else's thoughts at the same time they're thinking of you. Of course, it's quite different when you know *who and why* the person is calling . Then it's paranormal—a psychic intuitive response.

This is how mental telepathy works. When a person is about to phone you, that thought is sent out into the universe. That thought occupies a place in space. Each thought has energy, and if you are lucky or intuitive, you can tune into that thought. Having attended the psychic workshop for many months, I noticed my psychic awareness was increasing.

One evening a woman was awakened in the middle of the night by the sound of the phone ringing. At that time, she had only one telephone, and it was downstairs in the kitchen. She jumped out of bed and started running down the stairs with her husband following close behind.

"Who could be calling at this time of night?" he shouted as he followed his wife down the stairs.

Without hesitation, the answer spewed from her mouth. "It's Andy."

The husband didn't notice that she called out the man's name. He was too busy wondering why the man was phoning. "Andy! Why is he calling?"

Again, she answered spontaneously. "He's in jail."

The phone call confirmed her statement. The police had arrested Andy for driving erratically. The husband informed the officer that Andy didn't drink. He was diabetic and was most likely having an attack. They should give him some orange juice and when he felt better, assist him home safely.

Even though the woman was amazed by the incident, she let the matter go rather than trying to explain something she didn't understand.

This story explains the saying; Thoughts are things occupying a place in space. It's clear that Andy had, in desperation, projected the thought of phoning his friend, and the wife had picked up on the man's message. If this has ever happened to you, perhaps you are psychic as well.

MENTAL TELEPATHY

Mental telepathy is a way of communicating mind-to-mind. It's important to know how to sense a positive thought from a negative thought. Being in tune with thoughts will help in your daily life. This may require practice to use your extra sensory perception wisely.

Try this experiment. You and a friend will agree on a day and time, then mentally send a thought. It's best to try this experiment just before going to sleep because your body will be relaxed and your mind cleared of daily responsibilities. Person One will be the sender. Person Two will be the receiver. Person One will mentally send the thought of a color. It may be a picture of the actual color, the name of the color, or the spelling.

Person Two will quiet her brain waves to receive the message. She will concentrate on her forehead—the mind's eye—and allow the messages to present itself. Distance isn't a barrier. Your friend can be next door or miles away. Even a wall cannot stop the message. It isn't necessary to repeat the message. Just send the thought for a few seconds. By repeatedly trying to send the same message, you may increase tension, thus placing negative energy around your body. The aim is to relax.

The next morning, phone each other to see if you correctly identified the color. On your next attempt, switch sides. Try to receive the message. Are you best at sending or receiving? Thereafter, send different images, such as an object, an emotion, or the image of a personal friend. Attempt sending different images until you are successful. Practice makes perfect.

MÜNCHHAUSEN

Münchhausen syndrome by proxy is a mental disorder in which a person deliberately and repeatedly causes physical or mental harm to another person. They either fake symptoms about themselves or cause someone else to be sick. Medical books often refer to Münchhausen syndrome by proxy as a mother who causes harm to her own child. Now that brings us to mischievous imps who are drawn to people who have Münchhausen syndrome by proxy.

As my awareness grew, I began to realize it was not a coincidence when I was guided to be at a certain place at a certain time. While visiting my friend Colleen, she explained her problem.

"I suspect I'm being poisoned. I get sick every time my friend Angie visits. On the last visit, Angie brought a pie, and within minutes of eating the pie, I became nauseated and ill.

Immediately, I sensed her friend had Münchhausen, but listened to be sure my intuition was correct. "Tell me more."

"Every time Angie visits, I get sick. I think she's poisoning me. Will you come over tomorrow and meet her? Find out if my suspicions are true."

I agreed, and the following day I went to Colleen's house to meet Angie. Outwardly, the woman appeared normal, pleasant, and unusually talkative. But what I sensed beneath her cordial smile was a dark and menacing personality.

Colleen turned toward Angie. "This is my friend Marie. She's a psychic."

Angie raised her eyebrows curiously. "Do you do readings?"

"No. It's something I was never interested in. Besides, if I tell people something they don't want to hear, they get angry with me. They usually don't follow my advice, anyway."

Colleen interrupted. "What do you see about me?"

"There are many excellent readers who can give messages from the deceased. It wasn't something I was guided to do, but I'll try." I took a deep breath and slowed down my brain waves. "I see a man standing next to you. Oh my God! He has a hole in his forehead. Do you know of such a man?"

Colleen frowned. "Yes. The law firm where I work recently handled that murder case."

"I guess that tragedy is still on your mind. At least it is still clinging to your energy field. This is what many psychics call a 'direct hit.'"

"What does that mean?"

"A direct hit is when the psychic gives' information that applied to only one person. Not many people would have such a morbid memory clinging to their aura."

Angie interrupted. "Do me! What do you see around me? What you see at my house?"

"Okay." Again, I took a long, deep breath, slowing down my brain waves until images began to form in my mind's eye. "I see negative energy in your basement. Do you have a basement in your house?"

"Yes. What else do you see?"

"Well, it's not good. I see imps and gremlin-like beings in your basement. They're mischievous pranksters."

Angie smiled, pleased that impish beings were hanging out in her basement.

"How did they get in Angie's basement? Where do they come from," Colleen asked.

"I've read articles that claim drones and imps exist in the fifth dimension. I haven't had much experience with imps, so I don't know much about them."

"What dimension do we live in?" Colleen asked.

"We live in the third dimension. The article says that imps and drones live in the fifth, a lower dimension."

Colleen took a large gulp of coffee. Within minutes, her face contorted, and she writhed in pain.

A faint smile slipped across Angie's lips as she watched her friend suffering.

The obvious answer flashed across my mind. *Angie slipped something in Colleen's coffee.*

Angie seemed amused as she watched Colleen holding her stomach in pain.

Again, my spirit guides flashed the word Münchhausen across my mind. *Ah, now I know why I'm here. Angie could be suffering from Münchhausen. I wonder if she is being influenced by the mischievous entities in her basement?*

Colleen clutched her stomach. "I have diarrhea," she grumbled and took off running to the bathroom.

I eyed my coffee cup. *Glad I didn't drink it.* In my mind's eye, I viewed Angie's basement as a dingy, dark place. Imp-like creatures were jumping up and down with delight at Colleen's distress. *Hum, so this is what Angie has aligned herself with. Apparently, she enjoys the same evilness as the devilish imps.* I didn't intend to speak, but my guides took over and the words spewed from my mouth. "You better be careful. I don't see much joy in the future if you continue on the path you have chosen." Normally, I wouldn't have been quite so blunt, but my guide felt it was necessary to give the warning.

Angie glared spitefully as she grabbed her coat. She left the room in a huff, slamming the front door hard behind her.

After Angie left, I warned Colleen that Angie could have Münchhausen syndrome by proxy, and the imps were influencing her to cause all kinds of mischief. Now it was up to Colleen to either report the problem to the proper authorities, end the friendship, or live with the consequences.

Now, why do I tell this? My visit didn't solve the problem. First, my job was done when I informed Colleen of the truth. Second, it was not my place to solve Colleen's problem. She has free will and would have to decide what steps should be taken.

I glean from this experience that some imps are kind and helpful. However, the imps in Angie's basement were incorrigible and uncontrollable.

They enjoyed watching Angie inflict pain to others. So, we wonder, were these imps drawn to the basement by Angie's mental defect? Like draws like. It's possible that Angie's illness had attracted like-minded entities who enjoyed watching someone in pain. It's also possible that the imp's presence had accelerated Angie's disease. It's not known if immoral creatures are drawn to people who have Münchhausen, but it certainly applied in this case. Now that you, the reader, are aware of Münchhausen, you will be able to alert another potential victim.

As to impish entities, I accept there is a fifth dimension—a reality that exists outside of the earthly world we live in. And I accept that some creatures are multidimensional. Even though they exist in their own fifth dimension, they can materialize in our third dimension. Imps, gnomes, and goblins may sound like folklore, but having visualized them in my mind's eye and observed their destructive behavior, I now accept that they can manifest physically or metaphysically into our earthly dimension.

MÜNCHHAUSEN AND THE CAR DEALER

Since my guides have brought my attention to Münchhausen disease, they have nudged me to be in a certain place at a certain time to further expose this disease. This time, the victim had been guided to me by spiritual intervention.

I had taken my car to the dealer for a tune-up. Since it would be several hours before they could start the job, a mechanic was assigned to drive me home. At the time, I was unaware that I had been guided to be at this place to help this man. I had never met him before, and while driving me home, he began blurting out his problems.

"Every time my brother visits me, I get sick to my stomach."

I declined to answer right away, recognizing that his spirit guides were prompting him to speak.

"I wonder why I get sick?"

"Do you eat when your brother comes over?" My spirit guides directed me to counsel him on Münchhausen as his brother's problem.

"Yeah. We always have something to eat, or at least have a drink."

"Have you ever heard about people who have Münchhausen syndrome by proxy?"

The man frowned and shook his head. "No. What is that?"

"It's a mental disorder, a disease that causes a person to deliberately and repeatedly harm another person."

The man cocked his head curiously, recognizing what his brother could have been doing.

"When you get back to the dealership, look up the word Münchhausen. See if this applies to what is happening to you."

My job was done. The guides had directed me to the place where I was needed. I can only hope the man followed up with his research. Now it's up to him to solve his problem.

THE POWER OF IMPS

Just viewing an object or a scene can affect your physical body. A pleasant picture can make you feel happy or serene, while a repulsive picture will make you feel upset, angry, or even raise your blood pressure. There is also a paranormal effect. Pictures with negative images give off vibrations of caustic energy that can affect the viewer.

Many years ago, I felt prompted to purchase a book of fairies, elves, and imps. Being an artist, I considered drawing fairies and needed a few illustrations to work with. Having no immediate use for it that day, I set it aside. Today, while teaching meditation in my home, I felt guided to place the book in the center of the room. It wasn't a coincidence that I chose to present this book to my class. I was ready to learn about the powerful energy given off by negative images and its effect on a group of students.

Today I was teaching a class to see images in the mind's eye and had placed the book of faeries in the center of the circle. I opened to a page with pictures of elves, drones, and imps. Little did I know I had been guided to do so. There was a lesson to be learned.

The students placed their chairs in a circle formation. They closed their eyes and began slow, deep breathing. After exhaling slowly, they were ready to visualize within their mind's eye.

As I sat quietly, I had mischievous thoughts running through my head. *How can I play a trick on my students? Whoa! It's not like me to think of playing tricks on students. Where are these thoughts coming from? This isn't my normal way of thinking. In fact, it's the opposite of how I think.*

Linda squirmed in her seat, giggled, then burst out laughing. She didn't mean to disrupt the class, but it was obvious she couldn't control her laughter. Within minutes, several members joined in the giggling. Their giggles turned to laughter. The laughter was contagious and spread throughout the room.

Where is this negative energy coming from? As I pondered the question, my attention was drawn to the book. The page was open to a picture of imps laughing. *So this is where the mischievous energy is coming from.* As soon as I realized the pictures of imps had infected the group, I jumped up and closed the book. I placed the book in a black plastic garbage bag, which, coincidently, had been placed on a nearby table. *The black color will prevent any negative energies from escaping.* I shoved the book in the black bag, carried it outside, and tossed it into the trash.

After I returned to the room, the members had quieted down, and calmness spread across the room. Before continuing the class, I took several minutes to explain how the negative energy on the page of imps had affected the whole group.

"The energy of the pictures had drawn elves and imps into the circle. Since the page showed several imps, their combined energy was strong enough to transfer their mischievous thoughts to the class. Each of you sensed the impish thoughts enter your mind. Let this be a lesson. Beware of what you bring in your house. Be cautious of antique, books, and pictures. They could have spirit attachments, as well."

We all gleaned a great lesson. The mere picture of devious imps had the power to change the student's behavior drastically. Since the members were prepared to receive a paranormal experience the images on the page was an effective presentation.

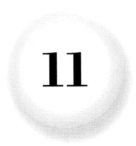

INTRODUCTION TO PSYCHOMETRY

Psychometry is the ability to read vibrations on an object by touch. You, acting as the reader, will hold an object in your hand. Begin by taking slow, deep breaths, then exhaling slowly until you feel relaxed. Concentrate on your forehead—the third eye. When the brain waves are slowed down, you, the reader, can sense or see an image in the mind's eye. Psychometry may be done with eyes open or closed. Objects, such as antiques, jewelry, mirrors, photographs, and clothing may be impressed with vibrations left by the previous owner. A spirit may hover nearby to protect its possession-the object being read, or there may not be a spirit present at all, just thought vibrations that are strong enough to be impressed in an object.

All objects contain vibrations of energy. A student holding an object may not see images or symbols on the first try. Some may not see within the mind's eye but will sense an image. They are sentient—meaning they sense. Those who see or visualize the vibration on an object are clairvoyants. The reader will attempt to analyze the images. If correctly analyzed, they will reveal information about the owner of the object.

Each psychometry reading should begin with a prayer for protection. It may be mentally or verbally spoken. The reader may call upon guardian angels, spirit guides, or God's white light. The prayer often used is as follows.

"We ask our guides for protection, guidance, and directions. We ask for the highest spiritual guidance we are capable of using."

However, if the reader exaggerates or gives false information, this creates negative energy and will block valid information. If the client—the person receiving the reading—mistrusts the reader, this often creates negative energy and obstructs communication between the reader and the owner of the object. A reader may also use psychometry to contact a deceased person by holding an object they once owned. Learning to use psychometry can be another tool for helping others.

THE BRACELET

Bonnie asked me to find a gold bracelet she had lost. She remembered where she had worn the bracelet and assumed it was lost outside the house.

"Yes, of course, I'll try. Let me hold something that you wear, like your watch or glasses. I can get impressions from them."

Bonnie slipped off her wristwatch. "I think I lost the bracelet outside."

I held the watch in my left hand.

"Why are you using your left hand?"

"Because the left side of the body is connected to the right side of the brain. Right brain is intuitive." I took a deep breath and slowed down my brain waves. I wasn't sure I could do this because it wasn't a serious matter. Usually, I did better if the request was important. Having known Bonnie for only a few months, I knew nothing about her personal life. With closed eyes, I fingered Bonnie's watch. Images began to form in my mind's eye. "I see a colonial house. Do you live in a large, white colonial?"

"Yes," Bonnie answered.

This confirmation proved I was on the right track and encouraged me to continue. "I'm in an upstairs bedroom at the back of this house. There's a closet to the right."

Bonnie interrupted. "My bedroom is at the back of the house, and my closet is to the right of the doorway."

"All right. Now I'm looking at the top shelf of the closet. There's a box or square container on that shelf. Inside this container is another container, something cloth with a pocket."

"I have a suitcase on the top shelf of my closet. Could this be what you're seeing?"

"I don't know. I can only describe what I see. This other container has a pocket, like a purse or something with a pouch." Within my mind's eye I saw a pocket against a black background. This pocket belonged to a smaller container. Now I saw a large, hard container. The images didn't make sense, and though it seemed strange, I relayed what I was seeing.

Bonnie again interrupted. "I don't keep my purses on the top shelf."

"Okay. Now I see white yarn. The yarn could be from a sweater. I see white yarn against something black."

"I don't keep my sweaters on the top shelf either," Bonnie insisted, sure I was making a mistake. "I wouldn't put a sweater on that shelf."

"All right. Try not to give me negative answers. They tend to turn me off." I took another deep breath, then exhaled slowly, searching the darkness of my mind's eye. "It's a white sweater in a pocket." It seemed illogical that a sweater could fit in a pocket, but I shrugged my shoulders and continued. "I see a gold bracelet caught in this white sweater. Hum, there's something about the yarn of the white sweater. I don't know what this means, but I think you will find your bracelet on the top shelf of your closet. I'm sorry. That's all I see."

"Okay. I'll look in the closet, but I never put purses or sweaters on that shelf." Bonnie was sure I was mistaken because the clues didn't make sense. There wasn't much hope in her voice as she said goodbye.

Later that day, Bonnie phoned me. "I found my bracelet. It was on the top shelf of the closet, just like you said. It was in a suitcase. Inside that suitcase was my missing purse. So, I looked in the side pocket of the purse, and there it was. The bracelet was caught on a piece of white yarn."

"That must be the white sweater I saw. The yarn, I mean."

"Yes. My bracelet must have snagged that yarn off my sweater."

By using psychometry, I had tuned into the energy attached to Bonnie's watch. Her subconscious had registered the bracelet caught on her sweater but dismissed it as inconsequential at the time. She had absentmindedly put the purse in the suitcase, something she wouldn't normally do. Her subconscious registered the bracelet in the pocket of the purse. This information was attached to the watch that she was wearing and revealed where the gold bracelet now lay.

The lesson I learned is to not get discouraged if you don't understand the clues right away. Look deeper into the meaning of the images seen in the mind's eye. The reading was not magical, simply a matter of correctly analyzing the impressions seen surrounding Bonnie's watch. Not very strange at all.

MOTORCYCLE DRIVER

Psychometry can be done by merely touching an object, such as the morning newspaper. I read an article in the newspaper about a man who took his fiancé's daughter for a ride on a motorcycle. Both the motorcycle driver and child were killed in an accident. By merely holding the newspaper, I received information. While reading the article, I mentally received a message from the man. He claimed the accident was his fault, and he blamed himself for the little girl's death. The next day, a friend and I were discussing the newspaper article.

"I wondered how it happened?"

Without thinking, I blurted out, "It was his fault."

My friend looked at me curiously. "What? How do you know it was his fault?"

"Ah. I mean, I wonder if it was his fault." I didn't realize I had blurted out what the spirit had told me. This friend wasn't into the paranormal, so I declined to explain further. *I must learn to think before I speak.*

There are times when my spirit guides inform me of things I would not ordinarily know, and I would blurt it out before I realize I was speaking. When these facts later prove to be true, I realize it was my guides speaking through me.

A similar incident occurred when I again misspoke out of turn. I was at a woman's house watching home movies of her family reunion. I didn't know her family well and had never met her grandparents, so I didn't know which of her relatives were alive or which were dead. On the screen, I saw an elderly man with wide suspenders and his pants pulled up high over his tummy. A gentle breeze swept across my face, indicating the presence of a spirit. I blurted out, "That's Grandpa Fred."

The woman looked at me curiously. "How did you know that? You never met him. Grandpa died years ago."

How was I to answer? I couldn't say, "because he just told me his name." Without revealing what the spirit had told me, I answered. "I just asked if that was your grandpa, Fred?" I heaved a sigh of relief when the woman was satisfied with my answer. From that time on, I was careful not to repeat so quickly what the spirits were telling me.

THE CRYSTAL BEADS

I received a phone call from a girl named Leslie, whom I remember as a quiet girl in her early twenties. I had met her briefly on several occasions, so it surprised me when she asked for help.

"Something is happening to me. My friend Sally said I should call you. I think I have some kind of a possession."

"What do you mean, possession?"

"I have an uncontrollable urge to swear. It's not like me to do this. I'm swearing all the time. Marie, can you help me?"

"Okay. Tell me what's going on."

"It's not like me to say 'son of a bitch.' I'm starting to swear when I'm angry. And I seem to get angry for no reason at all."

I agreed to meet with Leslie, but because she lived quite a distance away, I asked to meet at Sally's house, our mutual friend. Sally was waiting at the front door and led me into the living room. As I entered the living room, I sensed swear words coming at me from the kitchen. *A spirit is upset that I'm here.*

Leslie poked her head out the kitchen door. "Well, son of a bitch, you made good time getting here. How the hell are you?" Leslie slapped her hand across her mouth, astonished at her own choice of words.

Having met Leslie before, I was taken off guard by her coarse greeting. Sensing a spirit was influencing her, I made no further comment of her crude language and followed Sally to the kitchen. "Do you always talk this way?" I moved closer to make eye contact. *There's a definite grayish film over her eyes. She's possessed.*

"Hell, yes." Leslie paused. "God, Marie, I don't know why I said that. Words come out of my mouth before I realize it."

More swears bombarded my senses, followed by a threat. *"Stay away. Don't come any closer."*

I retaliated with a mental a protest. *"I'll come closer if I want to."*

Although Leslie didn't hear my comment, she backed away with a startled look on her face. She wasn't sure why, but something had frightened her enough to make her step back.

"Why does Leslie look so frightened?" Sally asked, as she watched Leslie backing away.

Leslie continued backing away. "What the hell do you want?" she muttered, slamming her hand over her mouth. It was apparent that the spirit had easily intimidated her.

I raised my hand, palm forward, toward Leslie and shouted in a booming voice. "Stand back!"

Leslie jumped back, startled at the thunderous command. She frowned, wondering why I was hollering at her. Sally jumped back also, confused at my boisterous demand.

As soon as the spirit slipped out of Leslie's body, the color of her eyes returned to their natural pale blue color.

Sensing the spirit was still hovering close by, I again shouted. "Stand back!" I moved toward Leslie and began a mental conversation. *"What do you want? You have no right to bother this girl."*

Leslie's eyes widened, frightened by my bellowing attack.

The spirit responded with more swears and again demanded that I mind my own business.

Sally, unaware of the spirit, didn't understand what was happening. "Why is Leslie frightened? What's going on?"

I sensed my spirit guides were about to direct me, and a calmness swept over me. Without answering Sally's question, I left the kitchen and entered the living room. I scanned the walls for a place to restrain the spirit. *I have to confine him, but where? Ah, I'll put him in the foyer by the front door.* With the power of my guides, I mentally drew the spirit into the foyer, then sent a strong mental message. *"You'll stay in this foyer until my next rescue session. Then I'll bring you to class."* Keep in mind that I, personally, don't have the power to confine the spirit. The guides directed the action, then channeled it through me, and the spirit had to obey.

Now subjected to the thought pattern of confinement, the spirit believed he was unable to leave.

I returned to the kitchen, where Leslie was smiling and casually chatting. She was her old self again—naïve and carelessly casual about the frightening event that had just taken place.

How easy it was to confine him in the foyer, I thought, smiling. "Let's find out more about your swearing. Do you know where this spirit came from?" I asked Leslie, accepted a steaming hot cup of coffee.

"I don't know. I just started swearing a lot, and I'm angry at things that never bothered me before."

"Try to recall what you did prior to these feelings. Anything different?"

Leslie shook her head. "Can't think of anything unusual."

"Did you use an Ouija board?" I asked, as my spirit guides prompted the question.

"Yeah. Sure. A group of my friends really got the board moving, too."

"Did the Ouija board spell out swear words?"

Leslie's forehead furrowed as she considered the possibility. "Yeah. That's funny. It did spell swear words. Do you think there's any connection?"

"That's probably where it came from. Psychic energy attracts spirits. Especially using the Ouija board. Too bad you didn't know how to protect yourself. From now on, don't fool around with psychic stuff until you learn what it's all about. Everything is under control for now. The spirit won't bother you anymore. I'm taking it to class next week."

"Where is it?" Sally asked, her eyes darting from side to side.

"He's confined in the foyer. Don't worry. He can't get out of that space."

"When are you coming back here to take him out?"

"I don't have to return to your house. I'll use mentally telepathy to draw him to the rescue circle next week."

The following week, as I dressed for the meeting, my attention was drawn to a gold chain necklace. *Hum. I guess I should wear this.* I wasn't sure why, but I trusted my intuition and slipped the necklace over my head.

I slid into the front seat of the car and took a deep breath to slow down my brain waves. With closed eyes, I directed my attention to my friend's foyer and mentally drew the spirit out, restricting it to the back seat of the car. *There! Now that's done.*

It was more than a seven-mile drive to the meeting place. Gray clouds blocked the moonlight, making the road unusually dark. A cold wind lashed rain against the window, making it difficult to see the road ahead. All the while, the spirit was hurling obscenities, protesting his confinement in the back seat. I had driven a short way when a fine mist began to settle on the inside of the windows. I turned the defroster on, but the fan refused to budge. *I'll roll down the side window. Maybe the air will dry the mist.*

The cold air barely cleared the glass, and the rain started pouring down with a vengeance. Cars whizzed by, splashing muddy street-rain against the windows.

I flipped on the windshield wipers, but they only smeared black streaks of mud across the window. Unable to see the road, I pushed the spray button repeatedly. But, without water, the wipers smeared more mud across the glass. Desperate to see, I leaned my head out the side window and continued slamming the spray button harder. *The wiper fluid is empty.*

The spirit continued cursing from the back of the car.

I gripped the steering wheel tighter and pressed on. I had never been afraid of a spirit before, but panic was beginning to set in. *This spirit is getting the upper hand. What did I get myself into?*

As I turned onto the main street, a heavy stream of traffic moved through the darkness. Headlight beams of the on-coming traffic sent glaring prisms against the wet window.

The mud is smearing the glass. I can't see the road. I have to get help immediately. Ahead, through the pouring rain, a flashing neon sign caught my attention. The blinking lights of the gas station were a welcome sight. Still blinded by the glare of on-coming traffic, I spun the wheel and ran over the curb with a hard thump. After easing the car to a stop, I heaved a sigh of relief.

The gas station attendant waved and shouted. "Need some window cleaner?"

With a grateful nod, I switched open the hood. *I'm safe now. I have only a few more miles to go.*

After the attendant filled the water container and wiped the mud off the windows, I started out again. A heavy mist still blurred the inside of the window, making it impossible to see. I stuck my head out of the window again. The rain pelted my face like sharp needles as the car crawled down the dark street.

The windshield wipers have plenty of water. I banged hard at the sprayer. The water sprayed the glass, smearing muddy street water across the window. Panic set in. I gripped the wheel tighter. *Could the spirit be causing these problems? I can't show fear. That will feed him negative energy. I'm determined to help him in spite of the trouble he is causing.* By the time I arrived at the meeting, I was exhausted.

June greeted me with a smile as she scanned the energy hovering beside me. "You brought someone with you," she said in her pleasant English accent.

"Yes. I locked him in the foyer last week until I could bring him here," I replied, pleased at my ability to control the angry spirit.

June frowned. "You had no right to do that. Spirits are people, just like you and me."

Oh, I didn't think of it in that way. I was glad June brought it to my attention and made a mental note to be more respectful in the future.

The women placed their chairs in a circle, the lights dimmed, and the meeting began. June opened the meeting with a prayer, and each woman mentally covered herself in white light. While June assisted other mediums, I mentally restrained the spirit away from me. As long as I didn't fear, he couldn't come close to me.

June, knowing I was holding a spirit at bay, knelt down in front of me, gripped my hands, and nodded. "Let him through now, Marie."

I took a deep breath and drew the spirit into my body. My forehead wrinkled and my lips turned down to a scowl. The male spirit used my voice and screamed aloud, "Son of a bitch."

June, sensing the spirit wanted to hit her, applied a slight pressure to my hands. "You cannot lift your hands," she chanted firmly.

This physical touch convinced the spirit that he was powerless against her. "Son of a Bitch! Let me go! What the hell am I doing here?" The spirit squirmed and tried to jerk my hands away from June's grip.

"You're dead! Did you know that, my dear?" June said in quaint English dialect.

"Yeah, I know. So what?"

"Can we help you?"

The spirit still using my voice shouted, "No!" With my mind connected to the spirit's thoughts, I sensed something suddenly frightened him. He had just become aware of the necklace around my neck. He reacted frantically, twisting and turning, trying to jerk away from the necklace. "Get it away from me," his masculine voice bellowed.

I felt my chest recoiling inward. *He's trying to get away from the crystal beads.* I felt the spirit's fear as it struggled to move away. *I'm determined to help him in spite of himself.*

"What are you afraid of?" June asked, applying a gentle pressure on my hands to assure the spirit.

Again, my body twisted, trying to separate itself from the necklace lying against my chest. My voice turned defensive as the spirit pleaded. "Get it away. I never felt anything like this before."

June took the necklace in her hands. "Why do you fear this necklace?"

"Get it away!"

June touched the necklace to my chest. "Let the love from this necklace flow through you."

My mind, still connected to the spirit's thoughts, sensed he had never experienced love before and had difficulty accepting the strange vibrations. Within minutes, the loving energy within the necklace had penetrated his consciousness. He began to cry. Tears streamed down my face. The calming effect of love had lessened his anger. "I never felt anything like this before."

June waited, giving the spirit time to release his fear. "Why are you here? Why didn't you cross over to the other side when you knew you were dead?"

My voice again turned masculine and answered in a repentant lament. "Because I did some terrible things when I was alive. I was afraid I would be punished."

"God understands all that has happened. Why don't you go with your guardian angels? They'll explain what to do. Now that you understand love, it will be easier for you to see your guides. There's no point in you staying earthbound any longer."

The spirit answered humbly, without a trace of fear or hostility. "I never knew love was that powerful. I never had love, not even as a child. I don't remember even knowing about love."

"Go with the angels. Let them guide you."

I sensed his mind was releasing a lifetime of hatred that he carried into his death. With eyes still closed, I raised my hands over my head and released the spirit. The spirit slipped out of my body and drifted toward two white figures waiting in the distance. Within seconds, I imaged him floating toward the glowing white figures.

When the meeting was over, June approached me. "Where did you get that necklace?"

"From my mother-in-law."

"She must think a great deal of you. That necklace is very powerful. It was given to you with love."

I grasped the necklace in my hand. "I never realized that love could be so powerful." During the mental connection with the spirit, I actually felt the power of love. It felt like a peaceful protection of motherly love. *Now, I understand why I had to wear this necklace tonight.*

On the ride home, the rain stopped, and the weather turned balmy. I pushed the button on the window wipers and watched the blades whisk away the last few raindrops. The mist had completely disappeared from the inside window and the vehicle had returned to normal.

As we examine this possession, we find that Leslie and her friends may have come in contact with this spirit while playing with an Ouija board. Unfortunately, they didn't know how to use the white light to form a shield of protection, nor did they have the ability to recognize they were drawing a dangerous spirit into their life. It wasn't revealed why this spirit chose Leslie. Perhaps he was guided by his guardian angels, knowing the mediumship contact would be made, thus freeing Leslie of the possession.

The spirit was earthbound by his own thoughts that God would not accept him. When the necklace transmitted an essence of unconditional love, his fear vanished. This rescue taught the mediums not to judge another person too quickly. While this man was alive, he never felt motherly love. The loving essence within the necklace touched his conscience, releasing the anger that held him earthbound. It appears that spiritual intervention was perfectly orchestrated to rescue this spirit.

The Ouija board was the catalyst that drew the spirits into the earth plane. There are evil, earthbound entities searching for a place or a person to attached themselves to. Most exorcist attack the malevolent spirits by accusing it of being evil, therefore reaffirming its belief. They often verbally condemn it burn in the fires of hell. This infuriates the spirit, and in fear of burning in hell, it lashes back with vengeance.

From my own experience, I have used the power of God's love to weaken a threatening entity. Love is more powerful than you can imagine. By presenting loving words in a mantra-like chant, the spirit was exorcised from its host. Evil exists in darkness, and darkness cannot stand in the light.

12

SPIRITS THAT COME WITH SCENTS

A medium concentrates on her third eye to visualize psychically. The third eye is at the bridge of the nose between the eyebrows. It's related to the pineal gland, which is in the interior of the brain. The medium will close her eyes and slow down her brain waves to see, or sense, within the mind's eye.

The right side of the brain is intuitive. It receives messages by symbols, images, and emotion. It imagines, dreams, and creates. When the right side of the brain is active, the left side of the brain becomes less active, allowing the intuitive brain to smell phantom odors.

The left side of the brain is logical. It's related to language, using logic and analysis. The left side of the brain counts, keeps time, plans, and draws conclusions. Each side of the brain usually work together to complete a thought or an action.

The nervous system crosses over as it enters the brain. The nerves from the right side of the body cross over to the left side of the brain, and the nerves from the left side of the body cross over to the right side of the brain. The left side of the brain operates the right hand, and the right side of the brain operates the left hand. The most common way to experience a spirit is by sensing it, visualizing it in the mind's eye, or feeling the icy chill of its presence. The most common way to experience a spirit is by sensing it, visualizing it in the mind's eye, or feeling the icy chill of its presence. There is also a paranormal way to detect a spirit, by smelling it.

VANILLA LADY

A group of students, ten or twelve, were seated in a semi-circle in June's living room, listening to a lecture on extra-sensory perception.

I closed my eyes and began slow, deep breathing. When I reached a deep state of relaxation, I sensed a presence in the corner of the room. *Someone is watching me.* With closed eyes, I envisioned a woman standing behind me. She wore a long, old-fashioned dress and a stiff poke bonnet. Sensing the spirit was curious, I mentally sent a message to the woman. *"Bless you."*

The woman seemed encouraged and, using the energy of my blessing, drifted closer.

I sat very still, raised my ethereal hand toward the woman, and again sent a message. *"Thank you for coming."* As my thoughts reached the spirit, a pleasant swirl of cool air brushed against my face. *The woman is acknowledging the blessing.* With eyes closed, I repeated the welcome. *"Bless you. Thank you for joining our class."*

The strong scent of vanilla drifted from the corner of the room where the spirit was standing.

She's wearing vanilla. I opened my eyes and glanced around the room. *Had anyone else smelled the vanilla?* Again, a waft of cool air brushed against my face. I smiled, pleased that the woman had responded to my thoughts.

The smell of vanilla grew stronger, filling the corner of the room where she stood.

No one seemed to notice the smell, so I interrupted June's lecture. "There's a woman standing in the corner. She's come to visit us. She's wearing vanilla for perfume. Does anyone smell the vanilla?"

The students turned toward the corner of the room and began sniffing the air.

June stopped the lecture, closed her eyes, then nodded, acknowledging that she also saw the entity. "Class, anyone who wants to smell the vanilla, go over to Marie's chair. Mentally bless the lady and thank her for coming. Your blessing will give her the energy to stay in our dimension a little longer."

The scent of vanilla grew stronger.

Several students crossed the room, sniffing the air. Those who were able to slow down their brain waves became aware of the scent. They were fascinated that they could walk in and out of the area where the scent was most prominent. This was the students' first experience smelling a disembodied spirit, and it was quite an awakening. During the next several weeks, the vanilla lady made two more appearances. Each visit reinforced the students' belief in phantom odors.

When the students slowed down their brain waves and closed their eyes, they were able to see the woman within their mind's eye. The phantom smell of vanilla stayed confined in a small area and never drifted throughout the room. This would have been impossible if real vanilla had been present. Aromas naturally drift and eventually fade away. However, the odor was smelled psychically, lasted only a few seconds, then disappeared without a trace, confirming the vanilla was a paranormal phenomenon.

MARY, MOTHER OF JESUS

A phantom smell may present itself before a meeting begins, thus identifying the spirit's presence. It's a rare occasion when the fragrant scent of flowers materializes. Mary, the mother of Jesus, often presents a blessing with the essence of roses.

Twelve members placed their chairs in a circle, in preparation for a rescue circle. But the spirit world had prepared a new experience for the students.

Laura looked curiously at her hands, then called out. "I smell roses."

Mandy, the student sitting next to Laura, leaned forward. "I smell roses on her hands."

"Roses are often associated with Mary, the mother of Jesus," I answered.

Within seconds, a peaceful, loving feeling permeated the room.

"The smell is fading. I can't smell it anymore," Laura whispered.

Carol, who was sitting next to Laura, looked at her hands. "Now I can smell the roses." she said, opening her hands, palms up.

Linda, who was sitting next to Carol, spoke next. "The roses are here now. I feel so special, like the roses are blessing me. Is that possible?

"Yes. Remember to thank the spirit who offered the flowers."

"Oh, it's fading," Linda whispered.

The pungent odor of roses materialized on each member's hand, pausing briefly to emit a peaceful feeling. The essence continued moving from one person to the next until it had made its way completely around the circle. When it came to the last person, the smell of roses faded away.

"We are privileged to have had a blessing from Mary, the mother of Jesus." I closed my eyes and took a moment to thank the Holy Mother for her blessing.

All members experienced the phantom odor. The fragrance didn't drift across the room as a smell would normally do. It remained confined to one person's hand until it moved to the next hand. If it had been a physical rose, everyone would have smelled it at the same time. Because the scent remained confined to only one area at a time, gives credence that the scent was paranormal. This experience reaffirmed my own Christian belief. A blessing from a sacred spirit is rare indeed.

AUSCHWITZ

June was holding a rescue circle in the living room of her home. Usually ten to twelve members would attend, but tonight more than twenty members showed up and placed their chairs in a circle.

Frowning curiously, I glanced around the room. *I wonder why so many mediums came tonight? The atmosphere feels exceptionally heavy. Is something special going to happen?*

June began with a prayer. "We sit with love and understanding. We ask our guides to stand by for protection and guidance. We ask for the highest spiritual guidance we are capable of using."

The women closed their eyes and began slow, deep breathing to lower their brain waves. With each breath, they mentally envisioned white light flowing into the top of their head, through their body, and out of their hands to the center of the circle. This white light would be their protection while interacting with the spirit world.

As the group meditated, a foreboding premonition of dread filled the atmosphere. The dimly lit room grew uncannily cool and eerily silent. The loathsome feeling continued building until the room felt oppressively heavy.

With closed eyes, I concentrated on my forehead and looked within. Though I saw no image, I sensed something moving silently toward the room from a great distance. *I've never experienced anything like this before. I can almost hear an eerie humming sound, like thunder roaring in the distance.* I cocked my head and looked deeper within. *Something huge is moving toward the room.*

June, sensing the oppression, scanned the room. Her attention was drawn to me. She moved quietly across the room and spoke softly. "Marie, I see a chalk-white face superimposed over your face."

I searched within the darkness of my mind. An emaciated, stone-white face with dead, expressionless black eyes hovered in front of me. "I see a chalk-white mask."

June knelt down in front of me.

With closed eyes, I squinted to see through the mist. "There are dark, oppressive clouds moving toward us."

The impression of heavy, gray clouds roiling and churning was felt by most of the mediums.

"I see a long string of boxcars approaching. They sound like thunderclouds rumbling in the distance. I can actually feel the vibrations moving through my body."

June nodded. She, too, saw the blurred image of boxcars materializing, creeping silently overhead toward the ceiling of the room.

When the boxcars reached the center of the room, they stopped and hovered in space. The room grew eerily silent. An eerie void of emptiness filled the room, and the atmosphere took on the morbid sensation of death. Suddenly, a blast of foul stench flooded the room. Some mediums covered their faces with their hands, gasping and coughing. Some opened their eyes, frantically searching for the source of the obnoxious smell.

The long string of boxcars hovered in midair, and the foul stench grew stronger.

I gagged and coughed. I wanted to put my hands to cover my face but sensed I shouldn't touch the death mask in front of me.

"Marie, you have someone with you?" June asked.

The emaciated face hovered in midair but gave no acknowledgement.

June started to reach for my hands but drew back as she instinctively realized she should not distract my concentration.

"Near me. Not in me," I whispered. My voice turned somber and subdued. "There is a spirit. . ." I stopped in mid-sentence. "No, not one spirit. . . Many spirits. Oh, my God, Auschwitz!" I blurted out aloud when I recognized the oppressive scene playing out before me. "They're taking them to the gas chambers." The hair on my arms stood up in confirmation as I witnessed the sickening scene of emaciated spirits hovering overhead. "I see body after body. They're packed like sardines, standing upright in the boxcars. Their flesh is rotting. *They have no presence of mind. . . No emotion.*"

The boxcars of lifeless bodies hovered overhead. The victims remained standing upright in death because there was no room for them to fall down.

In my mind's eye, I saw masses of bodies, as if the boxcar walls were no longer present. Men, women, and children stared into space with vague, expressionless faces, their eyes sunken from starvation and hopelessness, their minds deadened by deprivation, unable to focus on anything around them. *Have they escaped their own hell by withdrawing from their awareness?*

"My God, they don't even think about death. They've been deprived of hope for so long that they have become like mindless zombies. They're going to the gas chambers in Auschwitz. They don't have any purpose. Nothing matters to them. They just *are!*"

June knelt down in front and turned her palms up. "Ladies. Send peace and loving energy. Bless all those who have come to us."

The mediums placed their hands on their lap and turned their palms up. Each mentally projected a sincere blessing from their hearts. From the deepest part of their soul.

Time seemed to stand still. After several minutes, the oppressive heaviness began to subside. And the boxcars faded as well. As suddenly as the foul stench had come, it disappeared. Not a hint of odor remained in the room that only moments ago had been unbearably offensive.

"They're leaving," I said. "I see boxcars with masses of people rising above us. They seem to have no purpose, no state of mind. They just do as they're told. They travel, rising. They're being drawn toward the God light by a celestial force." I opened my eyes. "Oh, my God, I've never known such deprivation."

Now that the stone-white mask was now gone, June placed her hands on my hands. "Mentally create a beam of light on which they can travel. They're exhausted and need the energy of the God light. Mentally, tell them to go to the light."

In my mind's eye, I created a path of light. "They're heading toward the light. The victims are numb and emotionless. They travel like one state of mind."

The room grew eerily silence as he members quietly prayed. Several seconds later, a peaceful atmosphere permeated the room.

"They're gone," I said, then opened my eyes. "Oh, my God. I've never known such despair. They didn't have the will to fight, or even to stay alive."

"Bless them," June said, then closed the circle with a prayer of thanksgiving. "Thank you, God, for allowing us to rescue these victims and for directing them to the light. We understand the opportunity to help another, whether in this dimension or another, is a privilege. As we give to others, we give to ourselves. Thank you, God, for the opportunity to help."

The women quickly removed their chairs from circle formation, and the meeting came to an end.

All the members experienced the foul stench of the boxcars. If the smell had been a physical odor, it could not have dissipated instantly and completely without leaving a trace of odor behind. This offers additional credence that scents are particles of energy, just as thoughts are vibration of energy.

In retrospect, I look back at this humbling experience. It was truly the most unusual, rewarding rescue I had ever encountered. I believe the victims were divinely guided to the rescue circle for the sole purpose of immersing them in the God light, thereby cleansing the horrendous emotion from their memory. It is my belief that God often lifts the person out of the physical body before their actual death. So it's possible that the victims had already withdrawn from their own awareness and didn't realize they were dead. Because they appeared absent of emotion, they may already have been released to the God light. The positive power of prayer moved the victims toward the light. The God light was the power that allowed their entrance into the next dimension.

BEFORE VS. AFTER ENTERING THE GOD LIGHT

After death, most spirits pass into the God light without any difficulty. However, some spirits remain earthbound, unable to pass through the veil of darkness into the God light. Through many years of dealing with many earthbound spirits, I've found many reasons why a spirit does not, cannot, or will not enter the heavenly dimension of God's light.

1. Consider the spirit, Joseph, who didn't believe in an existence after physical death. His disbelief held him earthbound, unable to see the angels or the light of the next dimension. He simply didn't believe anything else existed.

2. The family who died in a house fire and the boy who hid in the toy box feared the fire. Their fear was so intense that it held them in thought pattern of *now,* therefore, unable to enter the light. The living residents believed their house was haunted, when in fact it was the spirits who were haunted by fear.

3. The woman who sought revenge on her husband for burning their stillborn baby was earthbound by grief and her need for revenge. Held

in a thought pattern of madness, she continued searching the grounds of the property she believed she now existed.

4. The swearing spirit hiding in a closet remained earthbound because he believed he wasn't good enough to enter the light. Only when he was touched by the unconditional love pouring through the half-open door was he able to enter the light.

5. The negative energy in the doll house had never existed in human form, therefore had no reason to enter the light. Destructive energy is often neutralized or cleansed by fire.

6. The friendly spirit that came to help Robbie, claimed she was not earthbound. She had already passed into the light and had the ability to return, only temporarily, to the next dimension at will.

7. The man under the effect of drugs was unaware of his own death. The drugs left him dazed and incoherent of his demise, therefore earthbound.

8. It's possible that the event at Auschwitz was so traumatic that its energy continued as an echo in the ether. It's also possible that the Holocaust victims had already been released to the God light, but the scene needed to be played out so the mediums could complete the cleansing. It is my belief that the victims were divinely guided to the rescue circle for the sole purpose of completing their entrance into the God light.

THE NUN

After physical death, most people are drawn by a brilliant light into the next dimension. After entering the God light, the person, now in spirit, is immersed in a heavenly dimension and may experience the infinite power of pure love. Some become enlightened, having the gift of omniscient knowledge.

Before entering the God light, some spirits remain earthbound for a wide variety of reason, such as being unaware of their own demise. For them, death is not final until the medium releases the thought patterns that hold the spirit earthbound.

A group of ten mediums were seated in a circle formation, ready for the rescue meeting to begin. All lights were turned off, and the room became quiet.

I closed my eyes, and within my mind's eye, vague fragments of a battlefield began to take shape. I viewed a combat in progress through a soldier's eyes, as if I was sitting on the ground. Then, I watched the scene unfolding as if I was laying down. I felt the cool, moist earth under my body, and my nostrils smelled the musty odor of earth beneath me.

Silhouettes of smoke drifted over a field of wounded soldier. Soon, the landscape became more distinct. Wounded bodies lay scattered across the ground. The brown uniforms appeared to be Americans from World War I. Several men, with guns in hand, were running frantically in different directions, as if to escape the battle. The scene changed and I felt myself drifting, looking down at a battlefield.

An eerie silence encompassed the area, and the fighting appeared to have ended.

I sensed I was floating over a battlefield. In the distance were vague figures of wounded soldiers waving their hands in the air, pleading for help. My attention was drawn to a figure in the distance. I drifted closer.

A nun was bent over helping the wounded soldiers. She was dressed in a long white dress, a stiffly starched white headpiece, and a black cloak wrapped around her shoulders. She had been so preoccupied helping the wounded that she hadn't recognized her own death.

June, who was sitting across the circle, sensed the spirit's presence. She moved across the room and reached out to take my hands, and hesitated, aware that the spirit guides had directed the nun into my body. "My dear, do you know you're dead?" June asked the nun occupying my body.

"Oh my." The words came through my mouth in a meek, female voice. The nun looked up and viewed the scene before her. She reflected no fear, only a sudden realization of her changed condition. Then, with a swish of energy, the nun slipped out of my body and drifted upward, toward a brilliant light.

I raised my hands over my head as if taking off a sweater, and my body spontaneous shuddered, releasing any emotional residue from my body. My work was done. The nun had entered the brilliant light.

Not all spirits are earthbound by fear. The thought pattern holding the nun was her intense concentration to help, thus unable to recognize her own death. It was a new experience for me, and especially refreshing to rescue a spirit who was spiritually aware and knew exactly what to do.

THE HOARDER

I received a phone call from a reverend, asking me to examine a girl who claimed to be possessed. I was to evaluate whether there was a spirit attachment or a psychological problem. I agreed to assist in the investigation.

We arrived at a rundown frame house on the outskirts of town and made our way across a weed-infested lawn cluttered with trash to a porch equally littered. A young woman cracked the door open slightly and invited the reverend and I inside. We squeezed through a partially open door and entered a living room cluttered with ragged furniture and five or six bird cages. There was so much trash in the room that the door couldn't open completely, so we squeezed through the half-open door.

This was my first clue to the girl's fragile state of mind. I mentally prayed for spiritual assistance before entering the room. After moving several kitchen chairs to make enough space to sit down, I questioned the girl. "Tell me your problem."

"I have a spirit in my chest."

"Why do you think it's a spirit? What do you feel?"

"It's right here! I can feel it," she replied, thumping her chest firmly.

I closed my eyes and concentrated on my mind's eye. There was no spirit, only a dark aura around her head. The dark aura indicated negative reasoning or an illness. My attention was drawn toward the living room. Even though there was a wall between us, I saw a male spirit standing in the corner. He appeared frustrated because he was unable to help the girl.

This is her spirit guide. This took me by quite by surprise. I had never seen another person's spirit guide quite so clearly.

The spirit guide mentally explained his problem. *"My duty is to protect and inform this young girl of the best choices to make daily. However, she doesn't receive my messages. The child's head is confused. I can't help because she is mentally unhealthy."*

I opened my eyes and shook my head. "No. There is no ghost near you." I didn't comment on the unseen presence in the living room. It would have been too difficult to explain.

"How do you know?" the girl retaliated.

"I'm a medium. It's my job to help. I don't see a spirit in you."

"You don't know that for sure!"

"Yes, I do. If there was a spirit, I would have seen it. Have you talked to a doctor about your feelings?"

"You're just like my mother! She wants me to see a doctor. I'm not sick."

I nodded ever so slightly. "Reverend, is there anything you would like to say?"

The reverend took the girl's hand and prayed. When he was through, he rose and headed toward the front door. "Perhaps you should listen to your mother. There's nothing more I can do here."

On the drive home, I assured the reverend. "There were no spirits attached to the girl. An exorcism isn't necessary. The girl's irrational behavior, the hoarding, and the rundown condition of her house confirmed her mental confusion. I agree. The girl needs psychiatric help."

I didn't tell the reverend about the male spirit standing in the living room. He might not understand. Nor did I explain that most people have one or more spirit guides who have been with them since birth. This spirit guide may have volunteered, or perhaps he was assigned to guard this specific girl. He was to offer assistance by sending thoughts of helpful mental messages. However, because the girl had a mental defect, it was difficult to reason with her.

If a person believes they are possessed, there should be a complete analysis by a qualified medium, followed by medical professionals to evaluate, diagnose, and direct proper treatment if necessary. Regardless of medical beliefs related to spiritual afflictions or lack thereof, the phenomena related to a spiritual possession is real to the affected person.

THE DEMISE OF MY MENTOR

It was a cold winter day when I received the devastating news that my teacher, my friend and mentor, June, was ill with cancer. Many of her friends and I took turns caring for her while her husband and daughters were at work during the day. By the middle of the summer, her cancer had metastasized, and she was terminally ill.

One day, while caring for June, I was privileged to witness an extraordinary paranormal incident.

June looked up toward the ceiling and said, "I see my aunt. She's with other members of my family. They're surrounded by a large, gold cloud. It's beautiful." June had pierced the veil and was receiving a welcome from the family members who had passed over many years before. This visit signaled that she had finished her life mission and was preparing to make her transition into the next dimension. It saddened me to know that I was about to lose the person who changed my life for the better. June had awakened my psychic abilities, which allowed me to know who I was, and taught me to use my ability to help others. Several weeks later, June passed away. I feel confident she had passed into the God light quite easily.

Several months after June's demise, she came to me in a dream carrying several well-worn books. She handed me the stack of ancient books and gave me a message.

"This knowledge is yours. Now it's your turn to take over."

It wasn't long before I began teaching. Many nights I would lie awake mulling over the next day's lesson. After slowing down my brain waves, the spirit guides channeled knowledge as thoughts entering my brain. I was fascinated by the ancient wisdom, information I didn't know existed. Many nights, when nearly asleep, the information would pour into my mind for hours. The nightly information often came with a similar message from the spirit teachers.

"As you receive this information, a physical experience will be presented to verify this information is accurate."

On this specific night, the spirit guides had channeled messages past four o'clock in the morning. Realizing that a spirit doesn't tire like a human does, I sent a mental message. *"Please remember, I am human. I need to sleep."* As soon as I made the mental request, I was asleep.

Since my teacher's passing, my main interest has been rescuing earthbound spirits. I soon noticed that I was often guided to be at a haunting a house to rescue an earthbound spirit.

Many years later, I wrote a book, *Awaken Your Psychic Abilities*, an easy method to tap into your natural intelligence, awaken your spirituality and increase the connection with the spirit world. This will lead to a more peaceful existence in your daily life. The meditation and exercises have been tried and proven to be effective in the enlightenment of the God consciousness.

The book is based on the information I learned during the seven years as June's assistant, the information received in the middle of the night from the spirit guides, and the knowledge I acquired during more than fifty years of rescuing earthbound spirits. This was my way of replying to June's request to pass along the information I had learned. Now it is you, the reader's turn, to learn and pass along this information.

14

VIBRATIONS

Through many years of visiting haunted houses, I have learned not all hauntings are caused by spirits. What appears to be a haunting may only be a build-up of negative energy. A living person's angry thoughts can transmit negative feelings that can be sensed or felt by others. If the person's anger continues, those thoughts can accumulate and become powerful enough to activate a metaphysical phenomenon, such as eerie noises or moving objects. The resident may think a spirit is present, but it may not be a ghost at all. It is merely active energy. This phenomena would send the average person fleeing from their home in terror, thinking they were being attacked by a ghost.

SHAKING BED

Mary and Ed rented a summer home from their friends. Mary knew Mister and Missus Hally had been having marital problems for years and suspected their constant bickering could have left negative vibrations at their home. Mary was psychic and felt she could handle any problem should it arise. She decided not to mention her suspicions to her husband, who had little patience with the paranormal. He would not have believed that someone else's arguments could cause harm. Mary, on the other hand, was prepared for what might occur.

The first few days of the vacation, Ed enjoyed walking in the woods, unaware of the tension within the cottage. But it was not a calm setting for Mary. When she had time to sit quietly, negative thoughts crept into her head. *I hate it here! Can't stand it! Hate it! Gotta get out of here!* The thoughts invaded her mind night and day. She knew the disturbing thoughts were left by the feuding couple. Each time the distressing thoughts invaded her mind, she would clear them away by mentally covering herself in God's white light and filling the room with the same loving light. But the positive energy only lasted a day or two, then the negative thoughts returned. It was becoming difficult to block the intense thoughts.

Some mornings Mary would awake with thoughts rushing through her head. *Gotta get out of here! Can't stand it!* As the days passed, she found herself working harder and harder to neutralize the negative feelings.

By the end of the first week, the negative vibrations found their way into Mary's sleep. This night she had a frightening nightmare that something was attacking her. She tossed her head from side to side, trying to wake herself up. She tried to scream, but still in a deep sleep, was unable to utter a sound. After struggling for what seemed like a long time, she was able to force a moaning sound.

"Are you all right? You're dreaming," Ed grumbled, gently shaking his wife's shoulder.

Mary opened her eyes, relieved to be awake.

"Yes," she answered, still trembling from the nightmarish dream. "I felt someone was attacking me." She wrapped her arms around her husband and snuggled close to his warm body. She rested uneasily the rest of the night, waking several times, lifting her head off the pillow, sensing an uninvited presence in the bedroom. The morning sunshine brought a pleasant warmth to the house, and Mary set the incident aside.

The following evening, Mary awoke abruptly in the middle of the night by the feeling that someone was in the bedroom. She lifted her head off the pillow, scanning the dark bedroom.

A grayish blob hovered at the foot of the bed.

She lay her head back down, wondering what it could be. *It's not a ghost. I've ever seen anything like that before.* She studied the shadowy blob hovering in the darkness. *It doesn't look like a human. There's no shape to it at all. It must be a negative thought form of balled up in energy.* While concentrating on the peculiar shaped form, the same negative thoughts crossed her mind. *Hate it here! Hate every thing! Gotta get out of here.* Mary lay still, observing the image. Having years of experience in the paranormal, she was able to put her fears aside and analyze the nonhuman form. *If it's not a spirit, it must be a thought form.*

Suddenly, small lump began to form at the foot of the bed.

Mary's body stiffened. *There's something moving at my toes.* She felt a lump the size of a golf ball moving at her toes. Even though it crawled beneath the mattress, she could feel its movement. *It feels like a bulge moving beneath the mattress.*

Slowly, steadily, the sinister glob moved beneath the mattress. The room took on a gloomy atmosphere as the nonhuman blob crept steadily under the mattress.

Mary's muscles tightened, and her eyes darted anxiously from side to side. *It's crawling under my leg.* She lay motionless as the glob of darkness moved upward. *It's moving up my spine. What should I do? It's crossing the center of my spine.* Mary closed her eyes and searched for an answer in her mind's eye. *This thing must be a negative energy of some kind. I doubt it's an animal. The weight of my body has no effect on it. I can still feel it moving under the mattress.*

The sinister lump continued slithering slowly upward.

She had experienced many strange phenomena over the years, but this was different. She took a deep breath and expanded her chest, drawing in positive energy. *I'm sure it's not a spirit. It has no shape or form. It doesn't have the feeling of a ghost. It's more like an accumulated mass of energy. I've never felt anything like this before.* If she had felt an icy chill, or a heaviness in the atmosphere, she might have reacted differently. But, having experienced negative energy before, she assumed this was violent thought form.

The lump proceeded upward slowly, touching each vertebra as it traveled up her back. It stopped when it reached the level of her shoulders.

What now? Mary lay still, frozen with anticipation. Again, she took a deep breath, drawing in energy.

The lump slithered ever so slowly across her shoulders, then began creeping back down her spine.

I must not fear. I must not be frightened! She remained still, repeating over and over to herself. *Fear will only add energy to this thing. I will not fear!* She lay very still while the blob made its way down her body.

The bulge slithered under the mattress until it had reached the foot of the bed.

Mary lay motionless for a long time, anticipating what might happen next.

The blob disappeared, and the room returned to a calming normal.

After Mary was sure it was gone, she rolled over and intertwining herself in the warmth of her husband's body. She lay half awake and half asleep, expecting the thing to return while her mind played back the possibilities. *Maybe it was a mouse. A ghost I could handle, but a mouse. Oh no!* The thought of a mouse made her shiver. *There's no way I can explain this to Ed. He would be frightened and want to leave.*

The room remained calm and peaceful for the rest of the night.

Several days passed without an eerie incident.

Though Mary remained cautiously aware, she knew the negative energy was still in the house, and the strange phenomena hadn't disappeared completely.

One night, Mary was tired from a long afternoon walk and decided to go to bed early. Ed stayed up to watch the television in the living room. She had just fallen asleep when she woke to the slight movement of the bed shaking. She raised her head off the pillow.

A faint light from the living room barely lit the bedroom.

She scanned the room from side to side. *There's nothing here.* She lowered her head slowly, so as not to miss a sound or movement. She waited suspiciously, her eyes open, fully expecting something to happen.

The bed shook again, this time harder, as if someone had a hold of the mattress, and was shaking it back and forth.

Mary bolted upright, her heart racing wildly.

The movement stopped.

She pulled the blankets up to her neck and sat quietly in the dark room. *What's happening?* She searched for a logical explanation. *Had there been a small earthquake? Surely, Ed would have felt it, and would have been in there to tell me about it. Maybe Ed was asleep!*

The faint sound of the television and the crinkle of the potato chip bag drifted from the living room.

Mary slid down and snuggled under the blanket. *Maybe I was dreaming.* She lay still for quite a while with her eyes open, but the eerie feeling wouldn't go away.

The bed rocked gently for a few seconds.

Again, her muscles tensed with the eerie movement. *At least this time it was gentler.* She heaved a sigh of relief when she heard Ed turn off the television. He entered the room quietly without turning on the light and slid under the blankets beside her. Mary lay still, expecting something to happen. But the bed remained quiet. *Why wasn't the bed shaking now when Ed could feel it?*

The next morning, Mary decided to check the bed thoroughly, determined to find a logical explanation for the strange shaking sensation.

After Ed left for his morning walk, Mary set out to examine the bed. She inspected the heavy metal frame, then checked each bolt to be sure they were tight and in place. *There's no loose connection that could have caused the bed to shake.* Next, she lifted each blanket gingerly, in case a small animal jumped out. None did. After shaking them, she stacked them in a pile on the floor. Hoisting one corner of the mattress, she leaned it against her shoulder while searching beneath it for signs of animal droppings. The mattress was clean. Next, she ran her hand over the area where she had felt the lump moving. *There's nothing unusual.* After checking the other three corners, she let the mattress drop back in place. As a last check, she shook the bed frame, but the bed stood firmly in place.

Now that she was sure there was no physical problem, she decided to check for a metaphysical one. After remaking the bed, she sat on the floor, leaned her back against the wall and faced the bed. She closed her eyes and tuned in psychically. *Are there any spirits in the room?* As Mary meditated, she mentally requested God's white light to fill the room.

The morning sun poured through the windows, and the bedroom remained calm and peaceful. The sound a door vibrated through the house. Ed had returned from his morning walk.

Mary went to the door to greet him, still determined not to mention the shaking bed. There were only two weeks of vacation left, and as long as the house didn't bother Ed, she could handle it.

The house remained peaceful for several days.

Ed was enjoying the vacation, and the fresh air was a welcome change from his office routine. This day he had walked a longer distance than usual. The sun had been hot, and feeling tired, he retired early. This time, Mary stayed up to watch television. About an hour later, Ed appeared at the doorway, visibly shaken. "Something is shaking the bed," he whispered.

Mary turned the sound down on the television. She found it difficult to keep a slight smile from slipping across her face. Deep inside, she was glad Ed had experienced the vibration, but she could see he was really upset. "Yes, I know. It happened to me, too. I don't think it's anything dangerous. I think it's just angry vibrations in the room."

Ed stepped further into the living room. "Vibrations from what?"

"It's energy caused by arguments between the Hally's. I think the bad feelings in their marriage caused a disruption in the energy field, especially in that bed. Someone must have been very upset in that bedroom. But don't worry; it's nothing that can hurt us."

Ed glanced suspiciously over his shoulder at the dark bedroom, and the room seemed spookier than before. Though he was tired, he was too uneasy to return to bed. He made his way into the living room and sat down on the couch. He wasn't sure what had made the bed shake, but felt relieved that Mary had accepted it so calmly.

Mary could see her husband wasn't going back to bed, so she attempted to explain. "When we first arrived, I could feel Irma's hatred of this place. I got the feeling that she wanted to get out of here very badly. I picked up a lot of her negative thoughts. I didn't tell you because I know you're uncomfortable with these things."

"Well, what does that mean? Thoughts. What's that?"

"It means I could sense her desperate thoughts."

"Do you mean you know what she was thinking?" he asked, raising his voice to a squeaky pitch.

"No. Not what she's thinking. I simply picked up on the emotion of her thoughts."

"I don't want to hear about the paranormal," Ed grumbled, then got up and turned the sound up on the television. He wasn't going to go back to bed—not yet. When the program ended, he waited for Mary to make the first move toward the bedroom.

The next day, the house returned to a normal peaceful feeling, and the bed remained still.

Several days later, Mary felt the bed shaking ever so gently. She took a deep breath and mentally filled the room with white light. The bed stopped shaking. She hesitated to mention the new incident to Ed. It would only make him edgy and upset.

During the last few days of their vacation, the bed rocked gently while they were both in it. This time the movement was so mild that Mary noticed it only because she was watching for it. Either Ed didn't feel it, or he didn't want to mention it.

The vacation had come to an end. Mary began packing their luggage while Ed closed the house for the last time. It had been quite a vacation. She was glad her husband experienced something paranormal and hoped it would make him realize the importance of her psychic abilities. Mary doubted Ed would ever spend another vacation at that place again.

Even though Mary had lessened the vibrations with white light, she knew when the Hally's returned the arguments would continue, and the thought vibrations would return. Mary wasn't surprised when she heard several years later that mister and missus Hally had divorced.

In retrospect, the shaking bed reaffirms the saying that 'thoughts are things occupying a place in space.' Although this house appeared to be haunted, there were no ghosts. The haunting was caused by an accumulation of bitter arguments, angry thoughts, and negative feelings. The couple's continuous arguments had activated the phenomena.

The glob was an accumulated ball of negativity. It wasn't a physical entity because the mattress did not buffer the feeling of it creeping beneath the padding. If it was a spirit, Mary would have mentally communicated with it. She didn't fear it because that would have caused more friction, and the shaking would have occurred harder and more often. By remaining calm and using God's white light, Mary was able to neutralize the negative energy, if only temporarily.

IRON-CLAD SENTRY GUARD

I was invited to lead a meditation at a friend's house. She had asked me to come early and to check-out a room that was always colder than the rest of the house. Being the first to arrive, I followed Denise into a room off the living room.

"Sometimes this room is icy cold. What do you pick up?"

"There's a cool chill here," I replied, moving my hand over a desk.

Denice edged in closer. "This room is always cold."

I nodded, closed my eyes, and began moving my hand around the room, feeling for any change in the atmosphere.

"What are you doing?"

"Feeling the energy. This desk is so cold, it's like putting my hand in a freezer. Who sits at this desk?" My forehead furrowed into a frown, and I stepped back. *Someone is warning me to stay away.*

"My husband does his paperwork here. He's always checking on how much money I spend."

Moving my hand over the desk, images flashed across my mind's eye. "I see a man in a suit of armor. He's rigid. Cold like a piece of metal."

"You hit the nail on the head. That's my husband," Denise grumbled.

"He's powerful. He likes to take control."

Denise nodded. "Vince tries to control me. I have to give him every grocery bill. He checks the price of everything I buy."

"Hum. Don't cross him. He can get mean."

"He does get mean. I would divorce him, but he said I wouldn't get a dime. He laughed at me. Said I wasn't smart enough to go to work. That I'd starve to death."

Even though I sensed this man lacked any normal compassion, I didn't share my thoughts with Denise. I jumped back, startled by an icy wall of resistance blocking my way. "Ugh. He doesn't want anyone in his house." It was apparent that he viewed his wife as a servant, someone to clean his house and cook the meals. "Your husband's need to dominate has created a negative energy in this room."

"I didn't tell him I invited the ladies here today. He would be furious."

"He doesn't want you to have company?"

"Hell no! He's at work and doesn't know anyone is here. He never comes home for lunch, so we won't be interrupted."

In my mind's eye, I envisioned he man as a metal-clad guard on sentry duty. *This man is extremely materialist.* Again, I didn't share my thoughts, nor did I elaborate on my visual imagery.

Our conversation was interrupted by a knock on the door. Denise left the room, and when she returned, she was followed by three ladies. "Come in," she said, guiding everyone into the living room. After several minutes of small talk, the women closed their eyes and were ready to meditate.

I began the meditation. "Slowly take a deep breath. Hold it for as long as is comfortable. As you slowly exhale, release all your cares, all your concerns. Feeling very, very relaxed."

The room grew eerily quiet.

With eyes still closed, I sensed a presence at the front door. "Your husband is angry that we're in his house," I whispered.

"That's okay. He doesn't know we're here."

Suddenly, something struck my body, jolting me backward. A powerful force pressed inside my head. *Something is pushing at the right side of my brain. It's her husband! He's coming at me in full force. He's trying to enter my mind!* I felt the physical pressure of a living person's thoughts. *He's trying to get into the intuitive side of my brain.* The energy of his thoughts grew stronger. His dominance was assaulting me as physical matter. I resisted, mentally pushing back, trying to stop the thought form. This wasn't like a ghost attacking. I had felt that before. This was different. It was a dark, sinister thrust of domination pushing at one side of my brain. *Now I understood Denise's fear.*

The women, unaware of the thought form that was attacking me, continued meditating.

With eyes closed, I began receiving impressions. My view extended past the normal concept of space and time. I visualized a man so driven with the need to control that it had become his obsession. I continued mentally pushing back, forcing this negative thought form out of my mind.

The sinister force continued pushing. Threatening to take charge.

I took a deep breath, struggling to regain my confidence. *I must resist. Can't let him gain strength from my fear. He's furious. He thinks I've invaded his territory.*

The thought form grew stronger, pressing, forcing its energy to take control. This man's thought existed in a pattern of *now*, and his need to attack was *now*.

Understanding that the attack was a thought form, I was able to release my fear. I took a deep breath, raised my hands over my head as if taking off a sweater, and, with a mighty thrust, forced the thought form from my head. When I was sure it was gone, I opened my eyes and ended the meditation with a prayer. "Thank you, God, for your protection during our meditation."

The meditation ended, and the women opened their eyes, unaware of the terrifying attack I had just endured. I didn't explain to Denise or the ladies what had happened. It would have been difficult to explain something I didn't fully understand at the time.

Even though Vince wasn't physically present, his thoughts had enough power to guard his house while he was miles away from home. He wasn't consciously aware of trying to enter my brain, but his thoughts, which were a part of him, were strong enough to attack. This phenomenon was caused by Vince's obsession to control. Because his need to dominate was constantly on his mind, his thoughts had materialized into energy. These particles of energy acted as a catalyst, activating further phenomena, such as the icy chill surrounding his desk, and the unwelcome feeling in the room. Although the man's desk felt chilled, as if a spirit was present, there were no spirits involved. Fortunately, Denise was not psychically aware of the negative energy, so it didn't affect her quite so dramatically

The pressure I felt on the right side of my brain was his need to control. His thought of protecting his property was so powerful that it reacted as a physical entity. Though I didn't see his thoughts, I did experience them.

REPRIMAND FROM A SPIRIT

Allow me to explain by example how I came to know that spirits move as fast as a thought. Many years ago, while meditating, I saw in my mind's eye a woman watching me from about fifty feet away. Though I recognized her, I wondered how she remembered me, and why she was here. I had met this woman many years ago at a family wedding and seldom had contact with her family. So, I wondered, why had she come to me in spirit?

In my mind's eye, I perceived the woman watching me using automatic writing to receive information from the spirit guides. As I continued writing, I sensed this woman didn't trust anything psychic, but was curious.

All of a sudden, the woman was directly in front of me. There were no actual words, only her thoughts. "Tell my son I will be around. I'll visit him often." All at once, she was again standing more than fifty feet away. She had moved from one space to another, as fast as a thought.

I nodded and agreed to give her son the message. With a quick swish, she disappeared.

Several years later, I had an occasion to visit her son's home. While talking to him, I sensed her standing next to me. I hesitated to give the message that day, not sure how the young man felt about ghosts, and if he would accept the message.

The following year, I again had an occasion to be at her son's home. The son and his wife asked me to do a healing on them.

As I laid my hands on the man's shoulders, I felt a spirit's anger coming at me, reprimanded me. "Your mother is standing behind me. She's upset because I didn't give you a message that I promised several years ago. The message is, 'tell my son I will be around and check in on him.'"

The man's wife jumped up. "You mean she's here?"

"Yes. She's standing behind me. She's upset because I didn't deliver the message I promised."

"Can she hear us?"

"Yes. She can pop in at any time. Spirits don't usually stay very long. It takes a lot of energy to remain in the earthly dimension and check in on their loved ones."

"Does she hear what we say?" the wife asked.

"Yes, she can hear all your praises or complaints about her." With a smile and a nod, I said, "Maybe that's one small part of karma that we have to face our own shortcomings."

I gleaned from this encounter that spirits can move as fast as a thought. It also gives credence that this spirit knew who I was, and where to find me, even though we had met only once many years ago. The spirit was aware of earthly activity, and what was currently happening in her son's life even though she had been in the God light for many years.

15

HAUNTING

Some houses are haunted by spirits who have not crossed over into the God light. The spirit may frighten anyone who enters their space. Without the assistance of my teacher, I continued investigating hauntings even though it was difficult working without a co-worker. I was soon to learn there were some things I couldn't do without help from an expert parapsychologist.

OLD WOMAN IN THE HUT

Sarah, her husband, and three children moved into a house in the northern suburb of Michigan. The small frame house was situated among old historical homes. The street was lined with trees so huge it looked like they had been there since the pioneer days. This house had an unusual floor plan with a bedroom on each side of the living room. Sarah's two pre-school daughters occupied one bedroom, and the school-age son slept in the other bedroom. Sarah and her husband shared the larger bedroom at the back of the house.

Because the bedroom was small, Susie, three at the time, slept in a crib. Debbie, four years old, slept in a twin-size bed. The girls usually got along quite well, but within weeks of moving into the new house, they became irritable and refused to sleep in their bedroom. Each night Debbie helped Susie out of the crib, and they headed for their parent's bedroom. Within days, Susie figured out how to climb out of the crib and follow her sister.

At first, Sarah allowed the nightly visits, knowing a new bedroom could be frightening to little children. But after it became a nightly event, Sarah felt she must do something. She put the girls to bed with a warning to stay in their bedroom. But in the morning, she found they had crept out of their bedroom and were asleep on the floor at the foot of her bed. The next morning, Sarah found the girls wrapped in their blankets, sound asleep on the couch in the living room. The girls refused to sleep in their bedroom.

Several weeks later, Sarah found the crucifix on the floor of the girl's bedroom. She suspected Susie had thrown it, because her crib was against the wall that held the cross. After finding the cross on the floor several nights in a row, she decided to investigate. That night, she watched from the living room.

Susie stretched up, yanked the cross off the wall, and threw it hard across the room.

Sarah wondered why this sudden disrespect for the cross? And why was Susie rebelling at such a young age? She repaired the cross, reprimanded Susie, and moved the crib away from the wall. The next night, she again watched from the living room.

Susie rocked the crib until it scooted back to the wall. Again, she stretched out until she could reach the cross and heaved it across the room, smashing it in pieces.

This time, the cross was too damaged to be repaired, so Sarah reluctantly removed it from the bedroom.

Months passed, and the girls were determined not to sleep in their bedroom.

One morning, Sarah found the girls sleeping on the floor with their small bodies inside their bedroom, but their heads outside the doorway. Sarah felt a twinge of fear in the pit of her stomach. Something was terribly wrong. She was at her wit's end, and in desperation, she telephoned her close friend. "Marie, something strange going on in the girls' bedrooms. They cry when they're in that bedroom. They don't want to sleep in their own beds. They tell me they're afraid. I sent them to their grandmother's house for the day. Will you come over and checkout the bedroom?"

I heard the anxiety in Sarah's voice. "Put on a pot of coffee and I'll be right over."

When I arrived, Sarah was waiting anxiously at the half-open door. She greeted me with a faint smile and led her into the living room. She appeared unnerved and physically drained.

As I approached the doorway to the girls' bedroom, I felt an uncanny presence of fear. The blue walls seemed to emit an angry sensation. The sheer blue curtains cast eerie shadows against the wall. *There must be more than just the children's fear of their bedroom.*

"I meant to paint this room powder blue, but I picked the wrong color. It turned out to be this awful shade of blue."

"It certainly is a strange color. It's such an intense blue." I put one foot inside the room and sensed the color was having a strange effect on the room. "It looks like the walls are vibrating. Oh, repaint this room!" I shivered and stepping quickly out the doorway. "Someone in that room doesn't want it repainted. It's forbidding me to enter."

Sarah frowned. "What do you mean, someone?"

I took one step into the room and closed my eyes. "Oh, what a hateful old woman." I opened my eyes and stepped out quickly. "Repaint the room in a softer color and hang up a crucifix!"

"I had a cross in there, but Susie wouldn't let it alone. She kept throwing it across the room until I couldn't fix it anymore."

This time, I stuck only my head into the room. The angry feeling rushed at me, demanding that I leave. I backed away from the door quickly and turned toward Sarah. "This is worse than I thought. If this spirit is powerful enough to make your daughter destroy a crucifix, then we have to do something quick. Put another crucifix up... Today!" I moved further away from the doorway into the center of the living room.

"I don't have another cross."

"The best crucifix is one that is made with love. Let the girls make one. Use Popsicle sticks, tape, and tinfoil. But this time, hang it over Debbie's bed, and put it high enough that Susie can't reach it."

"Is there really a woman is in there?" Sarah asked as she peeked through the bedroom doorway.

"I sense a hateful, old hag of a woman." After talking about making a crucifix, I noticed the bedroom walls seemed to vibrate with a strange quivering motion.

Sarah stepped closer to the bedroom door, just close enough to peek in. "Is there someone in here?"

"This spirit gives me the creeps. There's a violent energy coming from the bedroom."

"Can you actually see her?" Sarah asked.

"Not as a physical person. I see her in my mind's eye, like a thought form in my head. She's angry. She doesn't want anyone near her."

"Can you get her out?"

I closed my eyes again and tuned into the woman. "No. I can't today. She's angry that I'm here."

Sarah turned pale and backed into the center of the living room. "Who is she?"

I mentally scanned the bedroom from across the living room and began receiving impressions. "The old woman lived on this property long before this house was built. I see a hut. The roof looks like thatches or reeds. It's round and low... A small hut. She doesn't trust people."

"What does she want?"

"She doesn't want anyone near her property. I sense this bedroom was built right over her hut. She hates anyone who comes near her. Because she lived alone in the wilderness, she was attack many times. She doesn't trust anyone, not even a child. Let the girls sleep on the couch for the time being. It's pretty bad in there. The old woman is too powerful for me to handle alone. I can't enter the bedroom, not today."

The aroma of freshly perking coffee wafted from the kitchen. The women sat at the kitchen table for a long time, trying to decide how to handle the situation.

Several weeks later, Sarah phoned, informing me that her friend Doris was flying in from California. "Doris asked to spend a month or two at my house. She filed for divorce, so she, and her three-year-old daughter, will be staying with me until the divorce is final. I'll have to put them in the girls' bedroom. Now we'll see if that room affects anyone else."

The son's furniture was shifted to a room in the basement, and the girls' furniture was moved into their brother's room. Doris and her daughter moved into the girls' bedroom.

Within days, Doris complained that the handmade cross had fallen off the wall several nights in a row, but each time she hung it back up. "Last night, it startled me awake. The cross fell right on my face," Doris complained.

Sarah was determined to keep the crucifix on the wall. She tied a strong string around the cross, then pounded a large nail in the wall, and hung the cross. "That should keep it from falling,"

Several days passed without an incident. One morning Doris came out of the bedroom with a strange look on her face. "That damn cross fell on my face again. Just leave the damn thing down!"

Sarah knew it was important that the cross stay up. She picked up a large, three-inch nail, pounded it through the cross, then hammered the entire three inches into the plastered wall. "There, that should hold it!"

Doris frowned, baffled by Sarah's drastic action. She wondered why Sarah was so determined to keep the homemade cross? Could it be something else? Maybe Sarah was really angry with her. Had she overstayed her visit?

By the end of the first month, Doris had grown increasingly irritable. It was apparent that something else was causing her extreme anxiety. Several days later, Doris shipped her daughter back to her husband in California, packed her luggage, and left. Although Doris made no comment about feeling unwelcome, her abrupt departure made it clear she was upset.

As soon as Doris and her daughter left, Sarah moved the girls' furniture back into their bedroom, but didn't insist that the girls sleep there. She telephoned Marie. "My company left this morning. Doris let her ex-husband have custody of her daughter. I don't know what got into her. How could she give up her only child?"

"I wonder if the old hag had something to do with her decision to leave?" I said, not surprised that the friend had left so abruptly.

"Doris told her husband she wants the profit from the sale of the marital home and other assets. It seems so selfish, trading her daughter for money. Can you come over and get rid of that spirit?"

I agreed to try again. When I arrived, I still hesitated to enter the bedroom. I had never felt this defenseless before and wondered if the old woman was more than I could handle. While standing outside the bedroom door, I sensed a message. *Something is warning me to be careful.* I cautiously took a single step into the room and relayed what I was feeling. "I can feel the woman's hatred assaulting me. She's screaming at me to get out!" I stood still, sensing, waiting. After a while, I gathered my courage and took a second step into the bedroom.

The atmosphere grew heavy, and the freshly painted walls appeared to quiver like heat radiating off sun-baked metal.

My intuition warned me this was too powerful for me to handle alone. *Oh, how I wish June was here to help.* A tremor of fear surged through my body. *This is the first time I've ever been afraid of a spirit.* The ominous feeling of fear held me motionless in the bedroom. I took a deep breath, struggling to regain my confidence as I moved slowly toward the bed.

The ominous warning grew stronger, more intense.

I sat at the edge of the bed, closed my eyes, and mentally blessed the woman over and over again. I knew that sending love was the only thing that would weaken the hatefulness that pulsated through the room.

Suddenly, a powerful force seized my neck. I clutched my throat. *The old hag has a tight grip on my neck.* Startled by the physical attack, I began choking. I opened my eyes and stared wildly about the room. I tried to scream, but only a small gurgle came from my out-stretched neck.

Sarah could see the fear in my eyes but didn't know what to do.

I covered my throat with my hands, but the choking pressure continued.

Sarah watched in fear, unable to move. Then she remembered that blessing a spirit will weaken its evil power. "Bless you. Bless you," Sarah repeated over and over again.

Still holding my hands on my throat, I opened my eyes and saw Sarah peering down at me while her hands moved quickly back and forth, and up and down, making the sign of the cross at a rapid rate of speed. After several minutes, I felt the spirit release her grip from my neck.

In an instant, I bolted to the door, with Sarah following close behind. As soon as I was out of the bedroom, I heaved a sigh of relief and regained my composure. I knew I would never enter that room again, not without a well-trained psychic to assist me. I have a great deal to learn before I attempt to rescue such a violent spirit.

Sarah, now understanding the danger, let the girls sleep on the couch.

Several months later, she and her family moved from that house. Perhaps the children were young enough to forget their fearful experience in that bedroom.

I was relieved that I wouldn't have to deal with the old woman again but regretted that I wasn't able to help her to the God light. The haunting in the bedroom remains unresolved. It would take several strong mediums, and a lot of prayer to exorcise the spirit from the house.

After Sarah and her family moved out of the house, I assumed I would never enter that house again. But, as fate would have it, I was introduced to the new tenant.

The new tenant was a young girl in her early twenties. Annie was dating a young man in the service, so the courtship was mostly by correspondence. She handed me an envelope and asked me to do psychometry on the letter.

I held the envelope face down, so I wouldn't see the print. I wasn't told who the letter was from, or anything about the contents. I slipped my hand inside the envelope, feeling the paper with my fingertips. I looked sternly at Annie and shook her head. "No! No! No! This is good from afar, but not here, not now! Annie, do you understand what I'm telling you?" Even as my spirit guides were prompting me to speak, I wasn't sure what the message meant.

Annie smiled. "Just tell me what you feel about the person who wrote the letter." Psychometry was just a game to Annie, and she wasn't ready to accept or understand the warning.

With closed eyes, I visualized an image. "I see a tall, dark-haired man. Lots of bushy hair. He's smirking, holding his mouth to the side like this." I moved my mouth to one side, in a lopsided grin. "I see something black under his nose. I'm getting the answer. No! No! Annie, do you understand what I'm saying?"

Annie smiled. It was apparent she had not taken the message seriously. "Boy, that's good." She pulled a photograph out of the envelope. It showed a tall, bushy-haired man with a smirk on his face, and under his nose he sported a large, dark mustache.

"Are you dating this man?"

"Yes. We might get married," Annie gushed.

Suddenly, words spewed from my mouth. "No! Listen to my words.

Liken unto his mother, so shall he be! Do you understand?" I had received this information from a spirit, and though I didn't fully understand the full meaning, I hoped Annie would heed the warning.

Annie laughed. "Oh, his mother is nuts."

"Do you hear the words you are saying? His mother is nuts. Please, don't marry him!"

"Well, we're just thinking about marriage. Nothing is final."

I left that day, unable to convince Annie to think twice about her relationship with this man.

Annie and Tony were married that summer, and Tony moved into Annie's rented house. Tony had always presented himself as a likable, polite young man, and he appeared sincere and honest while in the presence of his new in-laws. But it didn't take long for Annie to realize he was not as he appeared to be. Within months of their marriage, she began to see another side of her new husband. At first, she denied the telltale signs that he was an alcoholic. She hid the truth from her family and friends. As she witnessed the drastic change in his personality, she realized that this marriage was a terrible mistake.

Annie telephoned me late one evening. "Tony is missing. I haven't seen him since he left yesterday morning." Annie's voice faltered with fear. "I'm too embarrassed to tell my parents, and I don't know what to do."

"Just relax. Let me check." I put the index finger of my left hand on the center of my forehead and closed my eyes. I took several slow, deep breaths until I had entered a state of relaxation. Images began to form in my mind's eye. "Annie, I want you to calm down. Relax, so I can see what is going on."

Annie interrupted. "He went away yesterday morning. He didn't come home last night."

"Don't tell me anymore. Just let me tell you what I'm seeing." I frowned, trying to understand the images in my mind's eye. "I see a man coming out of. . . a pool. . . of dark water. He has on a black shiny suit. Black suit. . . Seems tight, like rubber or plastic." My voice faltered. "I don't understand this shiny, black suit."

Annie interrupted again. "He said he was going skin-diving. That's why I'm worried. He could have drowned."

"Oh, now I understand. That's a diving suit. Does Tony have a black diving suit?"

"Yes. He went diving. That's why I'm worried."

Knowing that I was on the right track reinforced my confident, making the reading easier. "He's okay. He didn't drown. I see him climbing out of the water. Dark water . . . That means trouble. He is in a sleazy, cheap motel room. He's laying on a bed. There are two other men with him. Beer cans all over the floor. The room is a mess. He's alright."

Annie accepted my information, not because she believed in extra sensory perception, but because it gave her a temporary relief.

Tony returned home several days later and begin drinking on a daily basis. His personality had changed into an unreasonable, raging bully.

Annie was not accustomed to this type of behavior. She tried to keep him calm and rational, even anticipating his needs to avoid angering him. She went to extremes to be a perfect wife, but he always found some excuse to start an argument. There was no valid reason to excuse his drinking. Tony was out of control.

Late one evening, after several days of steady drinking, Tony swerved into the driveway. The fender of his car smashed in. He stumbled up the steps and wove his way to the back door. Once inside, he reeled out of control and began slapping Annie. He hit her so hard that he broke her jaw.

After Annie's release from the hospital, she realized that Tony was not going to change. She packed his clothes and ordered him out of the house. By the end of the first year of their marriage, she had filed for divorce.

After hearing of the reason for the divorce, I wondered if the spirit of the old woman had affected Tony's personality or had influenced his drinking. Since Annie didn't believe in spirits, there was no reason to tell her of the spirits that haunted the bedroom.

Annie lived in the house for several more years. Fortunately, during that time, she had no use of the haunted blue bedroom, and had turned it into a storage room. Several years later, Annie remarried and moved out of the house. She had finally found her happiness and became the wife of a handsome gentleman and eventually the mother of three children.

I never had another opportunity to enter the house. Since the old woman had already disrupted two households, I wondered if the next tenants would be affected.

Let's look back at the effects of the haunted bedroom. Sarah's two daughters were very young, therefore their minds were still open to the spirit world. They felt threatened by the old woman's spirit. The second person to occupy the room was Doris. She had been physically attacked by the crucifix falling on her head. So, it is assumed that Doris' daughter felt threatened as well. After Doris had slept in the haunted bedroom for several weeks, her personality changed drastically. The third person, Tony, had a destructive change in his personality after living in the house for less than a year. It's not known if he already was an alcoholic, or if his drinking was triggered by the old woman in the hut.

I don't believe the old woman was evil. I sensed she had been abused by many and would attack anyone who came in her path. Because her struggle to stay alive was so horrendous, she was unable to release the fear of anyone entering her area. The old woman may still be locked in a thought pattern of defending herself. Perhaps, one day, several strong mediums will come to her rescue and will have the ability to channel enough love to lessen her fear and guide her to eternal peace in the God light.

Over the years, I thought a great deal about the old woman. She may still be earthbound, existing in a thought pattern of an ongoing now. I sensed I should make no further attempt to rescue her until I had an experienced psychic to assist me, or until I was prompted by spirit to do so.

Time in the next dimension doesn't flow from minute to minute, day to day, or year to year. Existence is a continuum wherever it happens. The soul is eternal. Whether a person experiences a lifetime on earth or in spirit another dimension, they have the opportunity to evolve spiritually. People are constantly changing in their climb up the spiritual ladder toward the light of God.

THE BARTENDER

I met Laura and her husband at a charity ball, and found that we both were members of the same country club, so we decided to play nine holes of golf several days later.

Laura had heard about my psychic ability and wanted to know more. She insisted we go to lunch after playing the ninth hole. After ordering lunch, Laura said, "I've always been interested in the paranormal. Can you tell me something about my future?"

"I don't do reading for the future, but I'll do psychometry. Let me hold something that belongs to you. Not your keys. They carry too many vibrations because they're used on different doors."

Laura set her purse on the table. "Will this do?"

"That's fine. I don't need to hold it; I'll just touch the metal clip."

Laura nodded. "I've never seen this done. Why the metal clip?"

"Metal is a good conductor of vibrations." I frowned, puzzled at what I was seeing in my mind's eye. "Well, this is strange. I see two little girls with blond hair. I know your husband has black hair, and clearly you have dark brown hair, so I don't know why I'm seeing blonds. Two girls with blond hair."

"That's amazing. We adopted twin girls, and they have blond hair."

"Oh, I didn't know that."

Even though the information was correct, I sensed the doubt in Laura's mind. She wondered if I had already known of her family and was lying just to impress her. As we continued to chat, I sensed a man standing beside Laura. *This must be her father.* "You had a close relationship with your father, didn't you? Has he passed on?"

"Yes. I did have a good relationship with him. He died many years ago."

"He's standing beside you."

Laura's aura dimmed. It was apparent she didn't trust my words.

"Your father has a large belly, and he wears suspenders. That's unusual. Most men don't wear wide suspenders."

The word "suspenders" got her attention. Her aura now glowed, and she responded with a smile. "How did you know that?"

"Because I see him standing next to you. He looks after you. He tells me you don't have a good relationship with your mother. Is that true?"

"You're right. I never did get along with her. I tried, but my mother doesn't like me." Because Laura was convinced that the information was accurate, she joined the psychic development class several days later.

As I look back at this event, it was unusual for me to tune into a spirit when the issue wasn't of a serious nature. However, my guides considered the message from her father very important. It gave Laura the peace of mind to know that her father is still around and watches over her.

6

2

Laura, her husband, and two daughters lived in the quiet suburb north of Detroit. Tall oak trees shaded the streets, and neat brick houses were surrounded by neatly manicured lawns. One would hardly suspect that behind the glistening windows of Laura's house lurked a malevolent spirit.

Late one evening, Laura was awakened by her nine-year-old daughter, Marian, hovering at her bedside. "What's the matter?" Laura asked her trembling daughter.

Tears trickled down the child's face. "I'm scared."

Laura comforted her daughter and invited her to snuggle next to her in bed. The next evening, Laura was again awakened by her weeping daughter at her bedside. Unable to soothe Marian, she again invited her into her bed. When Marian fell asleep, she carried her back to her own bedroom. After her daughter came crying to her bedroom several weeks in a row, Laura scolded her and insisted she return to her own bed.

The following morning, Laura found Marian's bedroom empty. Upon checking her other daughter's bedroom, she found Marian in her sister's bedroom. She hoped this was a childhood fear and it would soon pass. But within days, Laura's other daughter, Anita, began to complain about sharing her bed with her sister.

Marian refused to sleep in her bedroom. "There's something in my room, and it's scary."

"There's nothing to fear," Laura said and again led the child back to own bedroom. But the next morning, she found Marian curled up on the couch in the family room.

Laura, concerned about Marian's nightly fear, decided to investigate. After the children left for school, she went into Marian's bedroom, sat down on the bed, trying to figure out the reason for her daughter's fear. After sitting quietly for several minutes, she sensed an eerie agitation. Wondering if she was just caught up in her daughter's fears, she dismissed it from her mind. Several days later, Laura again investigated Marian's bedroom. This time, she sensed an eerie feeling. Yes, there was something strange about this room. She didn't sense this unwelcome feeling in any other part of the house. Deciding find the cause of her daughter's fear., she picked up the telephone and dialed. "Marie. Can you help me? I think there is something in Marian's bedroom. I've checked the bedroom several times, and there's definitely a strange feeling in there."

"Tell me more." I replied as I mentally tuned in to Laura's house.

"Lately, I get the shivers just looking down the hallway toward that bedroom. I've got to find out what's going on."

"I'll stop by to check it out."

"That would be great," Laura answered with a sigh of relief. She was determined to find an answer to the creepy feeling in Marian's bedroom.

The next day, Laura led me down the hall to Marian's bedroom. I stepped into the room, closed my eyes, and stood quietly. "Yes, there's an entity in here. It's not evil, but it's offensive." I opened my eyes and moved around the room, left hand out-stretched, feeling for an icy chill or a cold spot.

Laura stood at the doorway, hesitating to enter. "What is it?"

"It's a male spirit with negative vibrations. He isn't dangerous, but he could be very scary."

"How did he get here?" Laura asked, as she cautious took one step into the bedroom.

"I sense that he entered through the negative vibrations in this house. He was drawn in by some kind of anger or conflict. There's a disturbing energy right here," I said, waving my hand near the wall.

"Could it be because my husband and I are marital having problems?"

"Yes. Any mental or physical disturbance will alter the energy in his room. That could be why it was drawn in this house. But we have to find out why it's only in this room."

Laura thought a bit. "You know, when my husband is angry, he tells Marian to sleep on the family room couch. Then he sleeps in Marian's bedroom. We usually sleep with the bedroom doors open, but I've noticed that when he's in a bad mood, he closes himself in that room at night."

"Well, that could explain why the spirit is in that room. It was attracted by your husband's anger. Remember what I said about like draws like. Because this spirit is like-minded, it feels comfortable with your husband's anger and hostility."

Laura edged her way back to the door. "Who is this spirit? What does it look like? What does it want?"

"I sense a spirit leaning against the wall. He's a middle-aged man, fat, with a potbelly and a short gray beard. He's wearing a brocade vest and gaudy suspenders. Funny, those suspenders drew my attention. He looks like a sleazy bartender. He enjoys frightening your daughter." I turned toward Laura, who was now standing in the hall. "He definitely has low morals. He's laughing. No wonder Marian is upset."

"How did it get here?"

"It could have been drawn in by your husband's anger when he slept in this bedroom."

"It's not just our disagreements. I'm sure my husband is mixed up with some dishonest men. Could that attract this kind of spirit?"

"Yes. Whoever your husband is dealing with might have low morals like this spirit. Your husband's anger must have been intense enough to create a vortex for the spirit to enter."

Laura leaned against the door jamb and peek in the bedroom. "Can you get rid of him?"

"Yes. But he'll return if things don't change. I'll teach you how to exorcise this spirit. But as long as your husband is letting his anger get out of control and dealing with dishonest people, this immoral spirit won't go away."

"How do I get rid of him?" Laura asked, staring intensely at the wall.

"Communicate with this spirit." Since there was nothing I could do today, I left the bedroom and the spirit standing close to the wall.

"Do you really think I can get rid of him? Do you think I'm ready? After all, I'm just a beginner,"

"Yes. Here's what I want you to do."

"Let's get away from this room. I'll feel more comfortable in another room," Laura said as she made her way down the hall.

I followed Laura into the living room and eased myself down on the couch. "Before you begin each day, mentally place white light around yourself. Then go in the bedroom and mentally fill the bedroom with white light. When you feel relaxed, mentally communicate with the spirit. Tell him that he's not wanted here. You can't help him at this time, and he has to leave."

Laura plopped down on the couch and mumbled her replied. "Uh-huh. I can do that."

"Above all, don't show fear. The white light will keep you safe and will neutralize negative vibrations in the room. You'll probably have to do this more than once. Eventually, the spirit won't feel comfortable in the white light. He'll leave of his own accord."

The next day, Laura began mentally projecting white light in the room. She continued this for three weeks, eventually dropping back to fewer and fewer days.

During this time, I visited Laura weekly, each time checking the bedroom. "I see the spirit fading. One foot has disappeared into the wall. That's a good sign. He's beginning to leave." Several months later, the spirit was gone, and the atmosphere in the bedroom became peaceful once again.

From that day on, Marian began spending more time in her own room. Eventually, she stopped sleeping on the couch and returned to her bedroom without a complaint.

The father's rage had depleted the home's natural protection, thus allowing a vortex to open. Many nights, his violent thoughts ran rampant in the small bedroom, changing the positive energy to negative energy. This negativity attracted the spirit, and it felt comfortable in the room where the anger was most prominent. This experience made Laura look closely at her relationship with her husband and the severity of their disagreements, and eventually forced her to take action and resolved the situation.

BEGINNER STUDENTS

As a teacher, I had the responsibility of selecting students who could work together in harmony. Little did I know the spirits guides were about to teach me a lesson on the effects of disharmony. This story taught me to be more careful when selecting new students.

Several years after the demise of my mentor, June Black, I began searching for a group of women who were interested in developing their psychic ability. I found four girls who were interested; Sandi, a street-wise redhead who claimed to be a psychic reader; Doris, a quiet girl in her early twenties who hoped her psychic ability would advance her musical career; Sarah, a young girl who was uncannily accurate at psychometry; and Francis, a negative hypochondriac who insisted she had strong psychic abilities.

Francis insisted that the meetings be held at her house. She believed there was a ghost in the basement, and she wanted to exorcise it. Even though she lived the farthest away, the group agreed to meet at her house the following Monday at ten o'clock in the morning.

Because the girls lived in different parts of town, they decided to meet at my house and then drive together to Francis' house. Sarah arrived early, eager to be with like-minded students. Doris, who lived across town and had the longest drive, arrived an hour late. Sandi also arrived late, complaining about the long drive and the traffic. We all piled in my car and headed toward Francis' house. It was our first meeting, and we were already an hour and a half late.

Since the group was new, no one knew Francis' last name or her phone number. We were unable to let her know that we would be late. After nearly an hour on the road, we finally pulled into the driveway of Francis' house. The house appeared neglected, and a dreary haze had settled over the area like a malevolent shroud.

I sense anger being directed at us. "Girls, Francis is upset. She's really mad at us."

Sandi, being the aggressive member, took offense immediately. "Well, we had to drive clear across town, so she will just have to understand."

Francis opened the door, clenched her jaw, and glared. "Well, what the hell took you so long? I've been waiting for hours."

"We're sorry. Sandi and Doris came a long way." I stepped forward to apologize. "The girls had trouble finding my house, and the traffic was awful." By the look on Francis' face, I could see no explanation was going to calm her anger.

"Well, you better be on time next week!" Francis grumbled as her eyes narrowed defiantly. She turned on her heels and led the way into a dimly lit kitchen.

Oh, this isn't good! I thought, as a wall of venomous energy hit me like a ton of bricks. *Too much negativity. I don't think we'll ever meet at this house again.*

As soon as the ladies sat down, Francis insisted on having a personal reading from Sandi. This would take more valuable time, and we were already late starting the meeting.

Sandi was taken off guard by the request and found it difficult to refuse. She claimed to be an accurate reader, and because she lived in a rough neighborhood, her readings tended to be harsh and graphic.

I could feel the room filling up with negative resentment. *This meeting is getting out of control.* It was apparent that my guides were giving me a lesson on selecting compatible students.

Sandi had no rules about discretion and began blurting out intimate details. "You're too damn negative. You take too many sleeping pills. Why do you feel sorry for yourself? You always make things worse than they really are. You messed up your own life."

Francis glared resentfully. "What do you mean? I'm not to blame for my husband leaving."

Whoa. No one mentioned her husband or a divorce. It was obvious that this group of ladies wasn't going to work well together at all.

"Yes, you are!" Sandi shouted. "You drove him away. You never smile when he's around. You deliberately show how miserable you are. I think you want to punish him."

Francis and Sandi glared at each other, and their irritation had caused a turbulent energy throughout the room.

I interrupted, "No more reading!" I took a deep breath, and after mentally filling the room with white light, I began in a slow, mesmerizing chant. "Close your eyes. Relax. Release all your fears, all your resentment. Feel a peaceful energy surrounding you."

Francis interrupted. "There's a ghost in my basement. We've got to destroy it."

"No, Francis! We don't destroy anyone. That spirit, if there is one down there, is a person. We have no right to hurt anyone, not even a ghost!"

Sarah, who was very intuitive, closed her eyes and started snickering. "I see a man coming up the basement stairs. He isn't wearing pants."

With closed my eyes, I searched within. Sure enough, there was a male spirit halfway up the stairs.

Sara continued. "It's a man with a weird sense of humor. He's naked from the waist down. He's grinning."

I opened my eyes and turned to Sarah. "You're right. He's coming up the stairs."

A quizzical smirk slipped across her Sarah's face. "He's wearing a hat, a shirt, shoes, but no pants." Again, she burst out laughing, but this time a guttural utterance oozed from deep in her throat. The spirit is too close to Sarah, and was influencing her to laugh. The meeting was out of control, and since the ladies were novices, they didn't realize their bickering had drawn the spirit into the kitchen.

Sarah's eyes snapped open, startled by the raspy sound coming from her own mouth. She slumped down in her chair, and her eyes darted frantically from side to side. It was apparent that the spirit had taken full possession of her body. "This is not me laughing," Sarah whimpered, shaking her head from side to side, trying to force the spirit from her mind. She straightened upright in her chair and gripped the edge of the table to brace herself. Again, she closed her eyes and burst out in raucous laughter. "What's happening?" she shouted, shaking her head, fighting to regain control. Terror covered her face when she realized she couldn't control her own laughter.

Suddenly, my guides took over, and I was on my feet. "Stand back!" I shouted, raising my hand, palm forward in front of Sarah's face. I took a deep breath, expanded my chest, drawing energy in. Then, I mentally sent a beam of white light toward the spirit. *Got to stop this spirit. It's taking over Sarah's body.*

But it was too late. The spirit had already taken possession of Sarah.

"Take me!" I shouted, knowing it was my responsibility to get him out of Sarah's body.

Sarah opened her eyes long enough to project a stare of fear and helplessness. When she closed them again, her shoulders drooped, and she slouched deeper in her chair.

"Take me!" I repeated, taunting the spirit to leave Sarah. "Are you afraid of a mere woman?" *This is getting out of hand.* Again, my guides chanted through my voice. "Encircle this spirit with God's white light. Send him white light."

The ladies were momentarily calmed by the mesmerizing sound of my voice and began sending white light. Within seconds, the male spirit had succumbed to the calming effect of the light and slipped out of Sarah's body.

Sarah's face had turned ashen white, and the whitish film was gone from her eyes. Still shaken by the experience, she mumbled softly. "He's back downstairs."

Francis jumped up and headed for the basement stairs. "Let's get him. We gotta do something to him!"

"No, we don't," I retaliated, motioning for Francis to get away from the basement door. "This spirit doesn't understand right from wrong. It's up to us to forgive him—to send him love and peace."

"Let's get him," Francis bellowed.

"No! Not until you learn how to protect yourself. You saw what happened to Sarah. She couldn't stop him."

"How did he get in her body?" Doris asked, still trembling by the experience.

"Sarah didn't know how to protect herself. But the real reason is the positive energy was drained from this room before we began the meeting. This spirit isn't evil. He's mentally challenged." I turned toward Francis. "What were you going to do in the basement, anyway?"

Francis thought for a minute, then scowled and shrugged her shoulders. "What made him come upstairs? Why is he in my house?"

"He feels comfortable in your dreary basement. That's why he's here. He likes the negative feelings in this house."

"I'm not negative." Francis mumbled under her breath, then gripped the coffee pot and filled each cup.

It's useless to continue. It was apparent that this group was too inexperienced to handle a mentally challenged spirit. Since the positive energy had dissipated and the girls were still traumatized, it wasn't safe to continue. I ended the session with a prayer.

On the drive home, the ladies discussed the negativity in Francis' house. They were concerned that if they came back to her house, they could be possessed by the spirit. All agreed there would be no more meetings at her house. They were not ready to be mediums, at least not right now.

After we arrive home, Sarah and I decided to go out for an early dinner. We headed for a local restaurant and selected a secluded booth in the corner of the dining room. Sarah picked up the menu, held it up to her face, and peered over the top, giggling mischievously. "That man is near me. He's making me laugh." She cupped her hands over her mouth and giggled.

This spirit finds it easy to intimidate Sarah. I leaned close and whispered,

"Mentally demand that he stand back. Put white light around yourself. Build a protection."

A waitress approached the table and waited to take our order.

Sarah covered her mouth with her hand to hide her impish smirk.

"We're not ready to order," I told the waitress, giving Sarah time to regain control.

The waitress frowned, obviously taking offense at Sarah's giggles, and moved on to the next table.

I could see Sarah was having trouble keeping the spirit away, so I began working mentally, ordering the spirit to step back. I leaned forward and whispered, "Wrap yourself in a circle of light and an armor of love."

The waitress returned to take our order, causing the spirit to back away.

Sarah grinned mischievously as she ordered a hamburger and a cup of coffee.

The waitress frowned. It was apparent that she thought we were laughing at her. After giving my order, I waited until the waitress had left the table, then mentally began demanding that the spirit stand back.

The waitress returned, slid the dishes across the table, then left without saying a word.

Sarah grinned, picked up a slice of tomato and waved it in front of her as if making the sign of the cross. "Bless you. Bless you," she giggled mockingly.

I worked even harder, sending peace and love to the spirit, assuring him that he wasn't evil, and that he was a child of God. When that didn't work, I taunted him to leave Sara and come to me. All of a sudden, I burst out in a guttural laughter and I knew I had succeeded. The spirit had left Sarah, and had entered my body. I took a deep breath, drew in the white light, then huffed, forcing him out of my body. At the same time, I felt my spirit guides lifting him out. After he was gone, we hurriedly finished our meal and left a generous tip to make up for our impolite behavior. By the time we reached the car, the spirit was gone completely. Sarah, obviously shaken, wanted nothing more to do with spirits. She decided that she would be happy with her gift of psychometry.

The next day, while mediating, I asked my guides why the students were subjected to this frightening experience. The message came as the thoughts in my mind.

"It is important that the intention of the members be sincere. When students come for just excitement, this could cause the meeting to be uneventful and frightening. When a negative or self-destructive person attends the meeting, their negativity would siphon off positive energy. Therefore, be careful about whom you teach."

Now I understand why my guides allowed this experience. I learned an important lesson, to invite only stable, well-trained people to mediumship classes. As to the spirit, it meant no harm, and was content to remain in the darkness of the basement. It would stay in Francis house until she changed her negative attitude to a more positive demeanor.

16

EXORCISM

Possession takes place when a spirit takes control of a person's mind and/or physical body. A person can become possessed knowingly or unknowingly, willingly or unwillingly, occasionally or continuously. A spirit may completely possess, partially possess, or co-exist within a person. The person may not be aware of the possession, therefore unable to prevent it from occurring. I have exorcised many spirits by reasoning with them. I am only a channel, a connection between the physic world and the next dimension. The exorcism is accomplished with the assistance of spirit guides, angels, spiritual beings, and of course, God.

Most people have a natural protection against possession, such as the clear white aura surrounding their body. To protect yourself, I would advise my clients to walk in the light of the God consciousness. This means, do what you believe is right, and what is the best for all concerned.

The following possession deals with Jinn, a non-human spirit. I was soon to learn that being possessed by jinn is quite different from being possessed by a spirit who once existed in human form. Exorcising a non-human spirit requires a completely different application.

EXORCISM OF JINN

A person may be possessed by one or many jinn. To be partially possessed by jinn could cause a change that neither the host nor an outsider would recognize. If the possession goes unrecognized, the jinn may influence the host to act in an unusual manner. This could be misinterpreted by medical doctors and incorrectly diagnosed as multiple personality or schizophrenia. In that case, the person could needlessly be confined to a hospital or worse.

People think exorcism as a frightening experience that is physically harmful to the host. They may have seen scenes on television where the clergy argues with a spirit, then condemns it to the fires of hell. Threats only make a spirit rebel with vengeance, causing more stress to the host. Often the clergy shows fear during the exorcism. Fear feeds energy to the spirit. An experienced medium thinks of a spirit as a person. Therefore, she would *never* damn it or condemn it to the fires of hell. She leaves all judgment to God. An exorcist who threatens with damnation or the fires of hell is usurping God's authority.

However, jinn are non-human spirits. They have a constitution completely different from spirits who once existed in human form. I address this experience to demonstrate a proven method of exorcising a non-human spirit such as jinn. Hopefully, shaman or clergy will use this effective method.

A woman called upon me to exorcise spirits from her body. This possession was causing her physical pain and extreme emotional stress. The feeling of movement in her stomach was unbearable. She was frightened, and it was interfering with her daily life. In the past, she had called upon the clergy and doctors, but no one had been able help her. When she arrived at my home, she showed me a book on mystical rituals she had been reading. She claimed that after following the magical spells, she felt entities crawling inside her stomach. She was terrified and panicked when she couldn't eject them from her body. "What should I do?" she asked.

"Throw that book in the trash. I believe some mystical rituals have the power to open a doorway for dark entities to enter."

Sensing the girl was possessed by jinn, I knew they could only be subdued by flame. My spirit guides directed me, step by step, through exorcising the jinn. I intuitively picked up several sheets of carbon paper, lit a candle, and waited for my guides to prompt my actions. Gripping the carbon paper, I began moving the paper over her shoulders without physically touching her body. My hands moved down her body, lightly skimming over her aura. Then, placing the carbon paper directly on her blue jeans, I swiped the sheet down her legs, drawing the jinn out through her feet.

"They're leaving! I can feel them being drawn out my legs."

When I got to the bottom of her feet, I crunched the paper in a tight wad and held it over the flame until it was burnt to cinders.

Within minutes, the woman heaved a grateful sigh of relief and murmured, "They're gone."

I would never have known that the jinn could be drawn out by merely swiping carbon paper over her blue jeans, but it worked. From this experience, I had learned an amazing method of exorcising jinn from a human body.

But the jinn weren't done with the woman yet. Several weeks later, well after ten o'clock in the evening, the woman's lady friend phoned me from a shaman's office. The woman had hesitated to call upon me again, so she went to see a shaman.

"Marie! I've got you on the speaker phone," the woman's friend shouted. "The jinn are back. We're at the shaman's office. He's been trying for hours to expel the spirits, but his methods haven't been effective against this group of jinn."

Holding the phone close to my ears, I could hear the woman screaming. "Get the hell out of me! Leave me alone!"

Whether some jinn had remained after the last cleansing or new jinn had entered, I can't be sure. These jinn were determined to remain in her body. I had no idea how to handle this exorcism from a distance. The woman was miles away, and I couldn't use carbon paper nor light a flame to remove them. What was I to do? Suddenly, my spirit guides took over and began chanting softly. "The God light is entering your body. Feel the love of God flowing through your body. Allow the light and love. Feel the love of God flowing within."

Again, I heard the woman's voice through the telephone. "They're leaving! I can feel them leaving." Within seconds of introducing love and the God light, the jinn had fled from her body.

I glean from this experience that the power of the white light, and the love of God was so powerful that just the mere words of love drove the jinn from the woman's body. Whether a spirit is an earth-born soul or a jinn, the introduction of God's love is amazingly effective. Even though these jinn fled the woman's body, their energy may not have been destroyed. They're still out there.

Paraphrased from Wikipedia; "Jinn are a race of spirit beings that can be good or evil. One or several evil Jinn can possess a human. Jinn can feel human emotions, such as anger or sadness. When an evil Jinn possesses a human body, it may cause intense fear by moving within the host's body. The more fearful the host becomes, the more energy the Jinn draws from the fear."

In the past, I've used the power of the God's light and love to exorcise spirits. Projecting love or instilling the God consciousness by word will weaken the evil tendencies of most spirits. Love may be projected by word, thought, emotion, intention, or prayer. It is a noninvasive method of removing evil spirits from a physical body. The emotion of love is so powerful that it can actually be felt. It can be used to exorcise all spirits, whether they are earth-born or non-human jinn.

Please accept this lesson as given directly from the spirit world. Carbon paper is used to capture and restrain non-human spirits. Fire will neutralize the non-human spirit. I have no scientific answer as to the use of carbon paper on jinn, only proof that it does work.

Because jinn is nonhuman, we may assume it has no soul. Therefore, its energy is changed by fire. Don't confuse this with the human ceremony of cremation which is an act of liberating the spirit for its ascent into heaven. Many countries accept cremation as a beautiful spiritual service. The soul is divine, and upon physical death, the consciousnesses rises out of the physical body and into the light, whether it is cremated or not.

ORBS

A small orb is an energy form not usually seen with the naked eye. It may appear as a circle of light or a glistening speck on the wall. It may be as small as a flicker or larger than a basketball. The size, color, or varied hues may have a significant meaning. Though I have no proof, I suspect the color, hue, and brightness has a lot to do with the spirituality of the orb. I believe an orb could be a spirit, a visiting ghost, an intelligent energy form, a time traveler, an interplanetary visitor, or a soul observing the earth plane before reincarnation. Perhaps they can be more than I can imagine. On one occasion, during meditation, I have seen hundreds of brilliant sparkles of light. My spirit guide referred to these orbs as 'ardents of love.' An orb may be much more, but I've never found them to be threatening. Of course, there may be sinister orbs out there, but I personally haven't encountered them. A large orb in the night sky is often referred to as a UFO, unidentified flying objects, and appear to be operated by intelligent beings.

Further proof of an orb can be found in your own camera. Certain cameras can pick up by the subtle spectrum of light given off by an orb. Search your old photographs of family gatherings and you may see a small circle of light hovering near the ceiling. That orb may represent a deceased family member who has joined the gala occasion.

The following experience convinced me that orbs are intelligent beings.

Two of my lady friends were going to a retreat that claimed to have sighted orbs in the sky. At that time, I knew nothing of orbs except to have seen photographs of them. Yet the words spew from my mouth with confident authority as I told the ladies, "Communicate with them. Mentally call them to you. They understand you."

When the ladies arrived at the site, they mentally called upon the orbs. They took photographs of orbs hovering over their head, thus verifying the orbs had responded to their request. When the ladies returned from the retreat, they showed me photographs of the orbs. I then confessed I knew nothing of orbs prior to their going to the retreat. The message to communicate with the orbs came through me, not from me. Apparently, the spirit guides intended to show us that some orbs are intelligent beings and have the ability to understand a human request.

Orb in the field

This photograph was taken on a weekend retreat. The women mentally requested the orbs to make their presence known. The orbs were not visible to the naked eye but were captured on film. Because the women asked with sincerity, the orbs responded. Remember, orbs can read your thoughts, and if you are not sincere, they will not make their presence known.

*Very rare photograph of and orb entering the
head of healer in process of healing.*

This rare photograph was taken during a healing session. I have blocked out the faces to ensure privacy of those attending the healing session. The opportunity to capture an orb in action is almost impossible, yet there it is. An orb entering the head of a healer. Notice the white trail indicating the orb is moving toward the healer's head. Was it a coincidence that the camera took this picture at this exact second? Or did the orb make this photograph possible? Perhaps the spirit guide orchestrated the camera and orbs movements so this photograph could be taken.

Several years ago, a woman emailed me asking for help. She claimed to be recently widowed and was left alone to raise three children. Many nights she was frightened by the occasional appearance of a white ball of light hovering near her wedding picture, which she kept on the fireplace mantle. The woman was at her wit's end and didn't know what to do.

She claimed to have called upon the clergy to remove the ball of light. She thought it was an evil spirit, and so did the clergy. They proceeded to smudge the house with sage and threaten to banish the spirit to the fires of hell. Yet the orb of light remained.

I closed my eyes and felt a comfortable feeling flowing from the orb of light. I observed it in my mind's eye as I proceeded to answer her email. The orb was the soul of her deceased husband. He was trying to tell her that he was watching over her and the children.

Several days later, I received an email reply. She thanked me for the clarification. This made perfect sense, and she now feels comforted to know her husband is still watching over his family.

The exorcism of a spirit should *never* be done by threatening it to burn in the fires of hell. Look at how the clergy took it upon themselves to usurp God's will and condemn a loving soul that meant no harm. The clergy should have realized that not all spirits are evil. Spirits are souls of people that once lived on the earth plane and should be treated accordingly with love and respect.

A GIFT OF HEALING

Just because we can't see spirits with the naked eye doesn't mean they aren't present. So we wonder what else is out of our visual range that we are not seeing? Animals are able to see vibrations that humans cannot see. Dogs and cats have the ability to sense an emotion and are aware of subtle energies such as ghosts. Night vision binoculars and cameras are used to capture light spectrum's that are otherwise unseen by the human eye. But what if the psychic can see something that isn't a ghost or a spirit? Is it possible for a psychic to see entities from a different dimension? The following is my true experience dealing with an entity from another planet or dimension.

One evening, nine women met at my house to learn the technique of hands-on-healing. Pearl, a fairly new student knew what to expect because she had attended several meetings to develop her psychic abilities. Even though she felt uncomfortable with spirits, she was willing to participate because it was exciting, and her energy was needed. However, she insisted her main interest was to learn to use her energy for healing, and she wasn't interested in spirits.

The women placed their chairs in a circle formation and the lights were dimmed. They began deep, slow breathing to lower their brain waves, then mentally said a prayer to draw white light energy into the room.

I opened the circle with a prayer. "We sit with love and understanding. We ask our guides for the highest spiritual guidance we are capable of using."

Each member took a turn at healing another member. The healer would place their hands on the shoulders of the member being healed. The healer would mentally draw white light into her head, then release the energy through her hands. Hands-on-healing is not intended to be a cure, but is used to add energy to the person being healed, thus increase the person's ability to self-heal.

As the women meditated, the room took on a peaceful atmosphere.

Pearl's anxious voice whispered across the circle. "Marie. Do you believe in aliens?"

"Yes." I replied softly, searching within my mind's eye.

"Well, I think there's one standing beside me."

There was no need for me to close my eyes to see. I saw the figure quite clearly, "Yes. I see. He's standing near your right shoulder. He is slender with narrow shoulders and stands about four foot tall. He's wearing a tight-fitting shiny outfit. It's silver on one side and black on the other side. His face is covered with a narrow metallic-like helmet, and his eyes are like slits in the helmet. The top of the helmet comes to a point. It's shaped like a bullet. One side of the helmet is black, and the other is silver."

Pearl shifted nervously in her seat. "I don't believe in aliens!" she mumbled resentfully.

"It's an honor that this alien has joined the circle." Even though I didn't know who this entity was, I sensed he was friendly, and had come for a purpose. Pearl was protected by the white light energy within the circle, and no harm would come to her. "Don't worry Pearl. The alien has come with the approval of your spirit guides."

The room remained unusually quiet.

The women opened their eyes and turned their attention to Pearl. Several women closed their eyes and could visualize the silvery image hovering next to Pearl. Some sensed only fragments of the entity. Most students only sensed its presence, but saw nothing.

I sat very still, studying the foreign-looking figure standing beside Pearl, but made no further comment. *Why has he come? What does he want?*

Pearl's panic-stricken voice broke the silence. "Marie! There's a lump on my forehead. I can feel it growing."

My guides immediately spoke through my voice. "Yes. I know. The alien inserted something inside your forehead. It's a gift of healing power. Mentally thank him."

Pearl scowled as she fingered the lump on her forehead. "Well, I don't want it. I don't believe in aliens!"

"It's all right. Relax." I replied softly in an attempt to calm Pearl.

Pearl, irritated by her unexpected gift, squirmed nervously in her seat. Unsure of what to do, she remained silent.

Sensing it was time to end of the meeting. I closed the circle with prayer, then thanked God for His guidance and protection

The women removed their chairs out of circle formation. All eyes were on Pearl as they headed toward the kitchen to discuss the unusual alien guest.

Pearl entered the well-lit kitchen, rubbing her forehead. "Look! Feel that lump," she grumbled as she slid her fingers across her forehead. "It's smaller now, but it was much bigger a few minutes ago."

The reddened area on Pearl's forehead was a physical manifestation witnessed by all. Several minutes later, the lump had shrunk down, and now looked like a pea embedded under her skin. "It doesn't hurt, but I don't like this at all."

"You should feel privileged that you were chosen to receive this gift of healing."

"Well, they can have it back. I'm not so sure I want this. I don't believe in aliens, anyway."

By the end of the evening, the lump and redness had disappeared completely. There was no evidence that anything unusual had happened.

Several weeks later, Pearl noticed her ability to heal had increased. She found it natural to remove pain from other people by merely laying her hands on the afflicted area. As time passed, she became a proficient healer, but rarely spoke of her alien encounter.

As I look back at this day, I recall the alien had appeared clear and well-defined, so I wasn't sure if I was actually seeing a physical body, or viewing the image in my mind's eye. I sensed this alien was alive, not in spirit, and hat he had the extraordinary ability to change form, so he could be seen physically. Changing form would be impossible on the planet earth.

17

PROOF OF THE POWER OF THE WHITE LIGHT

The following is an extraordinary phenomenon rarely experienced by the average medium which confirms the literal power of the God light. I wouldn't have believed it was possible to create a wall of light so powerful that it became impenetrable, if I had not seen it with my own eyes.

Karen and her family purchased a three-bedroom home in a suburb of Detroit. Even though this house was well built and had been well maintained, it was constantly up for sale. All the previous owners never lived in the house very long. Most stayed only a year or two, then moved without an explanation. Karen learned that the recent owners lived in her house only a year, but was never told why they moved out.

Karen believed she had some psychic ability and felt frightened when she sensed the presence of a spirit. She often sensed a black slime slithering across the floor. On several occasions, upon entering her daughter's bedroom, she screamed when the unearthly slime had attached itself to her feet. Her only recourse was flee from the room.

Debbie, the teenage daughter, complained about the eerie presence, but was too busy to let it interfere with her daily life.

In the past, Karen had called upon clergymen and psychics to exorcise the spirit from her home. But after each attempt, the spirit's presence became more pronounced and more frightening. In desperation, she reached out to her next-door neighbor Connie, who also had some psychic ability. The two women attempted to communicate with the spirit, but since they had no training in the paranormal, their efforts only convinced them there was more than one spirit roaming the rooms.

Karen was desperate, so one summer evening, she again called upon a minister to perform an exorcism. The wiry old man walked from room to room with a bundle of smoldering sage, waving it in the air, mumbling hateful threats. He referred to the spirit as an evil demon and with a boisterous voice shouted, "I condemn you to the fires of hell." An hour later, he left and assured Karen, "They won't bother you again."

Several days later, Karen noticed the house had taken on an oppressive heaviness. Apparently, the latest attempt at exorcism had only intensified the spirit's anger. As the months passed, Karen found it uncomfortable to stay in her house for long periods of time. She had to find another way to remove the spirit from her house. She again confided in her friend Connie, who told her of a psychic medium named Marie.

In answer to Karen's phone call, I agreed to investigate. Sensing this was a serious matter, I immediate made arrangements for the following day. My friend Marian joined me in the investigation.

Karen led us into the living room and introduced me to her neighbor. "This is my friend Connie. She wants to watch."

"Let's see what's happening here," I said as I slipped off my shoes. "Having bare feet makes it easier to contact the spirit world." I closed my eyes and mentally scanned the room. "I don't sense an evil presence."

"What do you see?" Karen asked.

I opened my eyes and glanced around the living room. A card table was situated in front of a large window stacked with dozens of bottles of nail polish. The toxic fumes of acetone, and methyl ethyl ketone lay heavy in the air. "Do you use a lot of the solvents to remove nail polish?"

"Yes. I do decorative nails, as well. Are you interested?"

"No. Right now, I want to investigate why spirits are in your house." I took another step into the living room and coughed as the strong scent of chemicals smothered the room. *Oh, no! This isn't good. Those toxic chemicals could have drawn in negative spirits.* Immediately my guides took over and prompted me to speak. "Are either of you ladies a medium?"

Karen and Connie looked at each with a puzzled expression and shrugged their shoulders.

"I don't know what a medium is," Karen answered. "I can sense spirits and it scares me. Sometimes I can feel them pass right through me."

"Okay. Let's see what we have here." Again, I closed my eyes and searched within my mind's eye. "There's a tall, thin man standing by the basement door. He's looking at me, wondering who I am. He's a shadowy figure, not evil or threatening." I opened my eyes to explain further. "I sense spirits are coming from a dark vortex in your basement. They may fight back and attack us, not because they're evil, because they're afraid."

"What does he want?" Karen asked, staring at the open door leading to the basement.

"Are you sure you're not a medium?"

Karen shook her head. "Sometimes, when I go in my daughter's bedroom, I feel a big blob crawling up my leg."

"Okay. Don't tell me anything about the spirit. Don't threaten it. Don't accuse it. Above all, don't argue with it. That only gives it power. Let me investigate first. I'll ask questions later if I need to know more. I don't sense evil. I sensed fear."

"Can we start with my bedroom?" Karen said as she led the way to a room at the front of the house.

I followed Karen into the bedroom. Marian and Connie followed close behind.

The sunlit bedroom was neat and clean. A small fan, situated high on a bookshelf, blew a cool breeze across the room. I closed my eyes and sensed a strange, irritating vibration. At first, I thought the fan was making it difficult to tune into the energy in the bedroom. "I don't sense danger." I studied the room with closed eyes, then opened them and frowned as questions crossed my mind. *It isn't the fan giving off the irritating vibration. Something else is interfering. I just can't put my finger on it yet.* I sensed my spirit guides were directing the rescue. "This isn't the place to start," I said, having received the information intuitively. "Let's go back in the living room."

Karen rushed past me and hurried into the living room. She stopped abruptly and stood clumsily, as if in a stupor. Her eyes paled to a whitish gray. Her head began to roll slowly from side to side, and her lips curled, sneering in an arrogant manner. "You think you know!" Karen growled in a raspy, masculine voice.

Now my mind was working on two levels. The left side of my brain, the logical side, was putting the facts together. *Obviously, that wasn't Karen speaking.* While the right side of my brain was viewing intuitively. *The spirit has a burned face.* It took a few seconds for both sides of my brain to connect and reason the truth. *Whoa! Karen is possessed.*

Karen clenched her jaw, and stared aimlessly in space. She hunched her shoulders forward, and planted her feet as if ready to attack.

"What have we here?" I asked, speaking directly to the spirit who had slipped into Karen's body. As I approached, I noticed that Karen's eyes had turned a whitish gray. *Ah, another sign of spirit possession.* Karen's vacant eyes meant her consciousness had temporarily slipped out, and she would have no physical control over her own body. *Karen is a medium!* I wanted to ask if she had ever done mediumship before, but it was apparent that Karen could not have answered, anyway. *Karen's a raw medium. That means she has the ability to communicate with spirits but doesn't know how to protect herself. That poor girl doesn't know what's happening.*

"You don't know!" Karen taunted in as low masculine voice. "You think you do, but you don't," she snarled as her head rolled slowly from side to side.

Karen's body wavered back and forth, and her head rolled from side to side.

Hum, the spirit was having difficulty steadying Karen's head, I thought as I watched her whitish eyes glaring at me with suspicion. "Yes, I do know," I replied in a firm, but commanding, voice. "Let me take your hands." I reached out and grasped Karen's hands.

Karen jolted backward with a sudden jerk. The spirit reacted as if it feared the physical touch and yanked Karen's hands away. Suddenly, Karen's body reeled forward and shoved with great force.

The impact sent me stumbling backward. I landed, still standing, halfway across the room. *The spirit has full control of Karen's body.* After regaining my composure, I snatched Karen's hands. *I have to connect with this spirit. I have to communicate with it.* I felt Karen's hands slamming my hand hard against the edge of a table. I stepped back, shaking the pain from my hand. I wasn't accustomed to a spirit having this much physical control. Under normal circumstances, most mediums might have been too frightened to proceed, but I was being prompted by my spirit guides, and they had blocked fear from my mind. Again, I approached the spirit. "I'm going to take your hands." I grabbed Karen's hands. This time I held on tight, then turned toward Marian and Connie. "Mentally cover this spirit with white light. Send this spirit love-God's love."

Marian, having attended other spirit rescues, knew exactly what to do. She closed her eyes, bowed her head, and mentally sent a silent prayer while projecting white light toward the spirit.

Connie hesitated. She thought all spirits were evil, and she didn't feel comfortable sending God's love. But, not knowing what else to do, she began a silent prayer.

The spirit, terrified by the vibrations coming from the prayers, screamed pitifully. "No! Let us alone!" Again, the spirit hurled Karen's body forward, striking out with great force.

The power of the attack again sent my body reeling backward.

Karen planted her feet in a hostile stance and glared. Her lips turned down in a scowl and her eyes rolled upward, showing mostly the white of her eyes.

I moved close to Karen and grabbed her hands, then spoke in a commanding, forceful voice. "I want you to sit down." The intuitive side of my mind was analyzing the situation. *This spirit has physical control over Karen's body. It has too much power.* Since Karen was several inches taller and several pounds heavier than me, I was no match for this spirit. *This spirit could use Karen's hands and strike me again. I have to take control quickly.*

Karen's body twisted and turned, trying to wrench her hands free. A sneer crossed her face, and her head rolled from side to side. "No! I won't sit down," the spirit's raspy voice screeched.

"I said sit down!" I edged Karen toward a chair, guiding her backward until I knew the spirit could feel the chair on the back of Karen's legs. Then, with a mighty heave, I pushed Karen down onto the chair and tuned into the spirit's thoughts. *It doesn't want to burn in hell, Why does it fear burning?* Gripping Karen's hands tight, I was determined to rescue it in spite of its resistance.

"No!" Karen's voice screamed while trying to pull itself away. Her head was still unsteady, but it seemed more controlled.

This spirit is fighting for its very existence. Why does it fear burning in hell? Who gave it that idea?

Karen stood up and yanked at my hands, trying to wrench itself free.

I held on tight, closed my eyes to visualize the spirit in my mind's eye. *Its face has been burned.* I opened my eyes. "You were burned, weren't you?" I asked softly.

The spirit stopped resisting, stunned that I could see its burned face, but refused to answer.

My voice changed to a soft chant. "You're not bad-looking. You think you look bad, but your face is becoming more beautiful." I studied Karen's face, still not sure whether I was speaking to a male or a female spirit. I continued using positive words to change the spirit's thoughts. "You're very nice-looking. There's a mirror in front of you. Look at yourself," I said, encouraging the spirit to reflect upon itself.

Karen's head rocked slowly from side to side while sneering defiantly.

The prayers were beginning to take effect and a calm feeling began to penetrate the living room.

Working on a mental level, I imaged a shaft of white light flowing into the top of my head. I sent it through my body and out my heart chakra, while chanting in a soft, mesmerizing voice. "You're changing. You're becoming nicer looking." From experience, I knew that thoughts can prompt a spirit's actions. *I need to change this spirit's thoughts.* "You are no longer burned. Your face is okay." I edged Karen gently to a chair. *I have to control of this spirit.* "I'm here to help you."

The two women continued to send prayerful thoughts of love and God's light toward the spirit.

Suddenly, Karen let loose with a loud screech. "Let me go!" The spirit twisted Karen's body and struggled to free itself from my grip, but the power of the God light had weakened its resistance.

"You have no power here," I commanded, setting up a thought pattern that would overpower the spirit.

"You don't know! You think you do, but you don't," Karen growled while scowling defiantly.

"Yes, I do! I want you to go to the light."

"I can't." The spirit's voice turned apologetic. "They won't let me."

"Yes, you *can* go to the light."

"No. I'm not allowed," Karen's raspy voice pleaded.

"Yes, you can go to the light." I didn't ask the spirit why it wasn't allowed to go to the light. That would only add power to its fearful thoughts. I continued channeling God's love and light in a silent prayer. The prayers had been effective. The spirit appeared less irritated, but Karen's head continued rolling clumsily from side to side. *I have to act quickly while the spirit is ready to listen.* "Go to the light."

The spirit began to weep, heaving Karen's shoulders with each sob. It seemed less fearful and ready to listen.

"Go to the light," I repeated, keeping my voice compassionate, yet commanding.

Karen's shoulders slumped forward, and her head drooped down until her chin touched her chest.

The spirit is losing its will to fight. I gripped Karen's hands, mentally sending God's light into the spirit. "It's time to go. Follow the light." I raised Karen's hands over her head, making it easier for the spirit to withdrawal from Karen's body.

Within seconds, the spirit slipped out. Karen opened her eyes, amazed that a spirit had been inside her physical body. Now that the spirit was gone, she smiled as she realized she had just assisted releasing a spirit to the God light.

I leaned close and checked Karen's eyes. *Good. They changed back to their natural blue color.* "Are you all right?" I asked.

Karen nodded, but the look of amazement still covered her face.

I didn't take time to explain what had just happened. I sensed there was more to do. "Let's see the other bedroom," I said, prompted by my guides to go to the smaller bedroom at the back of the house.

Connie led the way. I followed, with Karen and Marian close behind.

I had taken only one step into the bedroom when I sensed an entity didn't want me in that room. As I scanned the room, my attention was drawn to a red quilt on the bed. It appeared to be giving off vibrations, similar to waves of heat streaming off the sun-baked metal. *The spirit is feeding off the red color. It's using the red as an energy source.* "This quilt on your daughter's bed has angry vibrations. Will you remove it before we start?" I flipped the corner of the quilt over, folding the red on the inside of the quilt.

Karen, having recovered from the last event, folded the quilt and removed it from the bedroom. She carried it to the laundry room, then hurried back, unaware that she had been prompted by a spirit to return to the bedroom.

My attention was drawn to a window at the back of the bedroom. Thoughts rushed across my mind. *Close the blinds. Close the blinds.* Immediately, my guides took over and spoke through my voice. "A spirit wants to close the blinds, but I won't. Keep them open." *Hum. Does the spirit want the bedroom dark?*

Karen edged her way into the room, then hesitated. A puzzled expression crossed her face, unaware that she was being prompted by a spirit sit on the pink bench. She started across the room.

I raised my hand, stopping Karen from crossing the room. "Don't sit on that bench. The pink color is giving off negative energy. Let's move to the other room. This spirit has accumulated far too much energy in here. It's safer outside the bedroom." The three women followed me into the living room. Sensing the spirit had not followed, I closed my eyes and searched within my mind's eye. When I opened my eyes, Connie was standing next to the couch with a vacant look on her face. *Has a spirit entered Connie's body? What's going on? Are both girls mediums?*

The spirit guides had known that Karen and Connie were mediums and were about to give them a lesson in mediumship. I marveled at the way the guides had orchestrated this meeting. Both women were raw mediums in need of training. What better way than to learn than to experience it for themselves, especially when they had a medium to protect them through the process.

Connie's eyes changed to an unnatural whitish-gray and her lips twisted into a snarl.

What! This is not the same spirit that was in the teenager's bedroom. This is a slender, tall female. She's mean and spiteful. I took a deep breath, slowed down my brain, and read the spirit's thoughts. *She's been threatened many times by clergymen and psychics. She believes she is evil and will burn in hell.*

Connie's clenched fists were another indication that a spirit had taken control. She backed up against the couch, then planted her feet flat on the floor in a combative stance. Her head rocked from side to side and her eyes stared aimlessly into a void. "Fuck you! Get out of here!"

I was taken off guard when this spirit had enough control to walk Connie's body across the room. I had seldom seen this, and, for just a split second, I felt fearful and intimidated. Immediately, my guides took over and blocked the fear from my mind. Even though Connie was taller, and physically stronger than me, I headed toward the spirit. With complete faith in my protection, I grabbed Connie's hands and mentally connected with the spirit.

The spirit, terrified by the physical touch, reacted according to the thoughts that had been imposed upon it. It believed it would be banished to the fires of hell, and pushed me away with a forceful shove.

I stumbled backward. The thrust had been so sudden, and so forceful, that it startled me. *Wow! This spirit is strong. How do I handle this?* My guides again blocked fear from my mind. I reached out and grabbed Connie's hands.

The spirit, reacting as if it feared for its very existence, thrust Connie's body forward, and again heaved a powerful blow.

The impact sent me reeling backward across the living room. Once again, my faith wavered momentarily. *What have I gotten myself into?* I had been struck by spirits before, but not quite as violent as this. There was no time to weigh the danger. The guides entered my energy field, and again, fear could not enter my mind. I rebounded quickly and headed toward the couch. This time, I gripped Connie's hands tight. "Sit down!" I demanded in a gruff voice.

Connie's body struggles to wrench her hands free.

Whoa. This girl is strong. I took a deep breath, then mentally sent God's white light toward Connie. After the spirit calmed down, I placed my hands on Connie's shoulders and gently pushed her down on the couch.

"Fuck you!" Connie's voice screamed. The spirit stiffened Connie's body upright in a threatening posture. It was so fearful of going to hell that it slipped out of Connie's body. A stunned expression appeared on Connie's face. "That wasn't me swearing," she said meekly. "I don't talk like that."

"I know," I replied, nodding my head in agreement. Now that the spirit was gone, I wondered what to do next. *How can I get it back? How can I rescue this spirit?*

Connie, still stunned from the experience, appeared to be back in control of herself. Her eyes were no longer veiled with the whitish-gray of a spirit possession. "I have to go to the bathroom," Connie said, unaware the same spirit was prompting her to leave the room. She headed toward a bathroom at the back of the house.

Even though Karen was shaken by the strange events, she wanted to continue. "We have some spirits in the basement. They scare me so much that I don't want to go down there anymore."

Suddenly, Connie's voice screamed from the family room at back of the house. "Help me!"

Karen's face paled when she heard her friend calling for help. She rushed to the room at the back of the house. "Marie, help! They have Connie locked in the bathroom."

I dashed to the family room, with Marian following close behind. My attention was drawn across the room, toward the closed bathroom door. *The same spirit has taken control of Connie's body. It made her lock the bathroom door.* I stood in the center of the room, wondering what to do. After a while, I approached the door and twisted the doorknob.

The doorknob remained tightly secure.

All this was new to me, and reacting intuitively, I gave the door a slight nudge with my shoulder.

"They won't let me out," Connie's voice pleaded from inside the bathroom.

For a split second, fear swept over me. *What am I supposed to do?* Immediately, fear was blocked from my mind and my guides took over. Reacting intuitively, I took several steps back, away from the bathroom door. I felt my feet flattened to the floor, and a powerful surge of energy rise from the earth. *I'm connecting with the earth's energy.* I felt enormous. Powerful. Even though I had never done this before, it all seemed natural, as if I had used the earth's energy many times in previous lives. I didn't think about what I had to do. Intuitively stepping back, allowing a powerful rush of energy to surge though my body. I pointed my finger toward the bathroom door and sensed a powerful shaft of white light rush from my fingers toward the door. "Open the door," I demanded firmly.

Silence. No sound came from behind the door.

I assumed Connie was under the influence of the spirit and too frightened to move. *I have to get her out of the bathroom.* Again, I twisted the doorknob, but the door remained locked. Without even a thought of what I should do, I took several steps back from the door. Once again, I pointed my finger at the bathroom door. Again, a forceful rush of power came from the earth, surged through my body and out my pointed finger.

The room grew eerily quiet.

Several seconds later, the lock clicked, and the door opened slightly. Connie peered out of the half-open door with a bewildered look on her face.

I grabbed Connie's hands and led her into the family room. After leading her to the couch, I pushed her down gently and grasped her hands.

A low growl rumbled from Connie's lips and her eyes turned whitish-gray.

I turned to Marian and Karen. "Send this spirit love."

The women imaged the white light, then mentally drew it into the top of their head. With their eyes closed, they directed the love toward the spirit who now possessed Connie.

"Fuck you," Connie's raspy voice yelled out.

Ah, it's the same spirit. I began to chant softly. "You are peaceful. God's love is filling you. You are becoming more peaceful. You are light. You are love. You are becoming peaceful."

"Let me go!" the spirit snarled as it struggled to free itself. After a while, Connie stood up on the couch and stared vacantly in space. Then slowly, her body twisted downward, shoving the cushions up in front of her.

Is the spirit was trying to crawl under the cushions? Does it want to hide inside the couch? Again, I mentally directed God's love and light toward the spirit. *I'm determined to help this spirit no matter how hard it resists.* "Go to the light," I gently demanded.

Connie's head wavered slowly from side to side. It appeared the shafts of white light had weakened it, and it didn't have the same strength as before. "They won't let me," her raspy voice wailed as she writhed her way, deeper into the cushions.

"Yes, you can go to the light." The guides channeled the request in a gentle voice. "Go to the white light. You are a child of God. Go to the light."

A panicked expression spread over Connie's face.

The spirit thoughts entered my mind. *It thinks it will be sent away to burn in hell.*

Suddenly, the spirit stood up and heaved Connie's body forward, shoving me with such force that I landed across the family room. Immediately my guides blocked the doubt from my mind. I grabbed Connie's hands, and keeping my voice firm, yet mesmerizing, I repeated soothing phrases. "God's love is filling you. You're becoming more peaceful. Feel how peaceful you are."

Connie's head drooped and her body slithered deeper into the couch. The power of God's light had taken effect. The spirit appeared weaker, less aggressive.

Now is my chance to save this spirit. "Love is coming to you, surrounding you. You're feeling peaceful," I chanted softly.

Within seconds, Connie's eyes closed. She slid down on and laid her head on the arm of the couch. She appeared exhausted.

I put my head near Connie's head. "Release your fears," I whispered.

Connie began to sob softly.

"When you're ready to go to the light, raise your hands over your head. Go to the light."

The spirit seemed weak, but it lifted Connie's hands up in the air. Within seconds, Connie's body slumped back on the couch. The spirit had slipped out.

Connie opened her eyes and sat upright with a stunned expression on her face. A smile slipped from her lips, along with a sparkle in her blue eyes. "That was beautiful," Connie said softly. "I'll never be afraid to die. I just felt the compassion of unconditional love inside the white light. I'll never be afraid of death again. Not that I'm eager to leave this life," she chided with a smile. "This life is beautiful, but when it's time to leave, a long time from now, I know I won't be afraid."

The moment of serenity was shattered by Karen's voice calling from the front of the house.

What now? There can't be another one! I had been so busy that I hadn't noticed Karen had left the family room. *This is unusual to have his many active spirits in one house.*

"They're taking them all away," Karen bellowed from the living room. Her voice seemed different, anxious and troubled.

Marian, Connie, and I rushed back to the front of the house and entered the living room.

Karen was sitting on the couch, staring down at the floor with a blank expression on her face. She didn't look up when we entered the room.

Even though I couldn't see Karen's eyes, I sensed a spirit had entered her body.

Karen began to lean forward until she had placed both hands on the floor. It was apparent by her actions that Karen was no longer in control of her own body, and that a spirit was moving her toward the floor.

"Why are you here?"

Karen stared blankly at the floor and a low snarl grumbled from her lips. Her body slumped forward until both hands and knees were flat on the floor. She was partly sitting on the couch, posed like an animal ready to leap.

"Who are you?" I asked, not sure what I was dealing with. *Could this be an animal?*

Again, the spirit snarled, but refused to answer.

"You must go to the light."

The spirit shook Karen's head slowly from side to side. "You don't understand. I can't," it whimpered submissively.

"Why can't you go to the light?" I now sensed I was dealing with a child spirit. I felt relieved. At least I wasn't dealing with an animal spirit. *This is the same spirit that was in the teenager's bedroom.* I started a conversation in an attempt to distract the spirit from its fear. "Why can't you leave?"

Karen's body began to lean forward until she was kneeling on the floor. *The spirit is searching the floor for darkness. Why darkness?*

"They won't let me," Karen's voice pleaded.

"Yes. You can go to the light," I commanded in a firm, but gentle, voice. "White light is coming to you. God's love is coming to you."

Connie and Marian again took the cue. They began mentally sending love and God's light to the spirit.

Karen slid off the couch. With her brown hair dangling over her face, she looked like an animal laying flat on the floor. She began squirming and twisting her shoulders."Don't do that!" Karen's voice snarled. It was apparent that the spirit was confused by the compassionate feeling of the God light.

Ah! The spirit seems irritated by the effect of the prayers and the God light. Is the spirit trying to get away from something? Ah. It doesn't like the white light.

Karen's head weaved from side to side as if searching the floor. After a while, she lay flat on her belly and began brushing her face against the carpet.

"I'm sending God's love." Again the spirit guides channeled instructions. "God's white light is coming. All the darkness is disappearing. All the darkness is gone."

Karen lay flat on her stomach and began slithering across the floor like a snake. She began prodding with her fingers, as if trying to grab something deep in the fiber of the carpet.

The spirit is searching the floor for bits of darkness. It feels protected by the darkness. I mentally placed white light on the floor. Within seconds, I sensed the darkness had disappeared. "There is no more darkness," I murmured.

The spirit moved Karen's hands across the carpet, scratching and digging, as if trying to pick up specks of darkness off the carpet.

"There's not even a speck of darkness left. It's all gone. Only God's white light is left."

Karen's body lay still, flattened on the carpet. The spirit seemed confused because it has lost the darkness. Several minutes later, Karen sat up slowly and moved back to the couch. She seemed frightened and unsure of what to do.

I knelt down in front of Karen and took her hands. *This is a small frightened girl.* My voice softened as I commanded in a melodic chant. "Go to the light."

The spirit shook Karen's head from side to side. "I can't. They won't let me," a child-like voice pleaded

Again, I sensed I should not to ask this spirit questions. It would only add energy to the thought that someone could forbid it to enter the God light. Holding Karen's hands firmly, I mentally projected love and light. *It's afraid to leave this house. It doesn't know where to go.* In all the years of rescuing spirits, I had never sent a fearful spirit out into the unknown. And I wasn't about to force this child spirit out without guiding it to its proper home. "You are becoming more peaceful. You can feel God's love," I chanted as I leaned forward, closer to Karen's body which was now slumped back on the couch.

The spirit responded to the closeness of my body. It rested Karen's head on my shoulder and began sobbing. "I want to stay here. I like the children," Karen's child-like voice whimpered.

My guides continued to prompt me with words to speak. "God has children. He wants you to help them. Will you go to the light and help God's children?"

Karen's head shook slowly from side to side. "No. I want to stay here." It was apparent that the spirit was frightened and didn't want to leave its familiar surroundings.

"We understand, sweetheart. But God needs help with the children. There's no more darkness for you to hide in. You must go to the light. Will you help the children?" While I pleaded with the child spirit, I mentally sent peace and loving thoughts to release its fear of the unknown. With Karen's head still leaning against me, she nestled deeper into my shoulder. I felt Karen's warm tears moisten my shoulder. "God loves you. Go to the light. When you're ready, all you have to do is lift your hands and you'll go to the light."

Karen's hands rose slowly over her head. Seconds later, the spirit slipped out, leaving her body slumped forward. Karen opened her eyes, and for a brief moment was unable to speak. When she regained her composure, a smile slipped across her lips. "I just helped a child cross over into the God light, didn't I?"

When I rose to my feet, turned around and saw Connie sitting on the arm of the couch with a blank look on her face. *Has a spirit entered Connie's body? Is there no end?* Within my mind's eye, I saw a shadowy figure of the thin, tall man. *It's the same man that was at the basement door. He has a long chin that juts out past his nose. He's upset because the spirits are leaving.* Sensing he was very mean, I opened my eyes and said, "You have quite a large chin."

Connie's eyes narrowed and forehead furrowed curiously. He appeared to be wondering how I was able to see his chin.

It's time to change his thoughts. "You're not as mean as you think you are. You're really not a bad person."

Connie rose from the couch and stood motionless. The spirit appeared to be contemplating. Suddenly, the spirit slipped out of Connie's body and was gone. Connie opened her eyes with an amazed expression on her face. She was still processing what had just happened.

Again, I closed my eyes and begin searching for the spirit in my mind's eye. *Where did he go? How can I get him back? Am I done?*

Karen, unaware she was being influenced by a spirit, slipped out of the living room and headed toward the kitchen.

Connie, noticing that Karen was acting strange, followed her into the kitchen.

I turned toward the kitchen when I heard Connie calling for help. *When is this going to end? Why are there so many spirits in this house?* I rushed to the kitchen where Karen was glaring defiantly at me. I sensed a large, heavy-set male spirit had taken control of Karen's body.

Karen had taken on a masculine posture. Her arms hung out at her sides as if she had a massive body. *What have I got myself into?* Karen was taller and much stronger than me. I am only five foot one and no match for her physically.

Karen's body plodded backward until she was leaning against the refrigerator door.

I headed toward Karen and demanded in a firm voice. "You must go to the God light!" *I have to speak with authority if I'm going to rescue this spirit.*

Karen's body stood firm, shoulders hunched forward with fist clenched, and her arms raised in front of her, ready for a fight. The spirit was in full control of Karen's body and it was not about to leave the kitchen.

"You are becoming smaller," I intuitively demanded. "You cannot move. You have no power over me."

The spirit took several lumbering steps forward in a threatening manner.

I sensed this spirit was huge and extremely strong. *This one is more threatening than the others.* My guides moved within my energy field, and once again, fear could not enter my mind. "You will go to your knees," I demanded firmly, being directed by my guides to use this phrase. The words spewed out of my mouth so quickly that I didn't have time to think about what I was saying. I had been instructed by my guides to send him to his knees.

The spirit stood firm. It shook Karen's head stubbornly from side to side and glared. It raised Karen's hands up in front of her, as if bracing for a battle. Karen stood in a defiant poise, refusing to go to its knees.

"You will go to your knees." This time, my voice was louder, more commanding. I reached for Karen's hands, gripped them firmly, and again tried to steer her down to the kitchen floor.

The spirit resisted and wrestled Karen's hands away.

Again, my guides pressed forward, encouraging specific words to speak. "You will go to your knees."

The spirit glared, but stood firm. "I'm going to the basement. It's dark down there," Karen growled in a deep, masculine voice.

"You can't go downstairs. There's no darkness in the basement. I've filled it with white light." The words poured out without hesitation.

Marian and Connie took the cue. They closed their eyes and began directing white light into the basement, neutralizing the darkness.

Karen's lips curled into a snarl and responded in a booming gruff voice. "I'm going down!"

"You can't. I've put up a wall of white light in front of the doorway."

Marian and Connie again took the cue. They mentally imaged a wall of white light in front of the basement doorway.

The spirit, determined to leave the room, moved Karen's body toward the open basement door. Suddenly wham! Karen's body collided with the wall of white light. The blow hit with such force that it struck like a bolt of lightning. The blow was so forceful, that it catapulted her away from the basement doorway, sending her reeling backward with tremendous force. The impact slammed her hard against the side of the refrigerator.

Both Karen and the spirit were dazed motionless by the forceful blast light.

In the past, I had sensed the effect of the white light many times, but I had never seen it strike with such force on a physical level.

Karen's head meekly bowed forward as she slid down until she was crouching on her knees. It was apparent that the jolt of power had stunned the spirit into submission.

Now it's safe to approach the spirit. "When you're ready to go to the light. Raise your hands over your head. Go to the light. Reach for it. Go!"

The spirit raised Karen's hands slowly upward, and the spirit slipped out. Karen, still on her knees, slumped forward. When she opened her eyes, she was sitting on the floor dazed and amazed. She sat motionless for a moment, still trying to shake off the tremendous shock of the white light. Within seconds, she regained control of her body and her conscious mind.

I heaved a sigh of relief. I wouldn't have believed that the white light could have been that powerful if I had not seen it with my own eyes. I glanced around the kitchen, then closed my eyes, searching in my mind's eye for counseling from my guides. "I think there is one, possibly two, spirits left," I said to Karen. "I know you can take care of them. You saw how we did it today. You can do it, too. My guides say they were preparing both of you. They gave you these experiences so you would know how to rescue a spirit. It's a way for both of you to learn how to have compassion when rescuing earthbound spirits.

Karen, still shaken by the impact, nodded, acknowledging the divine intervention. She hesitated momentarily, unaware that a spirit had mentally prompted her to leave the room. "I have to go to the bathroom,." she mumbled as she headed toward the front of the house. Several seconds later, she shouted in a frantic voice. "Marie, they've got me. I can't move."

Marian, Connie, and I rushed into the living room.

Karen was standing in the hall with a frightened look on her face. Her back was pressed flat against the wall. "They won't let me go. I can't move away from the wall."

I glanced at Karen's eyes. *Good. They hadn't lightened in color.* This meant the spirit had only partial possession of Karen's body. "Karen! I want you to push this spirit out. Try! Huff inside yourself," I said, making a huffing sound with my voice. "Like a breath of air, force it out."

Karen drew in a deep breath and huffed. *"It won't come out."* She pushed with her mind, but even that didn't work. "I can't. It won't go." It was apparent that Karen had some control over the spirit, because she was able to think for herself without the spirit's thoughts interfering. Even though she sensed it was a female spirit, and she had mentally communicated with it, she still couldn't move her back away from the wall.

Standing directly in front of Karen, I kept my voice calm and controlled. "Tell that spirit to stand in front of you."

Karen mentally communicated the message. "Okay," she said with a nod.

"Do you see her?"

Karen shook her head. "No. But I sense who she is."

"Good. Now, mentally tell her to go to the light. Be firm. Remember, she's a frightened person. She doesn't know where to go. You have to tell her to go to the light."

Karen relayed the mental message. "She's too frightened to travel into the unknown."

"Marian," I called out. "Come here! Help me lift this spirit out of Karen."

Marian rushed into the hall and placed her hands several inches from Karen's legs. She began, starting at the knees, raising her hands slowly, drawing the spirit up and out.

I placed my hands several inches away from Karen's feet, then slowly raised my hands up while mentally drawing the spirit upward. When I reached Karen's head, I raised her hands over her head. "Push it out."

Karen huffed one strong breath. "It's out!" Karen whispered, then heaved a sigh of relief.

I sensed the session had ended for the day. Though I didn't know why, I knew there wouldn't be enough time to release this spirit into the light. "That spirit is out, but it might come back. Remember, these spirits need your help. This is something you must learn to do." I had just finished giving the final instructions when I heard the back screen door slam.

Karen's daughter and son had returned home from school.

Ah, this is why the session is over. The guides knew there wouldn't be time for any further spirit rescues because it might frighten the children. This certainly was a valuable lesson. I wondered how many more lessons we were to learn that day. Synchronicity was in effect, and the guides had been instrumental in preparing the women to challenge more spirits in the future.

Karen stepped away from the wall. "Thank you. Thank you. I didn't know what to do."

The teenage daughter passed through the hall, heading for her bedroom, and the session ended.

As soon as I arrived home, I journaled this amazing experience in detail. I wanted to remember how each spirit was rescued, and how each spirit was treated with unconditional love and compassion, no matter how threatening they appeared. Spirits are people who once walked this earth. Therefore, we should do all we can to lessen their fear. A copy of this experience was mailed Karen and Connie to be used for their future reference. The proof of the power of the God light should never be forgotten.

The wall of light was the most awe-inspiring physical phenomenon I've ever witnessed. The light was a physical entity, so concentrated, so powerful, that it became impenetrable on a physical level. The power that lay within the white light is beyond human comprehension.

We don't know how many spirits are still confined in the vortex of darkness, nor do we know how long they had been there. While they were there, they were existing in the *now*. Time is different in the next dimension. To them, there was no yesterday or tomorrow. There's only *now*. When this vortex opened, the spirits saw a ray of light and rose from the darkness into the basement. However, they were afraid to venture further, held earthbound by their own imagined fear of being damned to hell.

Spirits see energy, vibrations, movement, and color. Possible, they were attracted to the whirling movement of the vortex and headed toward the earthly light. A vortex is an opening through which spirits can come and go. It's not known how many years this vortex had been open, nor how many spirits had moved in and out of it.

The huge, mean male spirit didn't see the wall of light. If he had, he would have approached the basement doorway with caution. He did not. He was locked in his own impression of being evil. When he made contact with the light, it struck him like a bolt of lightning. The force literally knocked Karen's body against the side of the refrigerator and brought the spirit to his knees as well.

Now we understand why the residents believe their house was haunted. The spirit's fear of burning in hell was transmitted to the residents. The earthbound spirits existed in the darkness because their fear was, in part, deep-rooted by the unqualified clergymen while cleansing the house. It's not known how many times the spirits had been accused of being evil, and mistakenly believed they would be damned to hell. If the exorcist had known that spirits respond to thoughts, they might have acted with more compassion.

Compassion and unconditional love were the catalysts which released the earthbound spirits' to the God light. Notice, I never attack the spirits or argued with them. I never told them they were evil even though all the spirits presented themselves as mean and ready to fight for their very existence. When the power of the God light touched each spirit, it was able to release its fear and cross over into the light.

When the guides and/or angels took over, they coexisted within me. I became one with the God consciousness, therefore dealt with each spirit with unconditional love and understanding of their condition. I wasn't the one who controlled each rescue. I was only the channel through whom the angels and spirits worked. That is why fear was blocked from my mind. Over many years of working with spirit guides, I have full confidence that they will protect me mentally and physically. Asking for help from spirit guides requires sincere intent. A sacred force, such as the light, cannot be generated by demand. White light can only be created by offering compassion and unconditional love to all.

This whole day was arranged by divine intervention, making it possible for me to help each spirit separately. Notice that no two spirits were being rescued at the same time. The guides organized the time so the spirits were released to the light before the children arrived home from school. I could not have arranged this. It would have been beyond my control.

Most people have an aura of light around their body. This glow of light is a natural protection from possession. However, Karen and Connie were raw mediums, and were sensitive to the spirit world. They had not learned how to prevent the spirits from entering their physical bodies. Being psychically aware is the ability to see and sense more than the average person. That's why Karen and Connie sensed spirits but didn't know how to use their psychic ability to release them to the God light.

Most families that moved into the house thought the spirits were evil. This is because fear begets panic. Panic begets retaliation. The spirits were fearful, so they fought back by frightening the family. The child spirit pretended to be a black slime because it had learned to use the energy given off by Karen's fear. The more frightened the family became, the more the spirits absorbed the energy, similar to a battery recharging itself.

Many people consider a spirit evil, simply because they're afraid of what they can't see. Not all ghosts are evil, and not all hauntings are bad. Now that you're aware that some spirits only appear to be evil, you might be more apt to treat them with respect, just as you respect a member of your own family.

18

ARCHANGEL

It was the middle of March 2017, during my stay at the hospital that I had an extraordinary, awe-inspiring spiritual experience. I had been in the hospital for several weeks recovering from a cancer operation on my jaw. The time had come for me to leave and go to the rehabilitation building. I was sitting in a wheelchair in my room, waiting for my daughter to arrive.

The male nurse was standing about five feet away and spoke to me. "We're going to miss you. You must be very high on God's list to have agreed to take on such an experience as this. You must be quite a warrior."

"Perhaps we will meet again on the other side," I replied.

"I'm sure we will, but not for a long time from now."

The male nurse's physical body did not move, and my physical body remained in the wheelchair. Our physical bodies were five feet apart. As I looked up at the male nurse, I sensed a huge aura of light surrounding him, like the wings of an angel. With this light emanated the most beautiful feeling of unconditional love. So overcome with a sacred emotion of love, that for a moment I couldn't speak. The only thought that came to mind was that I was in the presence of an Archangel.

While sensing the presence of an Archangel, I experienced an immense feeling of unconditional love permeating the room. This lasted only a few seconds, but while it was present, it was intense, all-consuming, unconditional, pure love. The love was so powerful that it was like a physical entity unto itself.

Now, one would think I would have knelt down, or bowed my head in the presence of this spiritual being. But I did not. Without saying a word, I felt my soul-my consciousness-slip out of my body, rise up and embrace this Archangel. At that same time, the Archangel's soul slipped out of the male nurse's body and embraced me in the same manner. It was as if we had a deep spiritual connection. As our souls blended together, I had the feeling we had a close friendship, and had known each other through eons of time.

The logical reason for such a spiritual experience might be blamed on the effects of the drugs or the medication that I had been taking. But that was not the case, because all this occurred at the same time that my daughter walked into the hospital room.

As she approached the doorway, she experienced a beautiful feeling of unconditional love emanating from my room. When she entered the room, she experienced the overwhelming love, and knew she was in the presence of an Archangel. My daughter did not tell me of her experience until days later, when I revealed my own experience to her.

I often wonder if an Archangel had slipped into the nurse's body and used it momentarily, so I could experience the Archangels presence, or if the nurse actually recognized this spiritual connection had occurred. The other explanation is that an Archangel has taken on a human form in the nurse's body to do God's work. Either way, I feel it was a privileged to have an Archangel working as a nurse.

ORANGE BALLOON

I remained in rehabilitation for several months while recovering from cancer. Every few days, the therapist would bring an orange balloon into my room for therapy. We would toss the balloon back and forth to increase my reflex ability. It was not an ordinary thin rubber balloon. It was the size of a beach ball made of thick rubber, which made it quite sturdy. One day, the therapist left the balloon on the dresser. There was nothing else on the dresser. There was nothing next to it or even near it.

That night, I was jolted awake by the sound of the feeding tube beeping, warning that the feeding tube was empty.

The nurse, hearing the beeping sound, hurried down the hall. She was just about to enter the room when the balloon burst with a loud cracking sound. She let out a loud shriek and stood motionless for a second or two until she gathered her wits about her.

The balloon, which had been sitting on the dresser, burst into two pieces. Half of the balloon landed on the floor at the foot of my bed and the other half directly on my chest.

The nurse entered the room and let out a startled groan when she saw half of the balloon laying on the floor and said, "I get frightened when these strange things happen." Apparently, similar metaphysical occurrences happen quite often in the rooms at the rehab center.

As soon as I felt a part of the balloon had landed directly on my heart, I sensed a loving presence. My niece, who had died several years before, was smiling down at me. Her message was clear. *"We're here with you, Auntie."* Immediately, a feeling of love filled my senses. She had placed the balloon directly on my heart to let me know she was protecting me. I didn't tell the nurse that I knew who had burst the balloon, she was too freaked out already.

WE ARE NEVER ALONE

It has been several years since I won my battle against cancer, and recently the United States of America has likewise battled the Coronavirus. It was quite an experience while the country was in lock-down and people had little physical contact. I was often asked, "Weren't you lonely when you couldn't be with people?"

My answer was always the same: "No, because I was never alone." I was always consciously aware of the angels and spirit guides who soothed my difficult days and brought joy by popping humorous thoughts in my mind. They have counseled and mentored me every day of my life.

Perhaps you wonder, how many spirits are with people. It is my belief that you, and most everyone, have spirit guides that pop answers into your mind almost daily. It may come as a thought in your head, and will direct you to what ever is best for all concerned. Beside spirit guides, it is possible that you are assisted by; guardians, guards, also known as protectors, totems (animal spirits,) and deceased loved one who visit from time to time. Perhaps there are more unseen visitors than I can name. Be assured, you are never alone.

Father Time has restricted my earthly journey. My hair has turned gray and my walk is a little slower. The spirit guides no longer bring my attention to haunted houses.

I now look back at the day I met the Spiritual Council, the white-haired men I saw hovering over me when I first began this journey. I feel honored and privileged to have been chosen to fulfill one part of my life's mission: rescuing earthbound spirit. It has filled my days with happiness, excitement, knowledge, and gratification. My reward is the precious memory of watching each earthbound spirit as it drifted into the God light. The joy and emotion of each experience remains deep in my heart, and I cherish each memory. This earthly journey has taught me to offer unconditional love, just as God intended. I've also learned not to judge others, such as the spirits who attacked me during a rescue. I learned to treat others as I would want to be treated.

Through this book, I share my experiences to all who search for spiritual knowledge. I hope the reader will be enlightened and realize that the opportunity to serve is a gift. Sharing whatever talent you possess is a gift given, and a gift received. I'm pleased that God has allowed me to experience these awe-inspiring rescues and only hope I've completed what task He has set before me. I thank Him for the privilege of helping others and offering His knowledge directly from the spirit world.

BIOGRAPHY

MARIE HARRIETTE KAY is a writer, author, artist, psychic, natural medium, and a teacher of parapsychology. She was born the seventh of eight children in Detroit, Michigan. Coincidentally, it is said the seventh child is often psychic. Marie was married and raised three children. She began her psychic training with June Black, a psychic medium who came to United States from London, England. Marie became Ms. Black's assistant and for seven years studied meditation, psychometry, healing, automatic-writing, spirit communication, past life regression, mediumship, and much more. For the past fifty years, she has mentored many students, taught, and lectured parapsychology.

Marie has published AWAKEN YOUR PSYCHIC ABILITIES, an instruction manual with class set-ups for novices and/or teachers demonstrating easy methods to develop one's innate sixth-sense and spiritual awareness.

Marie has also published HIGH SOCIETY MURDER IN DETROIT, a murder mystery sprinkled with paranormal. It is a historical murder mystery which demonstrates the human frailty of misinterpreting information and the destructive psychological effect of guilt. It challenges the reader to decide who is to blame for each tragedy as it occurs.

Printed in the United States
by Baker & Taylor Publisher Services